DARK AND DANGEROUS

Suddenly, the hairs on the back of Lexi's neck prickled. Clenching her hand into a fist, she whirled around, swinging with all her might at the huge vampire looming behind her.

There was enough power in her punch to knock a man silly—and it would have, she felt sure, if the man hadn't caught her fist with one hand then grabbed her wrist with the other in one smooth move. Before she had time to react, he twisted her arm and shoved her forward over Ironwood's body.

When he leaned into her, she felt the size and mass of his body dwarfing her and tried not to panic as he pulled back her hood. "You're determined to get yourself killed, aren't you? I bet you gave your parents heart attacks growing up."

Lexi froze. "Darius?" He pulled her back to her feet and released her, stepping away as he pulled back his hood. "How'd you know it was me under the hood?"

His gaze heated. "I'd know your body anywhere."

Other *Love Spell* books by Robin T. Popp:

TOO CLOSE TO THE SUN

IMMORTALS: THE DARKENING

ROBIN T. POPP

LOVE SPELL NEW YORK CITY

To Marlaine,
for her unwavering friendship,
support and ability to pretend that my
fictional world is as real to her
as it is to me.

LOVE SPELL®

June 2007

Published by

Dorchester Publishing Co., Inc.
200 Madison Avenue
New York, NY 10016

ISBN-10: 0-505-52702-2
ISBN-13: 978-0-505-52702-8

Printed in the United States of America.

ACKNOWLEDGMENTS

I would like to acknowledge the following Web sites, which I found very informative and which I used as references for the spells and witchcraft. Any errors are wholly my fault.

Enchanted Oak, www.ytown.com/oak
Ivy's Pentacles, http://members.aol.com/ivycleartoes

I would like to thank:

Jennifer Ashley for her creation of the Immortals.

Leah Hultenschmidt for bringing me in on the project and for being such a terrific editor.

Joy Nash and Jennifer Ashley for all their hard work and effort on this project, which extended beyond the writing of their respective books.

Michelle Grajkowski for generally being a terrific agent.

Donna Grant, Mary O'Connor and Georgia Tribell for being supportive critique partners.

My readers—above all—who make it all worthwhile.

Immortals: The Darkening

Prologue

So this is death.

The irony was not lost on Darius as flashes of brilliant light blinded him and pain drove him to his knees. With one hand braced against the tiled floor of the balcony, the other clutched his stomach as every nerve burned with a blistering intensity. He fought to stay conscious while nonexistent shards of glass pierced his skull.

There was powerful magic at work here—living magic that, perversely, was killing him.

"Sekhmet!" he roared. This was her fault. If his patron goddess hadn't removed his life force, the Calling spell would have transported him painlessly to wherever he was needed. Earth must be in dire straits if humans had broken a seven-hundred-year silence to Call the Immortals.

He fought the pull of the spell, drawing on his own power until he felt it rippling along his skin, causing his tattoos to lift and morph briefly into the items they represented before turning into images once more.

"Whitley!" If Sekhmet wouldn't answer him, maybe her priest would. Gritting his teeth against the onslaught of ever-increasing pain, he fell into a sitting position and wrapped his arms around himself to keep from being ripped apart.

Then, as suddenly as the attack started, it ended. Slowly the pain in his head faded, and he opened his eyes. Bright light blinded him, but he quickly realized it was merely the sun shining overhead. As his eyes adjusted, the rest of his surroundings came into view—the clear blue sky, the lush green woods on each side of the sapphire-blue water of Lake Pax. Darius studied the flight of a snow-white hawk as it flew low across the water, searching just below the water's surface for its next meal.

Ravenscroft—his home—was beautiful, and yet its beauty was lost on him.

At the sound of running footsteps, he pushed himself to his feet.

"Darius, I heard you cry out." Whitley hurried to him, putting a hand under his elbow for support. "Are you all right?"

"It appears I'll live," Darius muttered, repeating a joke that was so old it had ceased to be funny.

"What happened?" Whitley ran a critical gaze over him, as if he needed to reassure himself that Darius really was okay.

"It was a Calling spell," he said. "A very strong one. There must have been many witches working together on it." He rubbed the back of his neck, trying to ease some of the tension.

Whitley looked stricken. "Without your life force, you could have been killed."

Darius grimaced but said nothing.

"It's a good thing you were able to break their hold," Whitley commented.

"I didn't," Darius answered, remembering the way the living magic had suddenly been cut off. "Something interfered with the spell."

"A demon?"

"If there's a demon out there powerful enough to stand up against that much magic, no wonder they need the Immortals," Darius said thoughtfully. He paused to give his next words emphasis. "I can't ignore this."

"There's no way she'll let you leave," Whitley said.

"I'm not asking her for permission." Giving the priest's shoulder a gentle squeeze, he turned and strode back into the palatial building that was his home.

His mother, a favorite of Re's when the Egyptian god had ruled the world, was known for her fiery temper as well as her power for healing, which made her unpredictable at times. *Most of the time*, he amended. "Sekhmet!" Darius hollered, storming through the great hall. He headed for his mother's audience chamber, slamming through the gigantic double doors that dwarfed even his 6'5" frame.

At the far end was the low dais upon which his mother's throne chair sat—empty. Behind it, the backlit waterfall filled the room with the soft glow of light and the soothing sounds of running water that did little to calm his nerves.

Looking around, he willed her to appear. "Damn it," he growled when she didn't. There was no telling what problems the delay was causing on Earth. Ravenscroft did not exist in the same dimension as Earth; therefore, ten minutes to him could be days by Earth's standard. Given the strength of that Calling spell, he didn't think Earth had the luxury of time.

Unable to quell the sense of urgency pressing in on him, Darius paced back and forth in his mother's audience chamber, impotent rage seething beneath the surface of his otherwise calm facade. After several hours, he finally felt the shimmer of power behind him and turned to see his patron goddess materialize on her throne. Though she was centuries older, she appeared to be as young as Darius, and her beauty never failed to take his breath away. Today she was wearing a long, flowing aquamarine gown, cut low to show off her ample bosom—and around her neck she wore her diamond necklace, from which hung a simple golden orb that radiated such brilliance it could have housed the sun. In truth, it housed something far more precious to Darius.

"Where have you been?" he demanded without preamble, his eyes on the orb.

"I'm fine, thank you for asking," she said coolly.

"I'm needed on Earth," he continued. "It's urgent, so if you'll just restore my life essence . . ."

Her green eyes sparkled with the temper Darius knew too well. "It's a sad day when a son can't even be civil to his mother."

Darius bit back his snarl. "Good evening, Mother," he said with exaggerated politeness. "I must say, you are looking spectacularly beautiful today, as you do every day. Your smile brings sunshine to an otherwise dark and dismal existence. The songbirds' sweetest melody pales in comparison to your—"

"Stop—before I forget how much I love you," she warned. "I was with my sisters when you bellowed for me—and didn't feel like abandoning them so abruptly. They still mourn the loss of your brothers."

Darius heaved a sigh. "They aren't dead, Mother."

"They might as well be," she replied hotly. "To stay on Earth, fornicating with human females and pursuing other hedonistic activities . . . too busy, even, to pay Ravenscroft a visit." She paused, shaking her head. "It's enough to break a mother's heart."

Darius rubbed his head. It was the same old argument. "They're grown men. They're entitled to live however and wherever they want." He couldn't help wondering whether his brothers had felt the spell. Where exactly were Adrian and Tain, Kalen and Hunter? Had they abandoned their new lifestyles to answer the summoning? "No matter how misguided their choices might be," he added, because defending his brothers was not going to make Sekhmet more sympathetic to his request. "I, on the other hand, am very aware of my duties and responsibilities, which is why I summoned you. There's trouble on Earth. I've been Called."

"What?" He was relieved to hear the alarm in her voice. "But you're still here."

"My body is bound to my life essence. You know that as long as you wear that orb around your neck, I can't leave."

She seemed to relax. "Good." She held out her hand and he took it, helping her to rise and step off the dais. "Shall we dine?"

"What?" He let go of her hand, surprised. "Didn't you hear what I said? There's trouble on Earth. I need to leave."

Irritation crossed her face. "You're needed here."

He stared at her in disbelief. "For what?"

She had continued walking to the doorway that led into the dining hall, but seeing that he was no longer following her, she was forced to stop and look at him.

"Really, Mother," he pressed before she could say anything, "Ravenscroft is not exactly a hotbed of demon activity. There's not a breath of death magic in the entire realm."

"Don't be ridiculous," she scoffed. "Just because there are no demons doesn't mean you can't train."

"What do you think I've been doing for the past seven hundred years? I've done nothing but train—relentlessly—so that when I'm finally *Called*, I'll be prepared." He took a step forward. "Now, for the last time, restore my life essence."

"No."

He stood there, staring after her as she turned and continued to the doorway. "Why are you doing this?" he asked when he'd recovered his voice.

She stopped again and looked at him. "I don't want you to end up like your brothers."

He was so angry he had to clench his fists tightly to keep from doing something he'd regret. He fought to make his voice even. "I am not like my brothers."

She stared at him, her expression as fierce and unyielding as the lioness she was so often depicted to be.

He shook his head. "You're unbelievable. You'd let everyone on Earth suffer, so long as *you* get what *you* want."

"Do *not* try to make me feel guilty," she shouted, sparks of anger shooting from her emerald-colored eyes. "I will protect what is mine. When Re's life was in danger, did the Nile not run red with the blood of those I slew to protect him? Do you think I care about the lives of a few mortals compared to that of my only son? No, you will stay here—with me."

Her gaze burned with an intensity Darius had witnessed only a couple of times before, and though he knew she loved him, he also knew that she meant what she said. She was never going to let him leave. Ever. With his freedom went his entire purpose for being. His life stretched out before him—bleak, desolate, and never-ending. He would spend the rest of his immortal life training for a battle he'd never fight, go to bed every night with no reason to wake up the next morning, pray for an end to his imprisonment that would never come. Even paradise could be hell if you were stuck there long enough.

Walking up to Sekhmet, he placed his hands on her arms and gazed deeply into her eyes. "Mother, there are two things you should know. I love you as only a son can love his mother. And I would rather die than be stuck in this prison of yours for all eternity." Then, in a move born of desperation, he yanked the orb from around her neck. Ignoring her cry of pain, he hurled it against the far wall with all his might, hoping if he destroyed the orb he could end his life.

The orb shattered against the wall with a burst of blinding light. Darius was barely conscious of Sekhmet's gasp as he waited for his life to end. The golden light drifted across the room toward him, spiraling slowly until it formed a thin coil that eventually took the shape of a long, narrow serpent.

As it drew closer, the serpent began to twist about in the air, chasing itself in a figure-eight pattern until it finally caught its own tail.

Darius glanced at Sekhmet and saw her face turn ashen. He knew right away that something was wrong, but before he could do anything, the coiled golden serpent touched his skin just over his heart.

Tendrils of power spread out and gripped him,

growing stronger every second, pulling him. His mind started clouding over until he was barely aware of his surroundings. He was aware of shouting in the background, but he couldn't make out his mother's words.

Almost beside him, a pinpoint of white light appeared and quickly grew. He recognized it as a portal and felt himself being drawn inexorably toward it.

"No!" his mother screamed, though he could barely make out her words. "Not this way. It must be restored . . . vulnerable . . . must protect . . ." Her frantic voice faded, now sounding like it was coming from a far distance. "In . . . physical love . . . find . . . pleasure . . . forget . . ."

Sekhmet's spell died in her throat and she found herself alone in the audience chamber, staring at the spot where her beloved Darius had stood seconds before.

"Darius," she shouted. "I summon you to appear before me." She held her breath and waited, her heart pounding. When he did not appear, she felt an icy fear grip her. His immortal life force had not been properly restored, and he was as close to being mortal as he'd never been before. It was why Ravenscroft had expelled him.

"Whitley," she called. She knew she had to do something to warn Darius about his vulnerability, and she was hoping her levelheaded priest would help. She paced the floor, considering her options. She couldn't go herself—Re had made sure of that before he lost his powers—but once she explained the situation to Whitley, he might agree to let her send him back in a dream.

She heard the running footsteps of the man who had been her lover for thousands of years. It was ironic that she, a goddess feared by mortals and deities alike, would be afraid of the reaction of this particular man.

She quickly rehearsed what she'd tell him, stopping when she got to the part about the unfinished spell. Whitley, being a man, would not understand a mother's need to protect her child from the lure of sex.

How much of her spell had touched Darius before he vanished? Worse still, what would the ramifications be of the incomplete spell?

"Mistress, are you all right?" Whitley rushed into the room. When he saw she was alone, he dropped the pretense of being a mere priest and came to her, enfolding her in his arms. "What is it, my love?"

"Darius is gone. He broke the orb and was expelled to Earth."

"It's okay," Whitley consoled her. "He must protect the humans."

"No, it's not okay," she told him. "His life essence didn't absorb into his soul as it should have. Instead, it drew on his unique brand of magic and turned into a tattoo. He's lost his immortality, and there's no telling how it may affect the rest of his powers."

"And he's just gone to Earth where a powerful evil is waiting for him." Whitley scowled at her, and she bowed her head in shame.

"It's my fault," she said miserably. "I only wanted to protect him."

"Call him back," Whitley ordered.

"I can't—I tried," she replied.

He glared at her. "Then send me back to Earth so I can warn him."

Doing so would make Whitley mortal again, and she couldn't bear to lose both her men. But it warmed her heart to know he was willing to sacrifice his immortality for their son. "There might be another way, if you're willing to help."

"Of course I'll help. What do you need me to do?"

She quickly explained her idea, but when she finished, she found she couldn't look him in the eyes.

Whitley was never one to push, so he remained silent and patiently waited for her to continue. Finally, she took a breath and looked up into his face, genuine tears in her eyes. "There might be one other problem."

Chapter One

The blaring noise of the alarm roused Lexi Corvin from a deep slumber, and she awoke feeling drugged and irritable. She wanted to rip the offending timepiece from the wall and toss it through the window of her fifth-story apartment, but knew she couldn't afford to keep buying new clocks—or replacing windowpanes. So, instead, with great restraint, she merely slammed her hand down on the snooze button to quiet the obnoxious noise.

Resisting the urge to go back to sleep, she cracked open her eyes and found herself squinting against the bright sunlight slipping through the curtains, giving the room a disgustingly cheery warmth that was at complete odds with her mood.

The week before a full moon was always hard on werewolves. Their animal side grew stronger, and they had an urgent need to foster reproduction. Translated into human terms, it meant she was bitchy *and* horny.

If she had still been living in upstate New York with her pack, she would have simply shifted to wolf form and spent the next week hunting prey and frolicking with the available males. That wasn't really an option anymore, now that she lived in the city. She had bills to pay, food to buy. That took money, and people who took off a week or two each month to be a "wolf" didn't hold jobs very long. She wanted to keep her job. It was the first one she'd had that particularly suited her. Bounty hunter.

Shoving back the covers, she dragged herself out of bed. She took a couple of minutes to stretch, trying to loosen muscles that had become tight and sore after chasing down four skips the day before. Crime in the city was up by staggering numbers, which meant business was good.

She crossed the bedroom and turned on the TV, flipping through the channels until she found the news. Lately, it was more depressing than ever. The world—or at least her little corner of the Big Apple—was going to hell in the proverbial handbasket. Just last night there'd been another gang fight in Central Park, leaving five teenagers dead and another three seriously injured. In Murray Hill, a venerable neighborhood filled with old money, a fourteen-year-old boy had gone berserk and shot his parents and younger sister before turning the gun on himself. Down in Soho, a man had stabbed his girlfriend multiple times following an argument, killing both her and their unborn child. Plus, five more people were mysteriously missing—making a total of twenty-three in the last four weeks. The police had no more clues now about how the different people were related or what had happened to them than they did after the first disappearances. The number of random street muggings was up, as were the number of rapes, and the police were advising everyone to stay inside after dark—much to the annoyance of the local nightclub owners, who were fighting back by offering nightly specials.

Lexi flipped the station and watched a reporter standing outside the mayor's office giving an update on the rumor that the city officials were debating on calling in the National Guard to patrol the streets both day and night. But New York wasn't the only city suffering, and the National Guard was already stretched thin. Lexi shook her head and turned to yet another channel, this time finding a TV evangelist asking his congregation to petition their government for stricter Conversion Laws because he felt the number of vampires in town had dramatically risen in the last six months.

She turned off the TV and walked into the bathroom. Had she really thought that by moving to the city she'd escaped the raw animal violence that came from living with the pack? It seemed she'd only traded it for a new, darker kind of violence—though she couldn't remember it being this bad five years ago. Only recently, as far as she could recall.

She stood in front of the mirror and gazed at her reflection. The light gray eyes staring back at her looked tired. She'd let her friend Heather talk her into going to a special meeting last night. Like Lexi, Heather was a witch, but while Lexi preferred to operate on her own, Heather belonged to a group called the Coven of Light. They had stayed up too late, listening to the members discuss possible strategies for dealing with this dire outbreak of crime. The coven believed the growing problems were the work of a powerful demon, who was upsetting the delicate balance of living magic and death magic.

Lexi didn't know who this all-powerful demon was, and frankly, she found it hard to believe the coven's predictions of doom and gloom if the Big Bad wasn't stopped. Like most magical creatures, she'd learned the basic laws of physics at an early age. The world was comprised of two types of magic: living and death. The natural state was for both magics to exist in balance.

The Coven of Light witches were convinced that the Big Bad was somehow going to eradicate all living magic, even if it meant the world would be destroyed as a result.

Weeks ago, Heather had told Lexi about Amber Silverthorne, a witch in Seattle who had an encounter with the Big Bad while investigating the murder of her sister. She'd almost died too, but then some warrior called an Immortal had suddenly appeared to protect her.

At that point in the story Lexi had almost walked out on her friend. Was she supposed to believe the Immortals existed? Please. Demons trying to take over the world? Immortals? Myths and legends. Then again, people once thought werewolves and witches were just stories too.

She picked up a brush and started working the tangles from her long black hair.

Lexi would have dismissed the whole story as nonsense, but Heather had never lied to her, and she could see for herself the death magic increasing in strength.

When the coven found out the demon was being aided by one of the five Immortals, the members decided the only way for it to be stopped would be to hold a Calling and summon the other brothers to help. Heather had begged Lexi to participate. They needed as much living magic power as possible to make the spell work. Still not one-hundred-percent convinced, Lexi had nevertheless agreed.

To her amazement, the spell had almost worked. She'd caught a brief glimpse of at least one of the other Immortals in her scrying flame. Unfortunately, the spell had also Called the rogue brother, Tain, who appeared on the scene with the Big Bad at his side and helped break the spell before any of the other three Immortals could materialize.

Lexi put the brush down and held up her hands to look at the palms. Fire was her medium for casting spells, and that night of the Calling, she'd had to hold a fireball in her hands for longer than ever before. In the end, all she'd had to show for her effort were first-degree burns across her palms and fingers. But now, a week later, the only evidence of her participation was a slight pinkish tint to her skin where the burns had healed.

Last night's meeting had shown her that the witches were feeling at a loss as to what to do next. They'd played their ace and lost.

Lexi still wanted to find some way to help, but right now she had some big bads of her own to tackle. Working her waist-length hair into a braid, she secured the end with a hair fastener. When she finished, she pulled off her nightshirt that read "F*** You and Your Anger Management Class" and pulled on her working uniform of a black leather sleeveless shirt, pants, and Dockers. The outfit was comfortable to work in, but, even more importantly, she knew it made her look tough. A lot of times, taking down a skip was as much about psychology as it was sheer speed and strength.

As she prepared to leave her apartment, she felt the prickle of pent-up magic along her arms. She'd need to visit Ricco soon to help her siphon off some of it before the buildup of magical energy killed her—not that she'd ever let it get that bad. She smiled at the thought of all the wonderful ways the dark-haired, blue-eyed vampire gang leader had "helped" her before. Ah, Ricco.

Heaving a sigh, she left her apartment. Outside, she discovered a beautiful, clear May morning with just enough of a breeze that in the shade, one could actually catch a chill. She let the sun warm her and took in the bustling neighborhood. Hell's Kitchen in the morning was a place unlike any other.

She walked along the sidewalk, listening to the chatter of people on their cell phones as they hurried about their business. The smell of fresh-baked breads and pastries mingled with gas fumes from passing cars. Over the din of traffic, she heard the distant blare of a cruise ship's horn as it pulled out of dock. At the corner, she waited for the traffic light to change before crossing to the other side, where she stopped at her favorite kolache shop to grab a bite to eat. By the time she reached the office of Blackwell Bail Bonds, she was in a better mood.

"Morning, Marge," she greeted the secretary at the front desk. Then she crossed her arms across her chest and gave the petite older woman a reproving glare. "I thought you were going to quit?"

"I quit last night, honey," Marge said in her deep, gravelly voice. She took another drag off the remaining half-inch of her cigarette. "It worked so well, I might try it again tonight."

Lexi shook her head. "Those things'll kill you, you know."

"Yeah, well, at my age, there's not much point in giving up something I enjoy." She exhaled a puff of smoke and coughed a couple of times. "What's going on with you? You look like shit this morning."

"Late night," Lexi said evasively, not bothering to elaborate when Marge raised her eyebrows. She wasn't sure Marge would believe her if she told her some superdemon was trying to destroy the world. "Who are we going after today?" she asked, pulling the top case file from her in-box. She was hoping for a difficult rundown, or maybe someone who would resist arrest so she'd have an excuse to rough them up just a little. Such things were frowned upon, but she would relish a bit of a fight just to work off her frustration—sexual and otherwise.

She opened the file and read over the case. "You're kidding me, right?" She waved the file in the air. "This is a fucking fairy. I'm not going after him."

Marge tsk'd at her in disapproval. "Such language."

Lexi tossed the file back in her box and cocked her head in apology. "I'm sorry. Let me rephrase. I'm not going after that fucking *leprechaun*." She looked at the other in-box and plucked out the top file resting there. "What kind of skips does TJ have?"

TJ was the other bounty hunter at Blackwell. He was a year or two older than she was and six feet of pure muscle. Behind that muscle was a keen intellect, which made him deadly for a human. Despite her werewolf abilities, Jonathan Blackwell still typically assigned the tougher cases to TJ.

She opened the file. "Maurice Gonzales. Charges of spousal abuse. Seven priors. Substance abuser." She glanced at Marge over the top of the file. "I'm taking this one."

"Lexi, you know the rules. Jonathan assigns the cases, and he specifically gave that one to TJ."

"It's not fair," Lexi said. "The leprechaun's a lush. He's

probably passed out somewhere. He'll be easy to find, and he's so tiny that TJ can carry him in a backpack."

"If you don't like the cases you're assigned, you'll need to take it up with Jonathan." Marge's scratchy voice was firm as she stood up and came around the desk. Taking the file from Lexi, she set it back in TJ's box. "All I know is that I put it in TJ's box. Now, if you'll excuse me."

"Where are you going?"

"If you must know, that coffee went right through me. Have a good day," she hollered over her shoulder as she headed for the bathroom in the back.

Lexi's gaze found the coffee mug sitting on the desk, looking shiny and clean. She glanced over to the coffee machine and saw the carafe, sitting empty and dry on a hot plate Lexi would bet was cool to the touch. She smiled to herself and pulled the leprechaun's file from her in-box and placed it in TJ's box. She grabbed the Gonzales case, quickly thumbed through its contents, then dashed out before Marge came back.

Gonzales's apartment was only about a twenty-minute walk down to the far west part of 37th street. This close to the river, the buildings tended toward warehouses. Its emptiness gave it a bit of a spooky feel, even in broad daylight. Not surprisingly, Gonzales lived in a building where security was nonexistent. The lock on the front door was broken, so there was nothing to stop her from going straight to his apartment.

The young woman who answered held the door ajar and looked out warily. There were fresh bruises around her jaw and right eye that didn't completely hide the discoloration of her older bruises. She looked like she didn't weigh more than a hundred pounds soaking wet, and Lexi wondered what kind of scum her husband was to beat her up. She was almost eager to give him a try at someone who could fight back.

"I'm looking for Maurice Gonzales," Lexi said. "Is he in?" She tried not to appear too obvious as she looked past the woman's shoulder into the apartment.

"Who are you?"

"I'm from the bail bond agency. He missed his court appearance, so I'm here to take him back to jail."

It was hard to miss the look of surprise that crossed the woman's face. "He won't go. I tried to remind him the other day and . . ." She gave a small shrug, but Lexi didn't need her to finish the sentence. Her bruises told the story for her.

"I understand your concern, but I think he'll find I can be very . . . persuasive."

"He's very strong," the woman cautioned.

"Stronger than a werewolf?" Lexi asked, smiling when the woman's eyes opened wide in surprise.

A slow, tentative smile appeared across the woman's face. "Maybe not." She glanced behind her at the small boy playing with toys in the middle of the room before turning back to Lexi. "If you take him to jail, how long will he be there?"

"That depends on whether I think there's a chance he'll run again. If I do, he could be there until his new court date—which could be several weeks from now."

"Several weeks would give me time to pack up and leave." The woman stopped talking while she thought about it. "If I tell you where he is," she said finally, "will you call and tell me when he's in jail?"

Lexi nodded. "I will."

"Big John's Ice House."

Lexi smiled. The day was looking up. She thanked

the young woman, got her phone number, then left. Big John's wasn't more than five blocks away.

Inside, the bar was more crowded than she would have liked since it was almost lunchtime, but she spotted Gonzales immediately.

He was sitting at a table with several other men, playing cards. Despite the dim lighting, she saw he had stringy, dark, shoulder-length hair and a jagged scar across his left cheek. When he held up his cards, she saw the prison tats across his fingers.

Lexi thought about her strategy. According to his case file, he was a little taller than her own 5'10", and he outweighed her by a good fifty pounds. She had a couple of options for taking him in—all of which would be easier if she could get him someplace by himself.

Stepping behind a floor-to-ceiling column, she unbuttoned the top couple of buttons of her shirt and pulled the band from her hair, letting it cascade down her back. Under the circumstances, it was the best she could do to soften her appearance.

Stepping up to the bar, she ordered a drink. As she waited, she passed her gaze over the room, making sure to linger on Gonzales until he saw her. When their eyes met, she gave him the barest hint of a smile and then kept looking around the room, making sure she looked at Gonzales at least once more before turning her attention to the drink the bartender handed her.

She pretended to daintily sip it, though she had no intention of drinking anything from this place. After a minute, she rose and, throwing one last shy smile at Gonzales, walked out of the bar. If she were lucky, Gonzales would take the bait and follow her out.

She walked slowly to the end of the building and

stopped to wait. Just when she was about to give up and go to Plan B, the door to the bar opened and Gonzales stepped out. She saw him look around, and, spotting her, he gave a big smile. His teeth were heavily stained from tobacco use, and she wasn't sure he'd ever seen a dentist. She had to work hard to keep disgust from showing on her face.

As he came toward her, she eased around the corner. There was a narrow gravel driveway that led to a parking area behind the warehouse next door, and she walked along it, hearing Gonzales's hurried footsteps as he came after her. Briefly she listened for sounds of anyone walking nearby who might feel compelled to interfere.

The hand on her arm pulling her to a stop came sooner than she expected. He must be eager, which suited her fine. The sooner she put him behind bars, the better everyone would feel. Schooling her features, she turned and gave him an innocent smile.

"Someone as pretty as you shouldn't be in this part of town by herself," he said. "Maybe I should make sure you get home safely. Or, better yet, how about you and me go someplace we can get to know one another better?" His breath hit her in the face like a wet, moldy blanket, making her want to gag.

Instead, she laughed. "Not if you were the last man on Earth."

The grip on her arm grew painfully tighter as he yanked her forward. If she'd been a normal human female, she might have been in real trouble.

"Someone needs to teach you some manners," he growled.

"I know you don't mean you. Now—Let. Go. Of. Me." She enunciated the words, wanting to make sure there was no miscommunication, but she couldn't help adding with a mumble, "You stupid fuck."

He stared at her as if he couldn't believe what she'd said. As the comment finally registered, she saw him get mad. *About damn time.* She had a full second to brace for the impact when he backhanded her.

The blow was still hard enough to knock her head to one side and split open her lip. As pain lanced through her, she felt the wolf in her rise. She was dangerously close to shifting, but she managed to keep everything except her eyes from changing.

"What the hell . . . ?" He sounded confused.

"Maurice Gonzales," she recited quietly, dabbing the blood from her lip with a finger, "my name is Lexi Corvin and I'm a registered bail enforcement agent. You missed your court appointment and jumped bond. I'm taking you in."

He jerked back as if he'd been hit. "Fuck that." He turned, but before he could run, she grabbed his collar and hauled him back.

He swung his arm in a wild punch she easily ducked. She fisted her free hand and hit him back as hard as she could. But he was a big man and didn't go down easily. Fueled by rage, he wrenched free and began pummeling her face and stomach with his meaty fists.

She did her best to ignore the pain and lashed out at him again, first hitting him with several quick jabs to the chest followed by a roundhouse kick to his kidneys.

She may have crossed the line of ethics in luring her skip into a fight, but her sense of justice couldn't pass up the opportunity to beat the crap out of a man who liked to hit women.

Lexi felt Maurice starting to tire, but before she could deliver the final blow, a sudden explosion of light off to the side flashed so bright Lexi had to close her eyes. A shock wave rippled outward, buffeting her with enough force that she had to fight to keep her balance.

When she dared to open her eyes, a concentration of smoke or mist was starting to disperse, and in the middle of it stood the figure of a man.

He was a giant, with dark, unruly hair that fell almost to the collar of his sleeveless black duster, which hung open in front, revealing well-muscled arms and chest, both covered with tattoos. His black leather pants hugged slim hips and muscular legs—and his boots seemed to be of a style much older than any Lexi had seen.

His striking features seemed familiar to her, and it was with a sudden shock that she remembered where she'd seen him before: during the Calling. He had appeared briefly in her scrying flame. At the time, his face had been distorted in pain, but there was no doubt. This was an Immortal.

Chapter Two

Seconds ago, Darius had been arguing with Sekhmet in her audience chamber. Now he was standing in the middle of a street between two large structures, staring at a man who had clearly been beating up the woman beside him.

Darius took in her appearance—the startling light gray eyes, her long dark hair, the soft features of her face, now bruised and bleeding. Rage filled him. He stormed over to the man, grabbed him about the neck and lifted him into the air with his left hand. The man weighed more than Darius had expected, but he held the thug easily while he slapped his right hand against his left forearm and came away holding a dagger.

"What are you doing?" the woman asked, rushing to his side.

"I'm going to kill him," Darius replied, his voice calm, yet cold.

"You can't," she protested.

He gave her a sharp look, wondering if she could

somehow see the slight lag in his strength. "I assure you, I'm quite capable."

She put her hands on her hips and glared at him. "You don't understand. I'm telling you not to."

He was surprised at her boldness. No mortal woman had ever spoken to him in such a fashion. "He struck you. For that, he should pay."

"He *will* pay," she assured him. "I'm taking him to jail."

He frowned. "It would be easier to destroy him."

He saw the spark of anger in her eyes. "Maybe so, but we don't typically kill our criminals straight out," she informed him icily.

"You're wasting your time with this one."

She moved forward and shoved him in the shoulder. "I agree, but do *not* kill him." He gave her a hard look, which she returned. "I mean it, Darius. Don't do it."

Her use of his name earned his undivided attention. "You know who I am?"

"Yes. You're Darius. One of the five Imm—"

He let the man fall to the ground and clamped his hand over the woman's mouth, ignoring the sensation of her soft lips pressing against his palm. "Quiet," he hissed. "It's better if no one knows I'm here."

Her eyes grew wide, but she nodded.

In that moment, while his attention was focused on the woman, the man he'd held captive scrambled to his feet and darted off. Remembering the woman's wish that the man not be killed, Darius slapped his dagger against his left forearm, where it once more melded with his skin to become a tattoo, and took off after the man.

Darius raced with the preternatural speed of the Immortals. Despite the other man's lead, he easily closed the distance. When he reached him, Darius grabbed him by the shoulders and threw him to the ground, where he pinned his quarry by putting his knee in the man's chest.

"What would you like me to do with him?" Darius asked the woman when she joined them.

"I've never seen anyone run that fast," she said, sounding so impressed that Darius fought to keep what was sure to be an idiotic expression off his face. Still, his ego swelled just a bit.

"The man?" he asked again, nodding toward his prisoner.

"Oh, right." She frowned as she looked around. "It'll take hours to get him booked and fill out the paperwork," she mumbled more to herself than to Darius. "I don't think we can afford to wait that long. There are people waiting for you. Still, I hate to just turn him loose. Too bad I can't just . . ."

Her words trailed off, leaving her thought unfinished, but Darius had caught the gist of it. Grabbing the front of the man's shirt, he hauled the man's head off the ground and hit him in the jaw as hard as he could. The man's head whipped to one side as his eyes rolled up into his head.

"He should be out for a couple of hours," Darius told her as he got to his feet. "Let's put him in there and you can come back for him later."

The woman turned to look at the large metal box he'd noticed against the side of the building. "The trash Dumpster?" A slow smile spread across her face, giving her features a radiance that transfixed Darius.

Taking that as agreement, he carried the man over to the Dumpster. While the woman held the lid, he unceremoniously dropped the man inside. They found a few cement blocks abandoned in the lot next door and heaved them on top to help keep the lid down in case the man should wake before they came back.

As they worked, he couldn't help noticing how her shirt fell open, offering a tantalizing sight of a generous cleavage. He'd definitely been in Ravenscroft too long, and as he breathed in this woman's intoxicating scent, he could hardly resist the temptation to drag her into his arms and take her right there and then. With considerable willpower, he forced his thoughts back to more immediate concerns.

"You said there were people waiting for me?"

"Yes. Your brother, Adrian, for one."

"Adrian! He's here?" The thought of seeing one of his brothers after so many years was exciting, no matter how dire the circumstances that brought them together.

"No, he's in Seattle with a witch named Amber Silverthorne, but I'm sure he'll want to tell you what's going on."

"Why don't *you* tell me what's going on?" he suggested.

A frown replaced the smile that had been there just moments earlier. "I can tell you what I know, but it's not much."

At that moment, two men appeared from around the corner and gave Darius and the woman curious glances as they walked past. The woman remained quiet until they had moved out of hearing range. She lightly grabbed the front of Darius's duster and gave it a small tug. "Let's go someplace where we can talk in private."

"I like the sound of that." He didn't bother trying to keep the suggestive tone out of his voice and received a sharp glance as he fell into step beside her. "What's your name?"

He'd followed her to a bustling intersection and came to an abrupt stop. It was unlike anything he'd seen before. A myriad of strange machines whizzed by, the spire of a huge building soared into the sky off to the right, and crowds of people bearing multicolored bags hurried past in both directions. The woman beside him paused, and he felt her gaze upon him.

"It's been a while since you last came to Earth, hasn't it?" she asked him.

His attention stayed fixed on the traffic as he answered. "About seven hundred years."

She looked around, perhaps trying to imagine what the world must look like to him now. "So much has changed," she mused. "I don't exactly know where to start." She waved her hand in the air and one of the contraptions shot across the street and stopped about a foot away. "Instead of relying on horses, mules or oxen for transportation, we have these." She pointed to the contraption. "They aren't alive—it's all metal and plastic. It's called—"

"A cab," he finished for her, earning another amazed stare. "I've kept up on things," he said, reaching out to open the back door.

He leaned in to look inside and then held the driver's gaze for a long time, assessing him. He wasn't worried about his own safety—after all, he was immortal—but he wasn't willing to trust the woman's life to just anyone.

"You comin' or what?" the driver asked.

"We're coming," the woman said behind Darius, pushing at his back. He stood aside so she could climb inside and then joined her.

She rattled off an address, and the cab shot into traffic. Then she looked at him. "My name is Lexi. Lexi Corvin."

Darius pulled his attention from the view out the window to look at her. He liked the way she spoke. Her voice was sultry, alluring. Like the woman. He silently vowed that before he left this place, he would get to know her—intimately. He turned his gaze back to the sights they were passing, but his thoughts stayed on the woman. How much had women changed over the centuries? he wondered. The way this one dressed, with tight-fitting clothes that perfectly molded to the shape of her body and the daring plunge of her neckline, suggested she was the type who spent much time pleasuring men. That might have bothered some men, but not Darius. In fact, it would make leaving her easier if she had no expectation of a personal commitment.

Feeling as if things were definitely looking up for him, he settled in and enjoyed the rest of the ride. It didn't take long, and, though Darius drew many interested stares when he got out of the cab, that was the extent of the attention he received. There were no crowds of men and woman rushing forward to welcome him to Earth as there had been in the past. He found the lack of attention a bit disconcerting.

"You okay?" Lexi asked after she'd paid the cab driver and he'd driven off.

He smiled down at her and saw her light gray eyes widen ever so slightly. "Yes."

They went inside her apartment building and rode an elevator to the fifth floor, another interesting experience for Darius.

"Are you hungry? Can I get you something to eat or drink?" Lexi offered as soon as they were inside her apartment. It was smaller than anything he was used to, which made him feel like a caged animal.

"Nothing, thanks," he said, studying her closely. "But you can tell me why I was Called."

"I think it would be best if you talked to your brother Adrian."

She picked up an instrument sitting on the table beside her couch and pressed several buttons on it before holding the instrument to her ear. A second later, Darius heard the voice of a woman on the other end of the line and guessed that this, then, was a telephone. He'd tried to stay on top of Earth's changes over the years, but most of his information had come from listening to the conversations of his mother and other gods and goddesses. He'd heard about many of the technological advances, but never seen them.

"Heather, it's Lexi," she said into the phone. Darius listened to her side of the conversation as he walked around the room looking at pictures hanging on the wall. "You're not going to believe this. The spell worked. . . . Yes, the Calling spell. . . . I know because I have an Immortal standing right here in my living room . . . because he looks just like the guy who appeared briefly during the ceremony." She paused and listened for a moment. "Okay. Wait a second."

"Excuse me," she called to him. "I need proof that you're really an Immortal," she told him when he turned to look at her.

She didn't apologize for doubting him, just stood there silently waiting. He wondered what she'd do if he refused. He wasn't sure there was time for such games, though, so he merely smiled at her, turned his back and gathered his hair so he could lift it up. On the back of his neck was the tattoo each of the five brothers had somewhere on his body, a cobalt blue pentacle.

"It's there," he heard her say into the phone. Then she was silent while the other woman talked. Darius let go of his hair and resumed his perusal of her room.

"Okay, Heather gave me the phone number in Seattle," she told him a minute later. "With any luck, Amber and Adrian will be home." She punched in another series of numbers and waited for several seconds.

"Hello. Amber?" Lexi paused. "My name is Lexi Corvin. I'm not a member of the Coven of Light, but I participated in the Calling spell last week, and, well, it worked. . . . Yes, one of the Immortals has appeared. Luckily, I was there and recognized him . . . Darius . . . I thought it would be best if you or maybe Adrian explained the situation to him? Great. I'll put him on the phone."

At this last comment, Darius had turned to her, and now she held the phone out to him. He stared at it a bit hesitantly, but he took it from her and held it to his ear as he'd seen her do. "Hello?"

"Darius!" The familiar voice of his brother boomed on the other end of the line. "I'll be damned. It's good to hear your voice."

"Adrian." He sounded just as Darius remembered him. "How the hell are you?"

"As well as can be under the circumstances," he said, his voice tinged with regret. "We thought when the Calling was interrupted there was no hope of reaching you. But I'm glad you're here. Things are not looking good."

"I would have been here sooner, but I ran into problems on my end."

"Problems?" There was worry in Adrian's tone.

"Nothing I couldn't handle," Darius assured him, not wanting to go into details at the moment.

"Glad to hear it. Now if this lead of Kalen being in Scotland pans out, there'll be three of us."

"Kalen's in Scotland?" After being alone for so long, he relished the idea of seeing his brothers again.

"We don't know for certain," Adrian continued. "There's a witch in the Highlands who contacted Amber just recently—a Christine Lachlan. She's pursuing a lead—we'll see what happens."

"And Hunter?"

Darius heard Adrian hesitate. "I thought he might still be in Ravenscroft with you."

"Still? Adrian, none of the brothers have been in Ravenscroft since the last time we were Called to Earth."

"What?" Adrian sounded surprised.

"I've been there alone these past seven hundred years." He couldn't help sounding a little bitter, but the last thing he wanted to do was get into an argument with Adrian. "What about Tain? Is he here too?"

Adrian didn't answer, and Darius could practically hear him struggling for the right words.

"Adrian, what's going on here?" he demanded.

His brother sighed heavily. "There's a demon—an ancient one, judging from his strength and power—who's determined to take over the world by destroying all living magic."

It was a familiar enough story. It seemed that dark forces were forever trying to rule the world—although there wouldn't be much of a world to rule if all living magic were destroyed. He didn't bother to ask if Adrian knew which demon it was; if he did, he would have already bound it by invoking the demon's name.

"And Tain?" Darius asked.

Adrian took a deep breath. "He's helping the demon."

There was silence while Darius tried to decide if he'd heard correctly. "What?" he finally asked. "I thought . . ." He stopped. He wasn't sure what he'd thought had happened to his youngest brother. "I don't understand."

"You remember the last battle? Where we were Called to defeat the Unseelie Host? That last onslaught of Unseelies was just a diversion to get me away from Tain. I found out that after the battle he'd gone off with a woman, but it turned out to be a demon in female form. Though I spent centuries looking for him, I couldn't find him—until now."

Darius shook his head. "There must be some mistake. Tain would never team up with a demon—especially to destroy the world."

He heard Adrian take a deep breath. "I saw him, Darius. I saw him and I talked with him. Over the centuries, the demon kept him chained and tortured him horribly. Once the demon had him beaten and bleeding, he would shift to female form and heal him with sex. After seven hundred years of that treatment, Tain's mind snapped."

Darius was almost numb with the shock and horror of what his little brother must have suffered. Tain had always been the gentlest of the brothers, never as strong-willed as the rest of them. That he should have suffered so wasn't right. Darius clenched his free hand into a fist, consumed with rage. "What's the plan?"

"Come to Seattle," Adrian told him. "I'm gathering forces, but I'm bound by Isis not to hunt for Tain until we're all together. Next time we face the demon and

Tain, I want to make sure we have all the living magic at our command that we can."

"How do I get there?" Darius asked, casting a quick glace at Lexi.

"You're going to fly on a plane. While we've been talking, Amber's been online getting you a ticket. Hang on a second while I see what she's found."

In the ensuing silence, Darius turned to Lexi. "Adrian's getting me a ticket to fly to Seattle—on a plane."

"Oh, good. If you'd like, I can go with you to the airport and make sure you get on the right flight."

Darius almost sighed in relief. This flying stuff was all new to him. But before Darius could tell her he'd like that very much, Adrian's voice came back on the line. "Okay. The best we can do is a flight out of LaGuardia at eight a.m. Do you think you can make that?"

"Yeah, no problem."

"Okay, then. I'll be there waiting when you land. I'm sorry I can't get you here any sooner, but I imagine you can find a way to pass the evening."

"Oh, yeah," Darius said, letting his gaze travel over Lexi.

He heard Adrian chuckle. "Seven hundred years is a long time to go without the pleasure of female company. Think you remember how things are done?"

"Some things are never forgotten," Darius assured him.

"Okay, well, be careful. I wouldn't want you to sprain anything important. I'll see you tomorrow. And Darius," Adrian added, "I'm glad you came."

Darius smiled. "Same here."

There was a click on the phone and Darius handed the instrument back to Lexi. The light spilling in from the window caused some strands of her jet-black hair to appear almost blue.

"So . . ." she said hesitantly. "I guess you'll be pretty busy for the next couple of weeks."

"I would imagine so." He slowly moved toward her.

"Do you think you might be back this way when you're done?"

He smiled because despite her attempt to sound casual, he heard the eagerness. The sexual energy radiating off her brushed his skin and ignited his hunger. "Absolutely."

He saw her reach into the front pocket of her shirt, and as her hand rubbed across her breast, he felt a rush of raw, sexual need course through him. He stopped directly in front of her and watched as she pulled out something small and white. "Here's my card," she said a little breathlessly, holding it out to him. He took the piece of paper from her and held it up, looking at the numbers printed on the front. She gestured to it. "It's my work address and phone, but on the back—that's my cell phone number." She shrugged. "You know, in case you . . . wanted to get in touch with me again."

He looked at the card for a moment longer, then tucked it into his pocket. Then he cupped her face with his hand and leaned in slowly, giving her a chance to pull away. He caught the faint catch in her breath and almost smiled. Then his lips touched hers.

She felt cool against his heated lips and tasted like the sweetest fruit after a lifetime of starvation. Nearly senseless with the need to be inside her, he fumbled one-handed with the fastenings of his pants.

"What are you doing?" Lexi gasped.

"Taking off my clothes," he said, shoving down his pants in order to free his straining member.

She pushed against his chest looking shocked. "Why?"

He smiled. "So we can have sex."

"What?"

Her indignation was so unexpected that an unlikely thought occurred to him. "Are you a virgin?" he asked, automatically reaching to pull up his pants.

"No, but—"

"Great," he interrupted, relieved. "Then there's no problem." Again he started to push down his pants.

"I'm not having sex with you," Lexi said forcefully.

He stopped undressing and looked up at her abruptly. "Of course you are. You find me attractive. I find you attractive. I can feel your need beating at me. The only question is: Do we do it here on the floor? Or should we take the time to find a bedroom?"

Her eyes sparked with indignation. "I'm a werewolf, and we're about seven days away from the full moon. Right now, I'd find a troll attractive, so don't flatter yourself."

He'd never forced a woman to have sex with him, and he wasn't about to start now. Clearly, he needed to brush up on his charm.

Fastening his pants, he gave her a knowing smile. Whether she believed it or not, she wanted him, and sooner or later, he intended to have her.

If seven hundred years in Ravenscroft had taught him anything, it was how to be patient. "I won't deny I'm disappointed with your decision," he said, "but I'll respect it."

He could tell his sincerity surprised her, but she recovered quickly and nodded. "Thank you."

He looked around. "So, now what?"

"Right now, I have some unfinished business lying unconscious in a trash Dumpster. You're welcome to stay here while I'm gone. I should be back in a couple of hours."

"I have a better idea," Darius said, walking to the door and pulling it open. "I'll go with you."

Chapter Three

It was six o'clock when Lexi walked back into her apartment after taking Maurice Gonzalez to jail. She and Darius had found him just where they'd left him in the Dumpster. Though she'd never admit it to Darius, she'd been grateful for his help. He'd easily removed the cement blocks and lifted Gonzales's two hundred plus pounds out of the Dumpster. When Gonzalez woke up and tried to resist arrest, Darius restrained him as effortlessly as if he were holding on to a butterfly.

Lexi knew she could have taken in Gonzalez by herself, but Darius had made it so much easier. He'd been so polite and helpful, she considered inviting him to spend the evening with her after all. It wasn't like he had anyplace else to go. But before she could ask, Darius told her he wanted to explore the city. She'd offered to show him the sights once she filled out the paperwork on Gonzalez at the station, but he hadn't wanted to wait.

She suspected he was looking for a woman who would be more accommodating than she had been.

The thought made the dying embers of her previous anger flame hot once more.

How dare he assume she'd have sex with him? It wasn't that she refused to have sex with a complete stranger—goddess knew that from time to time, she'd done just that—out of need, of course, she silently argued. No, it was more his arrogance in just *assuming* she would.

If she were honest with herself, she'd admit that not all of her anger was directed at Darius. The truth was that she had been tempted to have sex with him.

Forcing the Immortal from her thoughts was nearly impossible, so she headed for the kitchen to make herself something to eat. She felt restless and needed a distraction. But she couldn't help wondering where he was. What was he doing? *Who* was he doing?

When the phone rang, she welcomed the diversion.

"What are you doing tonight?" Mai asked with that not-so-subtle, hey-I've-made-plans-for-us tone of voice. "Feel like helping me do some research?"

"What kind of research?" Lexi asked hesitantly.

"I want to check out the Crypt."

"That new vampire bar?"

"That's the one," Mai said.

"Why?" Lexi asked, not sure she wanted to know the answer. Mai was not only a tenacious investigative reporter, she was a wood nymph with a gluttonous sexual appetite. The fact that she wanted to do research at New York City's newest and most-raved-about vampire nightclub couldn't be good news.

"I hear the back rooms are really hot."

Lexi heaved a weary sigh. "I don't know. I realize it's *the* place to go, but I'm pretty sure it's Vlads' territory.

Ricco's not going to like the idea of us going to a club owned and operated by his chief rival."

Mai heaved a weary sigh. "We always go to Ricco's place, and then you run off with Ricco and I'm left with someone boring."

"You never complained before. Did something happen?"

"No. It's just that I've been through all the regulars at Ricco's, except for Ricco himself. I'm in the mood for a Ricco, and I know that's not going to happen with you around. I thought that maybe at the new place, we might find new blood, so to speak." She laughed at her own pun.

"I don't know," Lexi repeated.

"Look, if you don't think Ricco will like you going to another club, don't tell him." Everything was so simple for Mai. "Besides, this isn't just for fun. It's work. I'm doing an exposé on the popularity behind the vampire nightclubs, but the article is going to be severely slanted if the only club I visit is Ricco's." She paused. "If you don't want to go with me, that's fine. I'll go by myself."

Lexi rolled her eyes. While Mai might have the spirit of a werewolf, she was built like a pixie, and her magic wasn't much stronger. If there were trouble, Lexi would never forgive herself for letting her best friend walk into it alone.

"All right," she agreed. "It's not like Ricco owns me. I guess I don't mind checking out a new place."

"Great. It'll be fun," Mai promised. "And, Lexi—try to wear something sexy." Lexi opened her mouth to protest, but Mai cut her off. "No offense, honey, but you know how you are. You dress in those black leathers all the time and scare half the men away."

"Fine," Lexi agreed, mentally searching her closet, hoping she owned something that would meet with Mai's approval. "I'll see what I can do."

"Good. I'll see you in a bit."

Almost as soon as Lexi hung up, she wished they were going to Ricco's club instead. Her energy levels were starting to get out of control. Ricco was the First Fang of the Bloods, the largest vampire gang in town. He was also the most in-demand male working the back rooms of his nightclub.

Normally, they should never have been able to come together—Lexi a creature of living magic and Ricco one of death magic. But there had never been anything "normal" about their relationship. That first night, long ago, she'd shown up at his club desperate with need, and he'd insisted on being her partner. It had been rough, but she'd been beyond caring, and he'd shown that he could easily keep up with the vigorous appetite of a shifter.

All he asked for in return was a little blood. Under the circumstances, the advantages far outweighed the slight discomfort of being that close to a death-magic creature.

She liked Ricco, but she didn't love him. She hated herself for using him the way she did, but she didn't have a lot of options. And the situation seemed just fine with Ricco. Over time, they'd built a comfortable relationship. And tonight, she needed that just as much as the sex.

When Mai arrived two hours later, Lexi had a pile of discarded clothes on her bed and was standing in front of her nearly empty closet, stark naked, wondering if anyone had invented a spell that could turn street-tough leathers into ballroom glitz.

"I see you're ready to go," her friend joked as she let herself into the apartment and walked into the bedroom. She looked stunning as usual in an emerald-green column-style dress that hugged her curvy body.

"I'm not going," Lexi told her.

"Of course you are," Mai assured her, placing a previously unnoticed department-store shopping bag on the bed. Reaching inside, she pulled out what looked like three feet of Lycra tubing in a bright sapphire blue. "Okay, Cinderella—look what your nymph godmother brought you."

Lexi instantly saw the possibilities and pulled the dress on. Standing in front of the full-length mirror, she adjusted the gathers of the material to show off her figure to its best advantage. It was tight, did nothing to hide any figure flaws—and she looked terrific in it.

"You like?" Mai asked.

Lexi smiled. "I like. Thanks."

"Okay—grab some heels and let's go. With the full moon on the rise, every bitch in the city is likely to be out tonight—no offense. I don't want to be the one going home sexually frustrated."

Lexi pulled her only pair of high heels—black, of course—out of the closet, grabbed her purse and left the apartment with Mai.

Twenty minutes later, they were stepping through the front doors of the Crypt. It was only ten o'clock, but the place was crowded. At the far end of the room, on the other side of the dance floor, a disc jockey was spinning CDs in a lighted booth. A second-story landing ran around the perimeter of the room, with tables and booths set up for small parties to gather. Lexi glanced up and noticed that several tables were occupied—mostly with couples well on their way to needing one of the back rooms.

Most club rules stated that heavy petting and groping were tolerated in the public area, but for more serious activities, guests were encouraged to find a private room in back. For those who wanted something a little different, theme parties were available—for a price.

The owner of the bar hadn't scrimped on giving the place atmosphere. Everything—flooring, furniture, walls and lights—was done in black or red. Panels of lush red drapes hanging on the walls helped foster a feeling of decadence. Strategically placed colored lights gave off a soft glow, making it possible to see without destroying the illusion of intimacy.

Lexi and Mai got their drinks and wove through the crowd, openly checking out the men they passed.

Mai, a natural extrovert, struck up a flirtatious conversation with a group of three males. Two of them were vampires, but Lexi wasn't sure about the third. He had a definite vitality that seemed more than human. When he smiled, Lexi found herself smiling back.

"My name's Josh. I haven't seen you here before," he said to her.

"No," she agreed. "I'm Lexi. This is my first time."

"Your first time to the Crypt? Or your *first time*?"

She smiled. "First time to the Crypt," she clarified.

"She prefers Blood Club," Mai interrupted.

The man smiled appreciatively. Ricco's Blood Club had a reputation for being a little rougher than most clubs. Lexi didn't think the rep was deserved, but then she was a wolf by nature. Besides, five minutes of heavy breathing and groping wasn't her idea of sex.

A flash of something caught her eye, and she turned. She could see nothing but the usual crush of people, so she looked back to Josh. Ten minutes later, she thought she caught the flash of something familiar once again out of the corner of her eye, and she turned to scan the room.

There, across the bar, still dressed in his long black duster and black pants, was Darius. As if he'd felt her staring, he turned and their gazes met.

The intensity of his look shot straight through her, causing her pulse to race and her body to hum with awareness. It was more than just his good looks that made him so irresistibly attractive. His whole demeanor spoke of male confidence and determination. This was a man who knew what he wanted and wasn't afraid to go after it. He would let nothing stand in his way. And right now, as he moved toward her, his expression made it clear what he wanted: her.

Annoyed by his arrogance, she forced herself to turn away. She was about to tell Mai it was time to go, when her friend stood on tiptoe to speak in her ear. "I'm going with Roger here"; she indicated the better looking of the two vampires. Before Lexi could stop her, Mai and Roger took off into the crowd, leaving her with the other vampire and Josh.

The hairs along the back of her neck tingled as Darius came closer, and Lexi suddenly became very interested in making conversation with Josh.

"You come here a lot?" she asked him.

He shrugged. "I've been here a couple of times," he admitted. "But now that I've met you, I'll have to make a point to come more often." He gestured to her glass. "Can I get you a refill?"

Before she could answer, he'd taken her empty glass from her and handed it to the vampire, who disappeared into the crowd. Somehow Josh had gained possession of her hand and lightly caressed it, which was very distracting.

Every fiber of her awareness tingled, and she didn't need to turn around to know that Darius was right behind her. He was standing so close, she could feel the heat of his body warm her back. She continued to ignore him, giving Josh a smile that was a little too bright and friendly.

"Leave us," Darius growled, placing his hands possessively on her shoulders.

Josh's smile faded, and he didn't look as confident as he had a few seconds earlier. "Wait just a damn minute," he started, but the rest of his sentence died in his throat when Darius gently but firmly moved Lexi to one side so he could take a step closer. "It was nice meeting you," Josh said hurriedly before practically falling over himself to get away.

Lexi turned on Darius. "You have no right to come in here and—"

"Do you know that man?" Darius interrupted.

She knew exactly where he was headed with this and stared up at him defiantly. "No—not that it's any of your business."

Darius gave her a disgusted look. "But you'd have sex with him." He gestured to the room at large. "That's the only reason anyone comes to this place, isn't it?"

Rather than answer his question, she asked her own. "Is that why you're here?"

He gave her a lascivious smile. "If the gods are willing."

She rolled her eyes. "I'm surprised you aren't already in the back rooms. What's the matter? Lose your touch with the women?"

He frowned and took her gently by the elbow off to the side where they could stand and talk in greater privacy. "The Calling spell is supposed to summon us to where we're most needed, where death-magic forces are greatest. So why did I end up in New York City and not Seattle?" He paused to give her time to draw the obvious conclusion.

"Because the demon is here?"

"That's what I wanted to find out. When I focused on finding the strongest concentration of death magic, I ended up at this club."

Lexi looked around, studying the faces around her, doing her best to sense an underlying evil. It was there, of course, everywhere she looked; vampires and demons luring humans and living-magic creatures into the back rooms. The vampires used glamour on their human companions to make them eager sexual partners, while the demons fed off the life force of their partners, leaving them with a high that was dangerously addictive. But these things were part of the thrill of coming to clubs like the Crypt and Blood Club. What Darius was talking about was something different. Something more powerful—and far more dangerous.

"Rest assured, if the demon is here, I'll find him." His gaze raked over her, making her conscious of just how snug and short her dress was. "Right now, I'm more interested in solving another mystery. Out of all the people in this city, why did the Calling spell bring me to *you*?"

Lexi wasn't sure there was any big mystery to it. "Probably because I helped with the spell."

"Were you the only witch from this area?"

"No, of course not. There were about three or four of us."

He nodded. "So why you?"

She shook her head. "I don't know. I'm not the

source of evil you're looking for, if that's what you're thinking. Maybe you appeared to me because I saw you during the Calling."

"I never left Ravenscroft—how could you see me?"

"Your face appeared in my scrying flame."

"You command fire." It was more a statement than a question, but she nodded anyway. "It makes sense," Darius continued. "Fire is Sekhmet's element to command also, so it runs in my blood. It's only natural that the spell would deliver me to a witch who commands it."

Lexi actually felt a stab of disappointment that there was no greater significance for why she was the one he'd appeared to, but before she could respond, a fight broke out across the bar between several male vampires. The crowd cleared from around them, like ripples in the water's surface after a stone has been dropped into a still pond.

The four vampires squared off, fangs bared and eyes glowing with an unnatural light. As if by unspoken command, they rushed each other at once, and it wasn't long before Lexi caught the faint odor of blood in the air.

"You should leave," Darius said abruptly. "It's not safe for you here."

Lexi had never been one to take orders, especially from those who thought to protect her. "I'm not ready to leave. I came here to have a good time, and I'm not leaving until I do."

Darius looked across the room at the dance floor, where the music still played and couples, oblivious to the fight, danced on. "Fine." He grabbed her hand firmly and pulled her into the crowd.

The colored lights gleamed off the sweaty bodies of the people pressing against them, pressing them together. Determined to ignore Darius and his chauvinistic attitude, Lexi let the throbbing music wash over her. She closed her eyes, raised her arms above her head and surrendered herself to the primal beat.

Then she felt his hand on her waist, felt it fan up over her ribs until his knuckles lightly skimmed the underside of her breast.

"You are incredible," he whispered. "Like nothing I've ever seen." The briefest touch of his tongue on the shell of her ear made her body pulse in a way that had nothing to do with the music.

She tried to put a little space between them, but he refused to allow it, molding his body against hers so close that she could feel the hardness of his erection through his leather pants and the thin Lycra of her dress.

The room was suddenly too crowded and her emotions too raw. Pulling away, she melded into the crowd without a word. She didn't even bother looking for Mai. They rarely left clubs together.

Compared to the stuffy warmth inside, the fresh night air was cool and refreshing. It went a long way toward soothing her emotions, but did little to help ease the ache inside her. There was only one cure for that, and she'd walked out on it. So she opted for the next best thing.

A short cab ride later, she walked into Ricco's bar, made her way to the back rooms and found the party hostess.

"Hi, Lexi," the woman said. "I'll see if he's in." She knew perfectly well Lexi only showed up when she needed to see Ricco.

Of course Ricco was in—though he was currently occupied with someone else. Lexi didn't care. When he was finished with his current client, he'd still be able to see to her needs. One of the nice things about vampires—they could literally go all night. They also couldn't contract or spread sexually transmitted diseases. Nor could Ricco ever get her pregnant. And when she'd had enough, she could walk out and not call or see him until she needed to again—in four weeks. In her book, that made him the perfect partner.

Lexi pointed into the outer room. "I'll wait in the lounge."

The hostess nodded. "I'll send someone for you when he's ready."

"Thanks." Lexi walked off. If this had been any other night, she might have gone home. She didn't like waiting and she was tired, but that damn Immortal had her wound so tight, she wanted to scream.

Walking into the small lounge, she looked around. There was a couch running along the wall where a number of others were sitting. This area wasn't part of the rest of the bar; it was specifically for people waiting for a back room.

She was searching for a place to sit when she heard a familiar voice. "Hello, Lexi—how are you?"

"Derrick." She nodded to her brother-in-law, who was sitting on the couch. "What are you doing here?" When he didn't immediately answer, she realized how stupid the question was. "Sorry," she continued. "It's none of my business anyway."

He made room for her to join him and she sat, feeling very uncomfortable. She'd only seen him a handful of times since her sister's funeral, and it occurred to her how difficult it must be for him to even be near her. She and her sister had been identical twins. Every time he looked at her, he had to see the wife he'd killed.

She shifted on the seat, unconsciously moving farther away from him. She hadn't meant for him to notice, but he did—she heard him sigh.

"When are you going to stop blaming me for what happened?" he asked under his breath. "If I'd been in a position to stop her, I would have. Bev was the most important person in my life."

Lexi heard the heartache and bitterness in his voice and vowed—again—to never fall in love.

A year ago, Derrick had been in a horrible car accident. He'd sustained considerable internal injuries, including the loss of both kidneys. Neither magic nor modern medicine could repair them, but they could be replaced. A new experimental procedure developed by a foreign wizard made it possible to modify the genetic makeup of any donor organ to make it compatible with the recipient. Time was of the essence, so to save Derrick's life, Lexi's sister, Bev, had insisted they give the experimental procedure a try—using herself as the donor.

The surgery had gone well, until the end. One of Bev's kidneys had been removed and successfully transplanted into Derrick. He had been wheeled into the recovery room when Bev started having problems. Her heart started failing before the doctors and nurses could even figure out what was happening.

An autopsy revealed that traces of silver had flecked off the magically enhanced surgical instruments and entered her bloodstream. From there, they had lodged in her heart—her half-lupine heart. It couldn't have killed her any more effectively had they shot her with a silver bullet.

What made the whole thing worse for Lexi was finding out that her sister had been aware of the risks prior to going into the surgery. The doctor had pointed them out to her. Bev had ignored them and insisted on proceeding to save her husband's life. By the time Derrick had regained consciousness enough to understand what was happening, his wife was dead.

Lexi couldn't understand the kind of emotion that had driven her sister to make the decision she had—to be willing to risk her life. If Bev had stopped to think about it logically, Lexi knew her sister would have made a different decision. She might have even found a way to save her husband without risking her own life. But now they'd never know.

Lexi never wanted to be so in love that she'd be willing to die for someone else; she didn't want her emotions to have that much control over her.

It was one of the reasons why she came to Ricco for her monthly sex fix. She was in no fear of losing her heart to him.

However, when she looked into the future, she saw a long progression of sexually satisfying but emotionally empty nights ahead of her. It was more than a little depressing.

"I can't do this," she muttered to herself, standing up. "Good night, Derrick." She walked out of the lounge and out of the club, not stopping until she got home.

Darius looked around, wishing Lexi hadn't left the bar the way she had. It had been over an hour, and his body still burned with the need to possess her. He tried to convince himself that it was a natural male reaction to a female in heat. A female *werewolf* in heat.

That alone should have been enough to keep him away from her, but it only intrigued him more.

He looked about the room, finding it curious how the vampires barely seemed to notice him. Considering that drinking Immortal blood vastly increased their strength, he would have thought the minute he stepped into the room, they'd be all over him. Instead, it was like his aura was no different from anyone else's. Like he wasn't an Immortal.

It was yet another mystery waiting to be solved—but not tonight.

"Are you looking for someone in particular?" a sultry female voice asked beside him. "Or just looking for someone?"

He looked down into the face of a petite woman with spiky neon-pink hair. Darius was having a hard time reading her magical aura and thought she looked enough like a pixie to be one. A very attractive pixie, at that.

As much as he wanted Lexi, he wasn't going to chase her down and beg. He smiled at the woman in front of him. "I was looking for you," he said, purposely letting his gaze run over her appreciatively. "Would you like to dance?"

She stepped closer and laid a hand against his chest. "I was thinking we could skip the preliminaries and find a nice private room in the back."

He cocked his head to one side and gave her a knowing smile. "By all means—lead the way."

She gave a delicate little laugh and, taking his hand in hers, led him through the crowd to the back of the club. He followed her through a bright red door. On the other side was a long hallway lined with doors—

some closed, some open. The pixie stopped at the first available room and, giving him a seductive smile, stepped inside. Darius followed somewhat cautiously, glancing back when he heard the red door to the bar open. He watched a couple walk through, but they didn't spare him a second glance as they moved directly into an open room and closed the door.

He turned back to follow the pixie and found her waiting inside the room, her eyes alight with desire. It fueled his own eagerness.

"I'm Daphne," she said, moving toward him with a seductive swaying of her hips.

"Darius," he said, wrapping an arm around her waist when she was near enough for him to pull her close. He kissed her, but it wasn't as exhilarating as kissing Lexi. He tried not to think about it.

"I love these tattoos," she said, tracing the outlines of several, sending shivers across his skin. She slipped her hands across his shoulders, easing off his duster. He needed no further urging and quickly undressed.

By the time Darius was naked, he looked up and saw that she'd already slipped out of her clothes. For a full second, Darius stood in stunned silence. It had been so long since he'd laid eyes on a nude female form that, for a minute, all he wanted to do was drink in the sight of her.

The young pixie, however, had different ideas. When she pressed her supple body against his, Darius lost all capacity for rational thought. The next several minutes were spent in a tangle of limbs until Darius, barely able to control himself, picked her up and carried her to the only piece of furniture in the room—a bed.

As soon as he laid her down, she opened her legs and pulled him to her. He entered her in a single thrust, nearly groaning aloud from the sheer pleasure of being buried deep inside her.

"You feel so good," she sighed, running her hands over his chest. Then she trailed her fingers through his hair, and he closed his eyes, tipping his head back, enjoying the feel of it.

The first prickle of power almost went undetected. It started at the tip of her fingers where they touched his head, and spread slowly down through the rest of his body until every nerve tingled as if on fire. A ringing started in his ears, and he was vaguely aware of the woman talking, though he felt no compulsion to listen.

Pain and pleasure rode him—just as he rode the woman beneath him. As his climax drew closer, the ringing in his head grew worse and his heart started racing faster than his exertions warranted. So much so that he thought it might burst from his chest.

His climax was nearly upon him when he finally recognized what was wrong.

He knew he should break contact, but even as he tried to find the strength to do it, she tightened the muscles sheathing his member. His orgasm ripped through him, tearing a roar from his very depths. A thousand tiny bright lights burst in his head.

And then everything went blank.

In the wee hours of the morning, well before dawn, Daphne began her journey through the tunnels beneath the Crypt. The evening had been a surprising success.

She thought back to the tattooed man full of untapped energy and smiled. He'd been oh, so talented in bed. If she'd been human, there would have been no keeping up with him. Fortunately, that hadn't been a problem, and the experience had been rewarding in more ways than one. Glancing at her hand, she saw the way it glowed, lit from within by the living magic she'd siphoned off the man.

Amadja would be pleased. Perhaps there would be even more sex in it for her. The thought carried her through the remaining tunnels to the set of heavy double doors at the other end.

Upon her approach, two vampire sentries opened the doors and she went inside to where the great demon lord sat on his throne. He was impeccably dressed all in black. It drew attention to his golden eyes and ebony hair, perfectly combed back. Daphne found Amadja sinfully handsome, but she couldn't help a little frown at the sight of Tain, who sat sullen and preoccupied beside the demon. It wasn't that the redhead was ugly, for he was, in fact, very good-looking. But Tain was an Immortal and not to be trusted.

As she approached the throne, she glanced to the side at the large collection pool set into the floor. It was filled with a brilliant opalescent substance that was neither liquid nor gas. Living magic.

The pool dimensions were six-foot-by-ten-foot, and it was nearly half full of the shimmering stuff. She had been collecting it over the past several months—at Amadja's request. It was hard work, not that she'd thought to refuse. She owed him her life. It seemed an eternity ago that the Mother Goddess had locked her away in a little-known dimension. If Amadja hadn't found her and set her free, she'd be there still—not alive, but unable to die.

"Hello, love," she purred as she stepped carefully onto the dais on which the throne sat. She made sure the slit in her long skirt fell open, revealing her shapely bare leg. She saw Amadja's gaze drop and knew she'd caught his attention. "I have something special for you tonight."

She trailed her hand lightly up his arm until he noticed the glow of her skin and snatched up her hand to examine it.

"What's this?" Awe filled his voice as he looked up into her face.

"I thought you'd like it." She pulled her hand from his grasp and crossed to the collection pool, moving her hips in deliberate invitation. When she reached the edge of the pool, she dragged her fingers down the length of her arm, letting the magic collect around her fingertips like cotton candy. When she had a handful, she held her hand over the pool and let the magic slide off.

She repeated this over and over, alternating arms. Her usual yield was four or five scrapings. By her eighth, Amadja rose from his throne and came to her. She flushed with pleasure under his scrutiny.

"What manner of creature did you take this magic from?" Amadja demanded.

"I don't know, exactly," she admitted. "At first, I thought he was human, but when I felt his energy, I knew he couldn't be. Then I thought . . ." She let the words die because what she'd thought still didn't make sense.

"Did you kill him?"

Daphne gave the demon lord a sharp look. "Of course not. Do you think I would destroy my best source of magic? He passed out after we finished, so I left him to sleep it off. When he wakes, he's going to be so high on life, he'll be back for more."

She dragged her hand down her arm again for another scraping and was about to let the magic slip into the pool when a hand grabbed her arm from behind. The hairs on the back of her neck prickled when she realized it was Tain. She shivered as he ran his hand along her arm. Everyone knew Tain was insane. She had no idea what he'd do to her.

But he merely rubbed the magic between his fingers. Immediately the substance seeped into his skin, giving his complexion a healthy glow. Even the wild light in his eyes seemed to calm. It was as if he'd been lit with an inner vitality and strength.

"It can't be," he muttered to himself before addressing her. "Describe the man."

She glared at him. Despite her fear, she had no intention of taking orders from him.

"Lilith, please," Amadja said in his velvety smooth voice. "This is important."

She turned to him, hating the way his voice made her want to do as he asked. "It's not Lilith anymore," she said defiantly. "It's Daphne." Lilith was the name she used before she'd been imprisoned, and she needed no more reminders of that time.

"Daphne," he corrected. "Please describe the man."

She spoke to Amadja, but it was Tain who reacted. "Darius."

She quickly turned to him, surprised. "Do you know him?"

"He's my brother."

Daphne felt her jaw fall open and quickly closed it. "An Immortal. I saw the pentacle tattoo on the back of his neck, but even with all the living magic, he didn't feel as strong as an Immortal."

"Are you sure, Tain?" Amadja asked, clearly concerned.

"Positive," the Immortal said, rubbing his fingers together again as if he still felt the magic there. "I recognize his essence. If he's here, the others could be here as well."

Amadja clenched his hands into fists, clearly not pleased. "Impossible. We stopped that spell."

Tain looked nonplussed. "Obviously not."

Amadja heaved a sigh. "We'll have to step up our plans, unless . . ." He turned to Daphne. "Did you say you left Darius sleeping in one of the back rooms at the club?"

She nodded.

"Take us to him." He turned to Tain. "Maybe we can take care of him here and now."

Confused, but unwilling to ask for explanations, Daphne led the men back down the tunnels and to the room where she had left Darius.

"He was here," she exclaimed when she found the room empty. "There's no way he could have slept it off that quickly."

"He could if he was an Immortal," Tain said. He didn't seem surprised that his brother was gone.

Amadja sighed. "It doesn't matter. If he suspects we're here, he'll be back, and we'll deal with him then." He glanced at Daphne. "Do you think you can handle that, pet?"

She gave Amadja her most seductive smile. "You know I can."

Amadja's soft chuckle filled the room as he came to her and pulled her into his arms. "Tain, leave us," he ordered, his attention fixed on Daphne's face.

Daphne felt Tain's glare like a knife in her back, but she was too engrossed with Amadja's tongue thrusting between her lips to care.

Lexi was in a dark mood the next morning when she arrived at work.

"Good morning," Marge greeted her cheerfully.

Lexi growled something in return.

"My, we're grumpy. I would have thought after beating up yesterday's skip, you'd be in a great mood." Marge's blue eyes sparkled with amusement. "Well, I don't know if this will make things better or worse, but you've got a visitor."

Curious, Lexi stepped over to the archway that opened into their waiting room and saw Darius sitting there.

Definitely worse, she thought, walking up to him. "What are you doing here?" she asked, not bothering to be polite. "Aren't you supposed to be on your way to Seattle?"

Some emotion flickered across his eyes as he looked up at her. "Do you know me?"

Chapter Four

Lexi rolled her eyes. "Look, I'm not in the mood for games, so if that's why you're here, you can leave."

She turned and started to walk off, but Darius jumped to his feet and, grabbing her arm, pulled her to a stop. She glared at the offending hand before looking into his face. "You might be immortal," she hissed, "but unless you can regenerate limbs, I suggest you let go of me."

This time she recognized the emotion that crossed his face as a combination of surprise and amusement. He let go of her arm and held up his hands to show he meant no harm. Then he slowly reached into his pocket and pulled out her business card. "Did you give this to me?"

She narrowed her eyes. "You know I did. What's going on, Darius?"

"My name's Darius?" He seemed to test the sound of the word in his head a couple of times. Then he blinked, and his attention was back on her. "I woke up this morning in a strange room with nothing but these clothes, that card and one hell of a problem."

Lexi studied him closely as it occurred to her that he might not be playing a game. "What kind of problem?"

"I have absolutely no idea who I am."

She stared at him as she let his words sink in. The look in his eyes told her he was telling the truth. "You don't remember anything?"

He shook his head.

"Do you remember me?"

He gave her an apologetic look, and she didn't understand why his forgetting her should upset her. The man couldn't remember his own name, she silently admonished herself. Why would he remember her?

"I know I was at the Crypt last night," he told her, "but that's only because I woke up there this morning."

"Come with me." She looked over at Marge, who had been listening to the entire exchange. "We'll be in my office."

"I'll make sure you aren't disturbed," the older woman said, giving a wink that Lexi pointedly ignored.

"Actually, could you bring us some coffee?" she asked as she grabbed a bag of bagels and cream cheese sitting next to a nearly full coffee machine and led the way back to her office.

As she laid out the bagels, cream cheese and some bottles of water from her mini-fridge, she said, "I don't see any bruises or cuts on you. Are you hurt in any way?"

"No. I feel fine." He downed some water, then took the bagel she handed him. "Thank you."

"You're welcome," she said, starting to work on another bagel. "So you don't remember a thing?"

"Nothing."

Marge knocked on the door and came in carrying a

pot of fresh coffee and two cups. Lexi ignored her curious looks as she set about pouring them each a cup.

After she left, Lexi said, "I don't know how much help I'll be. We met for the first time yesterday, but I'll tell you what I know." She told him as much as she could about who and what he was—and why he was there. "It bothers me that you don't know what happened to you last night after I left," she finally said. "Maybe we should call Adrian for help."

Darius shook his head. "Not yet. If this memory loss is some kind of demon attack, I don't want to expose him to the same threat."

She nodded and reluctantly agreed. "No evidence of physical injury makes me think it's magical in origin. Maybe you were hit with a spell. If that's the case, there might be something we can do about it."

"Like what?" he asked, his brow furrowed.

"I don't know—reverse it or find a counterspell, maybe."

"You can do that?" he asked, sounding impressed. She hated to disappoint him.

"I don't have enough formal training for something like that. But I have a friend who does. She might be willing to give it a try—if you are."

He looked hopeful. "I'll do whatever it takes to get my memory back."

Lexi picked up the phone and punched in Heather's number. After a second, her friend answered. Lexi described the problem, and Heather's offer to help was immediate. "Can you bring him out here?" she asked. There was almost a breathless excitement in her voice that made Lexi frown when she hung up the phone.

"Problems?" Darius asked.

"No." She tried not to sound annoyed. Now was not

the time to act like a werewolf-in-heat trying to keep the only available virile male to herself. "She'll see us, but she lives out in Jersey, so the sooner we leave, the better."

Leading him out of the office, she stopped at the front desk to get the keys to the company car from Marge. "We're going out."

Marge smiled knowingly. "Take your time. I'll tell Jonathan that you called in sick, shall I?"

"No, that won't be necessary," Lexi told her sharply. "I'll be back when I'm done." To prove her point, she grabbed the top folder in her in-box, opened it and then snapped it shut again. "Why is this back in my box?"

"Because TJ gave it back. He says he refuses to go after Irish mobsters."

Lexi swore under her breath but didn't put the folder back. "Fine."

After a quick walk to the parking garage at the end of the block, they reached the company's black Yukon. Lexi hopped in behind the wheel and turned to check on Darius—and smiled. The last passenger to ride in the SUV hadn't been as tall as Darius, and the seat was so close to the dashboard his knees were hitting it.

"Why don't you slide the seat back?" she suggested. "Reach down on the floor. Feel that lever there? Pull up."

She waited for him to comply, but wasn't too surprised when he couldn't find the lever. There were people who rode in cars every day, knew the lever was there and *still* couldn't find it. How could she expect a man who'd only been in a car once before to know where it was or how to operate it?

"Hang on." She leaned across the center console and tried to reach under his leg to reach the lever, but the angle was awkward. She couldn't help noticing the way his leather pants molded to his skin, clearly defining the muscles of his legs—and other parts. She was in a small quandary. Unless she wanted to get out and go around to the other side, she was going to have to reach between his legs, and that meant practically lying across his lap. Was she willing to sacrifice her dignity by putting herself in that situation?

She almost smiled. *Oh, yeah.*

Leaning across, she rested the upper part of her body against his thigh. Her breasts pressed against hard muscle, and she put one hand on his knee to keep her balance as she reached her other arm between his legs.

She felt her heart pounding in her chest and worried that he'd notice it too. It occurred to her that a man who looked the way he did probably had women throwing themselves at him all the time—which might explain his earlier behavior in her apartment.

Had he actually found her attractive when he'd suggested they have sex—or had that been seven hundred years of abstinence talking?

Once again she cursed the full moon that had gotten her emotions so out of whack that she couldn't do the simplest task without thinking of sex.

Her hand found the lever, and with a nearly desperate effort, she pulled up and the seat shot back.

Pushing herself to a sitting position, she offered him a weak smile. "That's better. Oh. Seat belt." She pointed to it and tried to explain. "That strap there—it's supposed to go across—buckles there—keep you alive."

He raised an eyebrow, and she knew she was rambling. He was immortal, and so there wasn't much point in him wearing a seat belt. "Except that I can't afford the ticket if we don't click it," she muttered. "Excuse me." She reached across him again, this time purposely not touching him any more than necessary as she drew the belt across his chest and buckled it.

She moved back behind the steering wheel, and they were finally ready to go.

"Hang on," Darius said just as she was about to start the engine. When she turned to see what he wanted, he smiled and leaned across her, his arm just brushing her breasts as he oh so slowly reached for her seat belt and dragged it across her lap. She was all too aware of the friction it created when it grazed her hip. Then he buckled it. "Okay," he said in a deep voice that held a note of amusement. "Now we're ready to leave."

Lexi's concentration was in shambles as she pulled out of the parking spot and maneuvered the Yukon through the garage. They were halfway across the George Washington Bridge before she could finally relax. "Are you all right?" she asked him. "You've been quiet."

"You seemed very focused on what you were doing," he replied. "I didn't want to bother you."

"I don't get a chance to drive very often," she explained. "I'm sorry if I made you nervous."

"You didn't. You are very comfortable to be with."

Comfortable, like an old chair. She gave him a wan smile and changed the subject. "It must be"—she searched for the right word—"disconcerting not to know who you are."

"It is," he admitted. "You tell me that I lived in an immortal realm for the past seven hundred years, and yet I remember nothing about it." He paused, seeming to get lost in his thoughts. "You said we were together last night at the Crypt? Were we searching for the demon?"

"Not exactly."

A knowing smile touched his lips. "I thought not."

She gave him a reproving look. "We weren't doing *that*, either."

"Then what were we doing?" he asked, confused.

"Arguing," she said dryly.

It wasn't the answer he'd expected, but after a moment's hesitation, he chuckled.

They drove on a bit, and he grew serious once more. "I've been thinking about what you told me in your office—about how I was Called. If the Immortals were born to protect the world, why weren't we Called before the demon acquired so much power?"

"My friend Heather knows more about this than I do. But she told me that as the human race matured, they learned to defend themselves. The Immortals were Called into service fewer and fewer times until they stopped being summoned altogether. Over the centuries, the Calling spell was completely forgotten. We're just lucky some witches in Europe were able to locate a copy of it."

"How'd you get involved?" Darius asked.

"Heather. She belongs to the Coven of Light. They're the ones Amber Silverthorne contacted when she and Adrian realized what the demon was doing and needed the extra help to perform the Calling."

"Are you part of the Coven?"

She gave him a smile. "Being a werewolf sets me apart from other witches. They like working spells around the time of the full moon, and I like to . . . well, let's just say the full moon isn't a good time for me to be around increased levels of magic. I like to practice on my own, but I can't learn it all on my own, so a couple of years ago, I asked Heather to be my tutor.

Now, we're friends." She gave him another quick look. "She's good. If anyone can help you regain your memory, she can."

"And if she can't . . ." Darius left the rest of his sentence hanging, and Lexi couldn't bring herself to complete it with empty words of reassurance. If Heather couldn't help them, they'd deal with it.

They both fell silent, and fifteen minutes later, Lexi was turning into Heather's driveway. She was more than ready to find some answers to Darius's problems.

As she pulled the Yukon to a stop, a young woman in a long, flowing, terra-cotta gown made up of multiple diaphanous layers came out to meet them. Her hair was loose about her head in a wild, chestnut tangle, and the thick glasses she wore made her eyes appear unusually large for her face. Instead of making her look mousy or bookish, Lexi thought it just added to her earthy beauty.

"There you are. It's so good to see you," Heather said, wrapping Lexi in a huge embrace.

"Heather, you act like I haven't seen you in months, when it's only been a week." Lexi returned her friend's hug and then pulled back to introduce her to Darius. "Heather, this is the Immortal, Darius."

Heather stood back, visually assessing him, and Lexi felt another uncomfortable stir of jealousy. Heather would have to be dead not to find the man attractive, and from the way he was looking at Heather, he clearly found her interesting.

"Come inside," Heather urged, leading them into her living room, which had floor-to-ceiling windows along one entire wall. It gave the room the feeling of being part of the wooded area surrounding Heather's home. The other three walls of the room were paneled, and the floor was tiled. There was little furniture in the room, but the few items sitting about were covered in earth-toned fabrics.

Heather led them down a hallway, stopping before a closed door. "We'll use this room. I've already purified it."

Lexi followed Heather and Darius inside and found herself standing in a large room with a packed-dirt floor. The four walls were painted a pale green, and the ceiling was a pale blue, emulating earth and sky.

The only lighting came from four dim lamps standing in the corners of the room, but it was enough for Lexi to be able to see the four white pillar candles sitting on the floor about ten feet apart, marking the four corners of an invisible square. Lexi knew the candles marked north, south, east and west.

The last spell Lexi had participated in had been the Calling, and the disastrous outcome reminded her of the type of forces they were dealing with. Maybe trying to break the curse on Darius wasn't such a good idea.

She turned to Heather, wanting to share her concerns, but already they had moved past her into the room. She opened her mouth to say something, but at that moment, she and Darius both turned and her gaze met his. An immortal man, brought to Earth to vanquish a demon too powerful to be stopped by the combined power of witches all over the world. If anyone was taking a chance here, it wasn't she.

"Lexi?" Heather asked. "Is there a problem?"

She swallowed and shook her head.

"Good. In that case, if you'll join us, we can get started."

Chapter Five

"Lexi, if you would sit there." Heather pointed to the south corner. "As your power lies in fire, we will use it to strengthen our energy." She turned to Darius. "Sit here, in the center," she told him. "So the energy of the four elements will flow through you."

They did as she asked, and watched as she picked up a bowl of soil. "I call upon Earth, the power to make," she intoned, setting the bowl down in front of the north candle. She returned to her collection of items and picked up a censer. Lighting a match, she touched it to the incense until it caught fire. Then she blew both out and carried the censer to the east corner and set it down. A small stream of smoke curled upward, and Heather waved her fingers through it. "I call upon Air, the power to take."

Next she turned to Lexi and nodded. Lexi conjured forth a small fireball and held it in her hands.

"I call upon Fire, the power to grow," Heather said.

Then she returned to her collection, picked up a bowl of what Lexi was sure had to be rainwater or water from a nearby stream and carried it to the west corner. "I call upon Water, the power to flow."

Earth, air, fire and water. The four elements had been called, so now it was time to cast the circle.

Heather picked up a large container of salt and, starting at the east candle, poured a small stream onto the floor behind it. She continued pouring as she walked in a Deosil, or clockwise, direction, making sure she stayed inside the circle she was creating.

"Green power and gold; red power and blue; here the power we do unfold; quarters' might, strong and true. Four the winds to weave the round, 'tween the worlds the power be bound. Till we send it at the last, guardians keep it strong and fast."

It was the chant for calling the elements; Lexi recognized the words from Rhiannon Ryall's *West Country Wicca*.

"The circle is now closed," Heather said when she was once again at the east corner.

She set the salt down and picked up an eloquently carved white pillar candle, which she placed in the center of the circle, in front of Darius, and lit. "Greetings, Mother Goddess. She who was, is and always will be. Maiden, Mother, Crone. We welcome you and beseech you, guide and bless our efforts here today. We ask your help as we try to break the spell on your son." She reached up and unclasped a necklace from around her neck. When she lowered her hands, Lexi saw there was a dark green stone with reddish-orange spots hanging from the chain. "We ask that you bless this moonstone, which will help to unblock his mind and allow him to reclaim his memories." She laid the moonstone at the base of the candle and then returned to her collection of items to get a bouquet of flowers. These she also laid at the base of the candle. "We welcome you, Mother Goddess, into our circle. The wisdom and powers is yours. So mote it be."

Then she picked up a cast-iron cauldron and carried it to the north corner, where she sat down. For several seconds, she sat there quietly, eyes closed, and Lexi knew she was grounding herself; gathering her energies. A prickle of magic skittered across Lexi's skin, and she found herself looking around to see if the others had noticed the increase of magical energy inside the circle.

Heather opened her eyes and looked at Lexi and Darius in turn. "Let us begin," she said quietly.

Pulling a black taper candle out of the cauldron, she held it up. "I have dipped this black candle nine times into white wax before covering it again in black. This represents how your attacker tried to hide his or her curse from you. Next, I will inscribe an uncrossing spell on its surface." She picked up a small needle and began writing on the candle, working quickly from the base of the candle to the top. When she was done, she lit the candle, let a few drops of wax fall into the cauldron and then quickly stuck the candle in the wax.

"Thy will I see and spells I bind. I banish you and all your kind. Thy work is done, there is no more. We vanquish thy power forevermore." Heather repeated the chant nine times, and when she finished, they sat silently until the candle burned down completely. Lexi wasn't sure what she expected to happen—or to feel. She looked expectantly at Darius, but his expression was unreadable.

At Heather's slight nod, Lexi let the fire in her hands go out and watched as Heather thanked the Mother Goddess for being there, got to her feet and extinguished the Goddess candle. "So mote it be," she said. She picked up the moonstone and fastened it around Darius's neck. The stone lay against his chest, where it was nearly lost in the tattooed artwork behind it.

Heather then went to the east corner and began dragging her foot along the circle of salt, this time moving in the Widdershins, or counterclockwise, direction. When she was once again back in the east corner, she turned to look at them and smiled. "The circle is now open."

"Do you remember anything?" Lexi asked, getting to her feet just as Darius was. At his perplexed look, she clarified. "Of your past; of what happened last night?"

When he shook his head, Lexi cast a quick glance at Heather, who merely smiled. "It would be great if it worked that way, but highly unlikely. Give it time and keep that moonstone with you."

She blew out the four white candles and led Lexi and Darius out of the room. "Can you stay for lunch before you go back?"

Lexi felt a tinge of guilt. "I thought it might be better if Darius stayed here with you. That way, he'd be in the protection of the Coven of Light."

They'd stopped walking, and Darius was giving her a strange look. Heather did a better job of hiding her curiosity. "Darius is, of course, welcome to stay here with me," she said, giving him a smile. "However, I think if that had been the Goddess's intent, he would have appeared to me in the first place." She held up her hand when Lexi opened her mouth to argue. "Besides, if he runs into trouble before his memory returns, he's better off being with a fire-wielding werewolf than with me."

Darius said nothing, and Lexi knew there was no

point in protesting. So she followed after them to the kitchen, where Heather, a vegan, fed them a fresh salad. Afterwards, Lexi hugged her friend good-bye, and then she and Darius got into the Yukon and headed back to the city.

Along the way, Lexi stopped at a fast-food place and ordered four cheeseburgers and two Cokes. Once they were back on the highway, she dug in the bag, intending to pull out a burger and hand it to Darius. She stopped as a thought occurred to her. "You eat meat, don't you?" she asked him. He was, after all, an Immortal, living with the gods and all that. Maybe they had some credo about eating only plants.

He had been staring at the bag, but now looked up at her, a quirky smile on his face. "Yes."

Smiling, she pulled out a burger and handed it to him. "Here you go—I think you'll like this. It's called a cheeseburger."

He took it from her and stared at it for a second while she pulled another from the bag. She used her knee to steer for a moment while she unwrapped her burger and then she bit into it, immediately feeling better.

"I love Heather and would never want to insult her," Lexi said around a mouthful, "but there's a limit to the number of fruits and vegetables I can eat. It's just not possible for a werewolf *not* to be a carnivore. It's our nature."

She glanced at Darius and saw him unwrap his burger. After only a slight hesitation, he took a bite.

His face lit up. "It's good."

She gave a slight chuckle. "I thought you'd like it." After that, the drive back to the city was done in companionable silence as they both finished eating.

In the parking garage, Lexi pulled into the empty Blackwell space and turned off the engine. She turned to Darius. "I don't suppose you've remembered anything?"

He shook his head.

"I'm sorry," she said. "I don't know what else to do. I guess we can go back to my place and wait. Or call Adrian?" she suggested hopefully.

"Or . . ." He picked up the file folder sticking out between the driver's seat and center console. "Didn't Marge say something about an Irish mobster?" He opened the folder and made a show of reading it, though Lexi had no idea if he could understand English.

"That's all right," she assured him. "It's just a delinquent leprechaun. I can do it later."

He gave her a dubious look. "I lost my memory, not my intelligence or my abilities. I've spent a millennium hunting down demons, vampires and other sources of evil. I've even, from time to time"—he held up the folder—"hunted down leprechauns. If you've ever hunted one before, you know how tricky they can be. You'll be glad I was there to help."

"How do you know you've hunted demons and leprechauns?" She didn't doubt it was true, but if he'd lost all his memories, how did *he* know it was true?

He cocked his head like he was thinking, and then gave a slow smile. "I just remembered. I wasn't trying to remember—I looked at the folder and suddenly the memories were there."

"Do you remember what happened last night?"

"No, nothing that recent. Just some old memories of hunting with my brothers." He smiled again. "I remember my brothers—Adrian, Kalen, Hunter and Tain."

"The spell's working," she breathed. "Don't try to

force it." She looked at the file clutched in his hand. The truth was that she *had* hunted leprechauns before, and the thought of having help was appealing. "All right. You can come with me."

She took the file from him and opened it, quickly scanning the known facts of the case and reading them aloud. "Patrick Darby—arrested two weeks ago on charges of public intoxication and lewd behavior. His lawyer secured bond for him, and Darby, in true leprechaun fashion, disappeared." She paused, flipping through the rest of the papers, looking for more information. "There's not much here."

"Every leprechaun I've known loves to drink," Darius offered.

"There are an awful lot of pubs around here, so I guess we'd better get started," she said.

Apparently the luck of the Irish was with them. It only took three stops before they'd found the right place. Several heads turned their way when they walked into O'Rourke's. Lexi imagined they made quite a pair. Darius with his tattoo-covered arms and chest, black duster and pants. She dressed in black leather as well, with her long black hair pulled back in a braid. They stood just inside the doorway while their eyes grew accustomed to the dim interior.

"What can I get you?" the bartender asked.

"I'm looking for a leprechaun calling himself Paddy Darby," Lexi said. "He's in his mid fifties, wrinkled eyes, bushy white eyebrows and thick hair. Know him?"

The bartender nodded to the far corner. Turning to look, Lexi saw a small man in a bright bottle-green coat, sitting alone at a table with a nearly empty bottle of whiskey in front of him. He was so short that his legs didn't reach the floor.

She and Darius moved forward quietly, so as not to alert the little man, who had obviously been drinking for quite a while and was singing loudly.

" 'Oh, the end is nigh, me bonny lass, so here's a kiss good-bye. We'll not fare well when they loose the hounds of hell, so lift the tankard high, love and drink until ye die.' "

It wasn't the rowdy drinking song one typically heard in bars. In fact, Lexi thought this one was a bit of a downer. Well, whatever reason he had for being upset, it wasn't her problem. What *was* her problem was bringing the little guy in.

She and Darius approached from different sides, hoping to take him by surprise. She was less than four feet away when he scrambled about on his chair and stood up.

"Friends and neighbors," he shouted, lifting his mug in the air. "The end is almost on us. Join me in another round, won't ye—"

He fell silent when he spotted Lexi, still quietly moving forward. She saw alarm register in his eyes and knew the instant he decided to run for it.

She raced forward just as he leapt off the chair and ran to the back of the bar. He was as fast as legend reputed leprechauns to be, and by the time Lexi and Darius reached the back of the bar, he had disappeared down a hallway.

Lexi and Darius exchanged looks, but neither knew where to start looking for the man. Then Lexi caught the stench of whiskey on the air.

"This way," she said, already moving to follow the trail. There were a couple of doors off the hallway, but the whiskey scent was strongest near the last door on the right, so that was the one she went through.

The leprechaun was there, panting and waiting to see if they'd find him. Seeing them come through the door must have rattled him, because he began racing around in circles, clearly confused and disoriented.

Suddenly he stopped his crazy circling and, giving them a mischievous smile, ran straight at the wall.

"Stop him!" Lexi cried. "If he teleports through, we'll never catch him."

Lexi and Darius leapt at the same time, arms outstretched, trying to catch the leprechaun. Before they could reach him, he hit the wall with a sickening thud and toppled over, like a cut-down tree.

Lexi stared at the unmoving body, stunned. "I guess he was too drunk to magic himself through the wall." She moved forward, pulling her cuffs from her belt. When she reached him, she bent over to slip the cuffs around his wrists.

In the blink of an eye, though, he rolled to the side, jumped up and raced for the wall again.

This time, he vanished through it, leaving behind a single shoe.

"Damn it," she swore, quickly clipping the cuffs back on her belt.

"Sneaky little devil, isn't he?" Darius sounded amused. "Still want to go after him?"

"Hell, yes," Lexi said, stooping to pick up the little shoe.

"Then we'd better hurry," Darius said from the open doorway. "Looks like there's an exit down the hall here."

She hurried after him, down the hall and out the exit.

Outside, standing in the alley, they looked around.

Unsurprisingly, there was no sight of the leprechaun. She strained to hear the sound of tiny, running feet, but all she heard was the blaring of horns and the rumbling of buses from the nearby traffic.

She walked up to the back wall of the bar, stopping at the spot where she thought the leprechaun might have come through the wall. "What do you think?"

Darius came up beside her and bent low to examine the bricks. He touched a spot and then pressed his fingers to his thumb several times, as if the little man had left behind a sticky residue, which was now on his fingers. After a second, he nodded. "That's the spot."

She held the shoe up to her nose and took a deep whiff. Memorizing the odor, she stripped off her clothes and, ignoring Darius's raised eyebrow, handed everything to him. "Try to keep up." Then she morphed into wolf form.

Immediately her perception of the world changed. Everything came into sharper focus; the smells were stronger and the sounds were louder. It was always this way when she first shifted, and she reveled in the heightened senses of her wolf form.

She sniffed the wall and caught the leprechaun's scent. Then, casting a quick glance at Darius to make sure he was paying attention, she took off.

She ran down the alley, but when she reached the end where the alley crossed the main street, she had to stop. The odor of exhaust fumes interfered with her ability to follow the scent, and the flow of traffic kept her from moving about to see where the trail might pick up again. Darius must have understood, because suddenly he was there, holding up his hands and stepping out into the middle of the busy street. Car horns blared and irate drivers shouted, but Lexi ignored them all as she trotted around, trying to locate the scent.

She was about to give up when a faint breeze stirred and she caught a whiff of the familiar scent of Irish clover and whiskey. Giving Darius a quick bark to let him know she'd found the trail, she took off running.

The scent led down four blocks, past pedestrians who turned to stare because the sight of a werewolf in New York City drew attention, though at least no one was running away from her screaming in terror. Lexi ignored them as she continued down the street, her focus on following the leprechaun's scent as it mingled with the smells of roasted nuts, hot dogs and car fumes.

She had to give the little guy credit. Even drunk, he certainly covered a lot of ground in a short period of time. She was starting to feel a little winded and couldn't help wondering how Darius was doing. A quick backward glance showed he was keeping up.

When the trail turned down another alley, Lexi knew the little man was getting tired. Without realizing it, he'd just turned down a dead end.

Slowing her stride to a walk, she focused on her other senses and was rewarded when her lupine ears picked up the faint sound of heavy panting. Her quarry wasn't too far ahead of her now.

"The trick in dealing with leprechauns," Darius said softly beside her, "is you must never give them time to think about what they're doing."

Lexi understood what he was telling her and moved into a trot as she followed the scent down the alley. There was a Dumpster up ahead, and she paused beside it to listen. A scurrying noise behind a nearby overturned box drew her attention, and she pounced on it.

The impact of her foot against the box sent the little man scurrying out. He was so intent on keeping an eye on her that he didn't pay attention to how close he was to the wall. He hit it with bone-jarring force and for the second time that night, bounced off and landed on his back. This time, Lexi didn't give him a chance to roll away from her. She pinned him to the ground with her paws, teeth bared and growling.

Darius appeared and slipped a golden cord around the little man's neck. "That should hold you," he said.

Darius was holding the cord loosely in one hand, and before Lexi could growl a warning, their prisoner jumped up and threw himself at the wall again. This time, some of him actually went through, but his head, neck and shoulders stayed behind, anchored by the cord.

"Ye can't hold me," the little man said in a heavily slurred voice. "I'll disappear." His laugh sounded like a cat coughing up a fur ball, and Lexi, even in wolf form, wanted to roll her eyes.

The leprechaun struggled to loosen the golden cord from his neck, and when that didn't do any good, he began hopping around, pulling back on the rope, looking much like a bass on the end of a fishing line—mouth open wide as he flopped around on the ground.

Darius held firmly to his end of the cord and watched the little man's attempts to escape with unveiled amusement. "He's not going anywhere," he said to Lexi. "You can change back."

He turned his attention to the sleek black wolf watching him so intently with those light gray eyes. Even in this form, she was stunning.

He knew he should look away, but he couldn't resist

the temptation of watching her morph. With the air still shimmering around her, she was a vision to behold. Her long dark hair fell around her like a sheer veil, accentuating her figure. His hands itched to hold the full weight of her breasts; his thumbs ached to stroke the dusky rose nipples that had beaded against the slight chill in the air. Her slim waist made the gentle flare of her hips all the more inviting, and Darius let his gaze travel down the length of her, pausing briefly at the dark curls at the apex of her thighs, and then traveling further down to the long length of nicely toned legs. Darius couldn't move, lost between awed reverence and thoughts of what it would be like to crawl between those legs.

"Saints almighty, but she's a rare one."

Startled from his thoughts, Darius furrowed his brows and glared at the leprechaun, who was also staring at Lexi. Feeling Darius's gaze on him, he looked up and winked. "I wouldn't be minding taking her for a wee ride."

Darius yanked on the cord, jerking the leprechaun forward until the small face connected with his fist. "Don't look at her."

The leprechaun clutched his nose, yelling obscenities. "What the hell? You can't tell me what to do."

Darius raised an eyebrow as he handed Lexi her clothes. Then he turned his attention back to the leprechaun. "I can do anything I damn well please. Now turn your head and give the lady some privacy."

"No," the leprechaun said with the defiance of a five-year-old. He puffed out his chest and took a step toward Darius, but the effect was more comical than anything because he only stood as high as the Immortal's crotch. Darius saw the leprechaun's intent clearly, and when the small fist came out to smash him in the balls, Darius slapped a hand to his chest and unleashed Fury.

The tattooed dragon's head came to life with a mighty roar, growing larger by the second until it was the size of a pony. The leprechaun's eyes widened in fear at the sight of the snarling beast with rows of razor-sharp teeth. At that moment, fire shot out of the dragon's nostrils, and the little man screamed, jumping as far back as the cord around his neck would let him—which wasn't far.

Lexi, who had changed back to human form and dressed, appeared at his side. Darius spared her a quick glance to see if she was frightened, but he should have known better. Instead she gave Fury a final look before turning to glare at Darius.

"I would appreciate it if I could deliver my prisoner in one piece," she told him. "Preferably still alive."

"Why take him in at all?" Darius asked. "You're wasting your time."

Taking out her cuffs, Lexi tried to grab Paddy long enough to secure his wrists, but he wouldn't stop thrashing against the cord. "What do you suggest?" Lexi asked between clenched teeth, giving Darius a frustrated look when she couldn't grab the little man's hands.

Darius shrugged. "I could let Fury eat him. I doubt anyone would miss him." At the suggestion, Fury swooped down, pinning the leprechaun to the ground.

Darius noticed that while Lexi kept a careful eye on Fury, she took advantage of the situation to move slowly toward the leprechaun. When she was close enough, she snapped the cuffs around his wrists. "Call off that thing," she ordered him. "I'm taking him in. He's not worth much, but I do have bills to pay."

Darius made a small gesture with his hand, and Fury shrank down to the size of his fist. Then he floated to the place over his chest where he had been moments before and slowly fused with his skin.

When Darius looked up, Lexi was glaring at him. He smiled—he couldn't help it. He enjoyed pushing her to get a reaction. Like the other time . . . he shook his head to clear away the fog and let the faint memory grow stronger.

"We've done this before, haven't we?"

Surprise lit Lexi's face. "Yes—I guess we did. Yesterday. You remember that? It was right after you appeared."

"Some of it." The memory of pain flashed through his head, and he remembered the Calling spell that had signaled the need for him to come to Earth. He remembered fighting with Sekhmet, then being pulled away to appear before Lexi. There were still some gaps, though.

"The rest will come," she assured him as if she'd known he was worrying about it. He gave her a grateful smile and walked with her to the end of the alley, pulling the leprechaun behind them. When a cab pulled up, he, Lexi and their prisoner squeezed into the backseat.

"I'll make it worth your while to let me go," Paddy Darby said after they'd been riding in the cab for several minutes.

"What?" Lexi looked at the leprechaun curiously.

"Ye said ye had bills to pay," he explained.

Lexi glanced at Darius, but he kept his expression bland, waiting to see if she could be bribed.

"I suppose you're offering me your pot of gold?" she asked. "No, thanks. It's probably Irish mob money."

"I don't have a pot of gold," the leprechaun mumbled so softly that Darius almost didn't hear him. He didn't try to make Lexi another offer, but fell sullen and silent, leaving Darius to wonder what kind of trouble he must be in.

More serious than simple public intoxication, he thought. A leprechaun's pot of gold was his life's fortune and so much more. It represented what it meant to be a leprechaun. A leprechaun who had lost his pot of gold was a failure and a disgrace.

Darius would have liked to question the little man about it, but just then the cab pulled in front of a large building and came to a stop.

"We're here," Lexi said, opening her door to get out.

"Where's here?" Darius asked her.

"Jail. We're going to leave our friend here, so he can think about whether or not he wants to jump bail in the future," Lexi said, pulling the leprechaun out of the car.

"I won't be here long," the little man said. "I have friends—powerful friends—who will get me out."

"Maybe so," Lexi said, pulling him up the steps of the police station. "Let's hope they like you enough to be willing to post bail again."

At that, the leprechaun's face paled considerably. Darius had seen that look before on men's faces. It was the look of someone who, given the choice between the task before him and death, would have chosen death.

Chapter Six

The sun was just starting to go down by the time Lexi finished the paperwork at the station and she and Darius were able to catch a cab to her place.

Lexi had no sooner walked in the door than her cell phone rang. She answered it and heard Mai's voice.

"Hey," Lexi said. "How are you?"

"Great."

Lexi heard the satisfied smile in her friend's voice. "Good time, was it?"

"Oh, my God. It was fabulous."

She sounded so excited that Lexi was actually surprised. "Really? You got a lot of good stuff for your article?"

"Well, no. That's why I have to go back tonight. Want to come with me?"

"Can't," she said, sneaking a look at Darius, who was walking around her living room, inspecting the knickknacks on display around the place.

"Why not?" Mai asked. "The full moon is less than a

week away—I know you need to relieve some of your magical angst."

Mai was right. Lexi could feel the pressure building inside her. It was bad enough trying to function in a state of extreme arousal all the time, but now she'd compounded the problem by bringing Darius home with her. Although maybe that wasn't a bad thing. "Not tonight," she told Mai. "I—"

"You can go if you want," Darius interrupted from across the room. Lexi clamped a hand over the receiver, but it was too late. Mai had heard his voice.

"Who was that?" she asked.

"I, uh, have company," Lexi admitted.

"That's my girl," Mai exclaimed. "Who is he? Is he hot? Did you meet him last night? He must be good in bed. I bet he's hung like a—"

"Good night, Mai."

Lexi disconnected the call, looking at Darius, who was standing across the room, giving her a knowing smile. She felt her heart speed up and found herself thinking that Mai had a point. A man who had centuries of experience under his belt, so to speak, would have to be good in bed, wouldn't he?

She tried to rein in her thoughts, but it was useless. Darius had a definite bad-boy aura with the duster on, but she was afraid to invite him to take it off because then he'd be half naked and that was too much temptation for her to resist right now.

Not wanting to be rude, but needing to put a little space between them, she headed into the kitchen and started searching the pantries for food. "Are you hungry?" she called to him, opening the fridge door to look inside.

"Famished." His low voice rumbled from right behind her, causing her to jump. She turned and saw that his gaze had been focused on her rear, and he was a little slow in raising it to her face. That show of interest kept her off balance.

"I'm afraid I don't have anything," she said hurriedly, closing the fridge door. "We can either go out or order in."

He gave her a slow smile. "If 'order in' means staying here, I choose that."

She thought about suggesting they go out anyway. She knew that as tempted as she was, and the way he was looking at her, if they stayed in tonight, they were going to end up between the sheets—assuming they even made it to the bedroom. As much as she wanted the sex, she really didn't want to make him even more egotistical.

As if he knew she was about to protest, he added, "I wanted to ask you more about some of the things I'm remembering. It's hard to know what's real and what isn't."

Damn it, she thought. How could she refuse a plea for help without coming across like a total jerk? "All right," she agreed. "We'll stay in. What do you feel like eating?" Between his knowing smile and her raging hormones, she heard the answer: *you*.

Ordering herself to get a grip, she tried for a casual tone of voice. "How about pizza?"

Without waiting to see if he agreed, she picked up the phone. It was a reflection of just how pathetic her life was that she knew the number by heart.

It didn't take long to place the order, and when she hung up, Darius had disappeared. She went looking for him and found him standing naked to the waist, his back to her, in the middle of the living room. She saw that even his back was tattooed. A broadsword angled from his right shoulder blade to his left hip was the most prominent image, though there were others as well.

At her gasp, he turned, and the sight of him left her totally speechless. She'd seen most of the tattoos despite the duster, but without it on, they were so much more obvious to her: the golden serpent over his heart, the dragon, the golden rope, the Chinese throwing stars and the various daggers and axes along his arms. The tattoos were the first things she saw, but then she saw the contours of a well-muscled chest that tapered to washboard abs and slender hips. He reminded her of a football player or that wrestler-turned-actor The Rock. "The pizza will be here shortly," she said, trying to stop staring. "Do you want to sit in here and watch TV?" She paused. "You've heard of television, haven't you?"

He smiled. "I've heard of it, but I've never seen it."

"Then come on." She gestured to the couch. "You're in for a treat."

She turned on her television set and found something to watch. Darius sat next to her on the couch, and she was able, for a while, to pretend that this was an ordinary evening spent with a casual friend.

When the pizza came, Darius ate with enthusiasm, making her glad she'd thought to order two large instead of her usual one medium. "I guess they don't have pizza where you're from," she commented, feeling a little silly to be so delighted that his first experience with pizza should be with her.

Darius, whose attention had been focused on the TV show, glanced at her and swallowed the bite he was chewing. "No. In fact, they don't have a lot of things in Ravenscroft." His voice held a note of bitterness. "I've only been here two days, and already I can understand why my brothers left."

"Do you have just the four brothers?"

He nodded. "What about you? Any brothers or sisters?"

"One sister. Beverly. We were twins." She felt the familiar ache she always felt when she thought of her sister.

Darius put down his pizza and gave her his undivided attention. "Were?"

"Yeah. She died a year ago from complications during surgery." She hadn't planned to say any more about it than that, but he listened with such empathy and attention that soon she was pouring out the entire story. Before long, she even lost her resolve not to cry, and a single teardrop rolled down her cheek.

Embarrassed, she brushed it aside and took a breath. "Wow—I bet that was more than you wanted to know. Tell me about you. These tattoos, for instance." She reached out to touch the dagger on his arm and then stopped short. "Is it safe to touch?"

"Probably not."

"I'm sorry?" He'd spoken so softly that even with her lupine hearing, she wasn't sure she'd heard him correctly.

"Nothing," he told her, holding out his arm. "You can touch it."

She laid a finger against the blade of the dagger tattoo. Part of her expected to feel cool metal, and she was a little surprised when she felt the warmth of his skin instead. Intrigued, she traced her finger along the length of the blade until she heard his quick intake of breath. She looked up, and the heat of his gaze nearly singed her.

She had to try twice before she could find her voice. "How do they work?"

"They morph into the real thing when I need them to. My mother, Sekhmet, has a bad temper, which makes for many enemies. For her, every day has the potential to be a battle, and she doesn't believe in going unprotected. She wanted me to always be prepared, so she made me a gift of these tattoos."

"Do they hurt?"

"You mean when they morph and become real? No. I hardly notice it."

She picked up his arm, wanting a closer look at the dagger. As she moved it this way and that, she was barely aware of how intimately she was touching him.

"Do you want to hold it?" he asked her, his voice sounding strained.

Her gaze snapped to his, wondering if he was actually referring to the dagger—or to something else. She decided it was only her depraved mind that gave the question double meaning.

"Yeah," she replied, unable to keep from sounding just a little breathless.

He chuckled at her reaction and placed his hand over the handle of the dagger. She noticed that the air above it shimmered slightly right before the image sharpened. Then he was suddenly holding the actual dagger in his hand. He flipped it around and handed it to her.

Its weight surprised her. Flipping it over, she watched the light play off the metal blade. It was as real a dagger as she'd ever seen, representing lethal power, danger and excitement all in one. Just like the man.

She knew it was the influence of the full moon making her all too aware of the man, but that didn't mean she could stop noticing.

She handed the dagger back and watched as he touched it to his skin, where it shimmered and faded until it was the tattoo once more.

"What exactly is that dragon on your chest?" she asked, when her gaze traveled over the small tattoo. "I think it scared Paddy sober." She gave a small laugh, but then saw him looking down at her with slightly raised eyebrows. "Okay, okay. It scared me too," she admitted. "A little. What is it?"

"It's Fury."

"Excuse me?"

He smiled. "That's what I call him." He turned toward her so she could get a closer look at the tattoo. Sitting this close to him, she was overwhelmed by his strength, his vitality—in short, by him.

She tried to hide her reaction by examining the tattoo. Looking closer, she was impressed with its detail. Even when it was small like this, no bigger than the size of her closed fist, it was intimidating.

"It's a demon."

Her eyes snapped up to his face in surprise. "A demon?"

"His real name is Fuhramek. He's the last of the Bocca demons. About six hundred years ago, he was terrorizing one of the Immortal realms, so I went to get rid of him. We were locked in battle for close to a year."

"What? Do you mean you fought off and on for a year?"

"No, I mean we fought—no breaks, no food, no sleep, no nothing—for a solid year."

"But how can that be? Without food or water you'd . . ." She suddenly realized how it was possible. "You were both immortal, so you couldn't die."

"Being immortal doesn't mean that by the end of a year of fighting we weren't in bad shape. We became too weak to fight any longer. We agreed on a temporary stay so we could recuperate, after which time we would return to resume the fight."

"You trusted him to show up?"

Darius smiled. "The Bocca demons aren't like typical demons. They lived by a very strict code of ethics. If Fuhramek said he'd be back, then I knew he'd show up." His eyes took on a distant look. "I left—went home, ate, slept and regained my strength. When I went back to resume the fight a year later, I found Fuhramek looking worse than I'd left him. He told me that when I left, the portal had shut, and because it had been created from the energy of living magic, he—a death-magic creature—couldn't open it without expending great energy—which he didn't have. He'd been stuck there the entire time."

"So you killed him and turned him into a tattoo?" Lexi asked.

He gave her a sharp look. "I too live by a code of ethics. No, I didn't kill him. I freed him from the dimension so he could regain his strength."

"Why? If you were just going to try to kill him, why help him get stronger?"

"Destroying an enemy too weak to fight is a slaughter—there's no honor in that."

She felt the conviction behind his words, appreciating for the first time what a man of conviction and morals he really was.

"What happened?"

"The extra year had made him too weak to travel home. Because all demons feed off the energy of living magic, I allowed him to feed off me to regain his strength. I knew he wouldn't try to kill me by taking all my energy, because there would be no honor in it for him. It was a slow process, and as time passed, we forgot our differences and talked. I guess we became friends. I learned that he was in that other dimension because he was trying to get home. So, in the end, instead of fighting him, I helped him get home. Only it turned out there was no home."

Darius took a deep breath as if remembering that time. "Sometime while he and I had been fighting, another demon race came along and destroyed his home dimension, leaving Fuhramek the last of his kind. I took him back home with me, but he wasn't comfortable being among the gods and goddesses of Ravenscroft. He was going to leave, and that's when we realized the harm I had done by allowing him to feed off my energy. Instead of restoring him back to health, I'd given him a life-long addiction to my immortal life force. Though he tried, he could no longer exist on his own. After a while, he started taking the form of one of my tattoos just so he could stay in contact with me."

Lexi stared at the tattoo. "Doesn't it hurt to have something that is death magic fused to your body?"

Darius smiled. "After all these centuries, I don't think there's much death magic left to him."

She mentally shook her head. It was just so different from anything she was used to. She dragged her attention away from his mouth and moved on to the coil across his stomach. "What about this? This is the rope you used on Paddy, isn't it?"

"Yes. The magic behind it allows it to assume and retain the shape I want it to, despite what others try to do to it."

"And this one?"

One by one, she touched the tattoos on his chest, listening to the stories behind their origin, though she was only listening with half a mind. The rest of her thoughts were focused on the feel of his skin, his scent and the sheer magnetism of the man himself.

"What about these?" she asked, touching the lightning bolts on his shoulder, unknowingly leaning toward him as he faced her on the couch.

His gaze met hers, and she could barely focus on his answer. "Those are a gift from the sun god, Re. They're some of his fire bolts."

Aware of just how close they were sitting, she wet her lips and tried to refocus her thoughts on the tattoos. "What about this one?"

When she touched the golden serpent over his chest, he shivered.

"It's new," he whispered, leaning forward to close the small space between them. "And I don't want to talk about tattoos anymore."

Chapter Seven

Darius's lips felt moist and warm as they captured hers. Instantly the hunger inside her raged out of control and she clutched at him, returning his kiss with a nearly frenzied intensity.

He grabbed her to him, and she ran her hands along his broad shoulders before embracing him.

"You taste so good." Darius's voice sounded husky. He let go of her long enough to reach between them and started working at the buttons on her shirt. The backs of his hands brushed against her aching breasts while he worked, and Lexi felt her nipples harden in response.

She couldn't stop a small groan from escaping, and it seemed all the encouragement he needed. Grabbing the front edges of her shirt, he ripped it open. Immediately she felt the cool air caress her overheated skin. He pushed her shirt back, baring her shoulders, then lowered his head to kiss the swell of her breasts. When he cupped her, his hands felt warm through the thin fabric of her bra.

She fought to free her arms from her shirt and then quickly unclasped her bra. As Darius pulled it off, she had a moment's hesitation. What was she doing?

As soon as Darius's mouth covered one of her nipples, all conscious thought fled and she could only react to the flicking of his tongue across her nipple and the tremors racing through her body.

He suckled her until she felt the moisture gather between her legs. Need pulsed through her, hot and insistent. She struggled to reach the waistband of his pants, but figuring out the foreign clasp was beyond her ability for rational thought.

"Off," she gasped.

He left her long enough to stand, and she watched unashamedly as he pushed his pants down his legs, much too slowly for her taste.

Lexi swallowed hard at the sight of his engorged shaft. Then the wolf in her rose, and inside her head she released a primal mating howl.

When Darius reached for her, she placed her hands in his and let him pull her to her feet. He made short work of her jeans, and when they pooled at her feet, he gathered her naked body close. She reveled in the hard warmth of him and felt the length of his shaft pressing insistently against her, throbbing with a need and life of its own.

"Bedroom," he demanded, lifting her into his arms.

"Hallway. Last door on right," she directed between a frenzy of kisses.

As soon as they reached her room, they fell onto the bed in a tangle of arms and legs. Almost immediately his shaft probed the juncture of her legs, and she opened for him. When he pushed into her, she gladly welcomed him. Still kissing her, he proceeded slowly, filling her inch by delicious inch. Deeper and deeper he went until she could take no more. Then, with aching slowness, he withdrew. She clutched his shoulders in a frenzy as the sensation of his length rubbing against her created a friction that nearly undid her. Every fiber of awareness centered on the tension building inside her.

Before he could completely pull out, he drove himself forward. Then once again, slowly, he withdrew. Each time he pulled away, he reached between them and began pleasuring her most sensitive spot until her inner core cried out for him to fill her once more. He continued this way until she thought she would burst into a thousand pieces. She fought against her impending orgasm, wanting this moment to last as long as possible.

When Darius began to slow his movements, she thought it might be another tactic to prolong the experience. She opened her eyes to glance at his face and saw that his eyes were glazed over—with passion, she presumed, and privately reveled in her effect on him.

Then, to her amazement, Darius flipped them over without pulling out. Now she was on top, straddling his hips as he lifted her up and then let her slide down his erection.

Though her eyes were closed, she felt him shudder, and when she rolled her hips, he released a groan of pleasure. Setting her own rhythm, she milked the experience for all she could. When her orgasm hit, it was like a tidal wave slamming into her, taking her breath away.

As she gradually came back to her senses, she noticed Darius had grown very still beneath her. She was fairly certain he hadn't found his own release and wondered if he might be allowing her this moment to enjoy hers to its fullest before seeking his own pleasure. It was an unexpected, selfless gesture, and she opened her eyes, wanting to see his face when she thanked him.

At first, she thought he'd merely closed his eyes too, focusing, like her, on the physical aspects of their lovemaking. After a moment, though, when he still didn't look at her, she noticed his low, steady breathing, and the horrible truth finally dawned on her. He was asleep.

Darius stood in the middle of an open mist-covered field on top of a mountain. He turned around, and everywhere he looked, the view was the same—acres of grass and an endless expanse of sky.

He was confused. Mere seconds ago he'd been in bed with Lexi. Then, suddenly, he was here—and he didn't even know where "here" was.

He started walking, picking a direction at random, but after taking several steps, he stopped because he realized that he hadn't really moved. Bending over, he plucked a few blades of grass and rubbed them between his fingers. Oddly enough, he felt only the friction of his fingers rubbing against each other. Intrigued, he lifted the crushed grass to his nose. There was no scent.

It was all an illusion. All of it.

He was in the dream dimension. There was magic at work here—incredibly strong magic if it was able to make him fall asleep in the middle of the best sex he'd had in seven hundred years. Someone was going to pay.

A prickling along his neck told him he was no

longer alone, and he turned to see the figure of a man approaching.

"Whitley!" He hurried across the grassy field, grabbing the man's upper arms in warm greeting when he reached him. "What are you doing here?"

The priest smiled as he returned the half embrace. "It's good to see you, son. Your mother wasn't sure if we would be able to contact you."

Darius couldn't help wondering if this was another one of his mother's tricks to get him to come back. "What's the matter?" he asked warily.

"Your life is in danger."

"What?" At first, he thought Whitley was joking. After all, Darius was an Immortal. His life was never truly at risk. But Whitley didn't look like he was joking. "I don't understand."

Whitley's expression was grave as his gaze traveled over Darius's nude body. At the priest's questioning look, Darius shrugged. "Your timing wasn't the most opportune. I'm sure I'll have some explaining to do."

Whitley gave him a sympathetic look. "Probably more than you realize." He took a breath and explained. "When you broke the orb, your life essence naturally returned to you. However, it wasn't restored properly." His gaze shifted to the golden serpent over Darius's heart. "As long as this tattoo remains intact, you are safe. However, the tattoo itself is vulnerable, and should something happen to it . . ." He paused as if he couldn't bring himself to finish. "Right now, you are as close to being mortal as you have ever been."

Darius tried to absorb exactly what he was being told. "Are you telling me that this tattoo *is* my life essence? That if it's harmed, I could actually die?" He raised his head to look at Whitley and saw the concern in the other man's eyes.

"We don't know how vulnerable you are," Whitley went on. "There was no way of knowing."

"Damn her," Darius muttered.

"Sekhmet never meant to hurt you—" Whitley began, but Darius held up his hand to cut him off.

"Don't. She never means to hurt the ones she loves—she just does. And you know exactly what I'm talking about."

Whitley's expression became guarded. "What do you mean?"

"You've lived with us my entire life. You know what she's like." Off in the distance, lightning flashed across the sky and it grew darker. "She wanted to protect me, so she stole my entire reason for existing. Now, because she wanted to keep me with her, she's placed my life—and that of everyone on Earth—in danger."

"Don't be that way," Whitley reprimanded. "She deeply regrets the danger she's placed you in."

Darius wasn't sure he believed that, but he knew it'd be wise not to argue. "Thank you for the warning," he said. "You can send me back now. I still need to find the demon responsible for all the problems on Earth." He purposely didn't tell Whitley about Tain, because he didn't want the information to get back to Ravenscroft where Tain's mother might hear about it. It would break her heart.

Whitley cleared his throat. "There's one more . . . little problem."

Darius knew, before he even heard it, that he wasn't going to like whatever it was. Another bolt of lightning streaked across the sky as dark clouds drifted in, an eerie reflection of his mood. "Better tell me what it is."

"Your mother was concerned that you might fall victim to the temptations available on Earth—specifically the temptations of the flesh, which she blames for your brothers not returning. She didn't want the same to happen to you, so she tried to cast a protective spell on you."

"She what?"

Whitley had the decency to look embarrassed and dipped his head. "It was supposed to help you not be distracted by sex—except that you were being pulled to Earth when she cast the protection, and you know the spell is only as good as the portion you heard. From what she remembers, um, I think it might be best if you didn't have sex while you are there."

The warning bells went off in Darius's head as he thought back to the words he'd heard his mother shouting: *In . . . physical love . . . find . . . pleasure . . . forget . . .*

A bolt of lightning cut across the sky again.

"She didn't want to keep you from having some fun," Whitley hurried on. "She just didn't want you to remember how much fun it was."

"Damn it, Whitley," Darius shouted. "Stop speaking in riddles."

Whitley sighed. "All right. Basically, it's this: If you engage in sex long enough to climax, you'll forget—everything."

Darius clenched his fists together. At least now he knew how he'd lost his memory that first night, he thought. "Of all the things she's done to me . . ." He swore. "Why would I want to go home?"

"Don't say that," Whitley said quietly.

"Is that everything?" Darius fought to keep his temper.

Whitley nodded. "Yes—that's it."

"I need to go," Darius said, noticing that the sky had grown very dark now and the lightning was getting worse. "Is this Mother's temper we're experiencing?"

Whitley looked around, a worried expression on his face. "No, I don't think so."

"I was afraid of that." There was the possibility that a demon was nearby, possibly even inside the dream realm itself. If that was the case, it was best that he and the priest leave as quickly as possible. "Can you release us?"

Whitley nodded. "Be careful, son. And keep that tattoo safe. I don't want to lose you."

"I'll be careful," he promised, stepping forward to give the man a hug. "Tell Mother . . ." He hesitated. "Don't tell her anything. I'm not sure I can forgive her interference this time."

Whitley took a step back and in the blink of an eye, he was gone. So was the grass and dark sky. Darius found himself lying in Lexi's bed once more. When he looked around, she was nowhere in sight.

Then he heard the clinking of dishes coming from the kitchen and caught the aroma of freshly brewed coffee. He glanced at the window, wondering just how long the dream had lasted, and saw sunlight shining through.

Not good, he thought. He'd not only fallen asleep, but he'd slept through the night. Sitting up, he noticed that Lexi had at least covered him. He pushed the blanket aside, got out of bed and, finding his folded clothes sitting on the dresser, put them on.

Then he took a breath and braced for the confrontation sure to come.

Lexi stood at the counter, vigorously dicing an onion. Each downward stroke of the knife accompanied a dark thought about the man sleeping in her bed. How dare he fall asleep right in the middle of sex? How tired would he have to be to do something like that? She didn't think anyone could be *that* tired. Had she bored him to a state of unconsciousness?

Yeah, she liked that explanation so much better. Not.

She put new effort into slicing the onion, trying to ignore the faint noise behind her indicating Darius was finally awake. She refused to turn around and acknowledge him. Frankly, she had no idea what to say. Even the scathing insults and put-downs she'd mentally rehearsed were forgotten.

"So I'm wondering," his voice floated to her in a very conversational tone, "just how mad are you?" She sensed him coming close and wasn't surprised when he appeared beside her. "I'm going to guess that you're pretty upset."

The last thing she wanted was for him to have any clue how upset she was. She didn't want him to think he had any control over her emotions. "I'm not mad," she said, surprised at how calm she sounded.

"Right. That's why you're destroying that defenseless vegetable."

She carefully set the knife aside and carried the plastic cutting sheet to the frying pan into which she scraped the onions. "I like it cut up small."

She set the cutting board back on the counter and picked up the green pepper. When she reached for the knife, though, Darius covered her hand with his. When he didn't immediately say anything, she looked up at him.

"Despite how it looked, I didn't fall asleep on you." He gave a half laugh. "Sleeping was the furthest thing from my mind, believe me."

"But you *did* fall asleep." She couldn't help sounding accusatory.

"Lexi. You're a smart woman—and a witch. You're familiar with spells and summonings."

"What are you saying?"

"It was lousy timing, to be sure, but I've come to expect that from my mother."

Lexi's eyes opened wide. "Sekhmet summoned you? To a dream world?" She considered the possibility and definitely liked it better than the alternative. "Why?"

He pulled the cutting board to him and, picking up the knife, began dicing the pepper. "It's a long story."

She gave him a look. "I have time."

He shrugged. "Okay. Well, our parting wasn't under the best circumstances," he said. "You know that Tain, Adrian, Kalen and Hunter aren't my brothers in the sense of our sharing the same parentage, right? Our mothers are different, but they're all aspects of the Mother Goddess. The last time the Immortals were Called to Earth, my brothers never returned home. It broke their mothers' hearts, and Sekhmet swore she would never let it happen to her. So one night while I was asleep, she stole my life essence from my body."

Lexi was shocked. "You're kidding."

He shook his head. "I wish."

"Did you ask for it back?"

He scowled at her. "Oh, gee, that never occurred to me." His voice held bitterness and sarcasm. "Of course I asked for it back."

"What did she say?"

"She refused, of course. And without my life essence, I was physically bound to Ravenscroft. I'd basically become her prisoner. Not that she treated me poorly," he quickly amended. "I could travel the Immortal realms, but I couldn't leave—not even when the Calling Spell summoned me."

That explained why he didn't show up the night of the ceremony, she thought. "I hate to state the obvious," she said. "But if you can't leave Ravenscroft"—she flipped her hand, palm side up, gesturing at nothing in particular—"what are you doing here?"

"That's a longer story."

He explained how his life essence was now contained in the serpent tattoo on his chest. Lexi found herself watching the way his hands worked as he continued to chop peppers. She remembered the way he'd stroked her body last night and quickly cut off the memory.

"So Sekhmet summoned me to warn me there could be complications," he finished, his expression unreadable.

"Like?"

He heaved another sigh, and she was beginning to realize he did that before he delivered bad news. "Like, the tattoo is vulnerable to attack, which makes me vulnerable too."

"How vulnerable?" He didn't answer, so she reached out and grabbed his hand, stopping him from dicing the pepper. "Darius, that tattoo is over your heart. Exactly how vulnerable are you?"

He gave her a tender, indulgent smile. "You sound worried."

She hated that he was right. "I *am* worried. If something happens to you, who's going to stop the demon and Tain?"

He set his knife down and gently took her by the arms, turning her until she had no choice but to look at him. He was standing too close, affecting her ability to think. "Don't worry about them. I'll take care of it. Now, I've put off leaving for Seattle too long and I must go."

She sighed, knowing he was right. "I'll make your reservation, and then we should call Adrian to let him know what's going on. I'm surprised he hasn't already called wondering what happened to you."

"Thank you for all your help," he told her.

She nodded, feeling self-conscious. She knew she should pull away from him, and yet she couldn't. He was studying her so closely, she felt herself drowning in his heated gaze. Then his mouth came down on hers.

Her lips parted on a surprised gasp and he took advantage of the small opening to slip his tongue inside. He tasted like danger and adventure rolled into one, and the intensity of his kiss robbed her both of breath and conscious thought.

Automatically she wrapped her arms around him, returning his kiss with the ferocity of the wolf inside her. She felt her passion rise, felt herself teetering on the edge of something more powerful. When he broke the kiss, Lexi was glad to see that he looked as shaken as she felt.

The kiss rocked Darius to his core. *When this is over, I'll be back for you.* He didn't say the words out loud. He couldn't. Not when there was a chance he might not survive the weeks to come. But the gods had brought him to this woman for a reason, and he was beginning to think he knew why. It wasn't just because she could put him in contact with his brother. He looked down into her face, saw her dazed from his kiss but not angry. He couldn't stop the small smile that touched his lips. "About the plane reservation," he reminded her gently.

She blinked several times, as if trying to bring the world back into focus, and then nodded. "Right." She stepped away, and he reluctantly let her go. "You should eat while I jump on the computer." She fixed him a plate of food, and he ate while she worked.

Twenty minutes later, Darius was on the phone, explaining to Adrian about his memory loss and missing the flight. He purposely omitted his newly discovered vulnerability. Adrian would refuse to let him help if he knew Darius's life was at risk.

Once Adrian had all the new flight info and they'd hung up, there seemed to be no more reason to linger at her apartment, so they caught a cab to the airport. Lexi helped him check in and then, because they still had a little time to kill, she stood with him outside the security gate, going over the directions one more time with him.

"No matter what, don't take off your tattoos. If you do, they'll not only kick you off the plane, they'll arrest you." She waited for him to nod that he understood and then went on. "You don't have any luggage to worry about, so just follow the flow of people getting off the plane and eventually you'll reach a public access area where Amber and Adrian will be waiting for you."

He gave her a patient smile. "I'll be fine. The airport can't be worse than the demon wars of the mid-twelfth century."

"No, I'm sure it's not," she agreed. "I just don't want you getting lost or feeling like you don't know what to expect."

"I like that you worry about me," he said, stepping closer to her. "I like knowing that you care."

He watched her lips form a denial and saw it fade. She was a study of contradictions. One minute she was acting as if she couldn't care if he lived or died, and the next, she was standing by his side like a protective mother, making sure he came to no harm in the strange, new environment.

Her appearance was another contradiction. From the way she dressed, one would assume she was cold and hard. Yet in his arms, when his lips touched hers, she turned warm and compliant. He didn't let himself think about whether she did that with every male. What was important was that she did it with him. He wondered if she'd do it now, there at the airport.

Looking down into her upturned face, he felt himself getting lost in those light gray eyes. He lowered his head, noticing that she wasn't trying to move away from him. He was so close, he could practically taste her lips already.

Then he caught a flash of neon pink out of the corner of his eye. It was so unexpected—and yet familiar—that he turned to get a better look and saw a young woman wearing a bright pink hat walk by. The image triggered the last of his missing memories and they came rushing back.

"I know where he is," he told a stunned Lexi.

"Who?"

Darius watched the woman in pink disappear into the crowd, then turned back to Lexi, who was not looking very happy. He wondered why until he remembered that he'd been about to kiss her. He was still holding her too close for polite conversation. The moment was over, though, and there were more important things to demand his attention.

"You remember the first night I was here? You walked out after we danced. I stayed behind. I remember now. I went into the back rooms with a woman.

She had bright pink hair—like that woman's hat." He pointed in the direction where the woman had vanished from sight. "You can't see her anymore, but she's not important. This woman I was with was a demon."

"So?" Lexi growled, giving him a dark look. "There are as many demons in these nightclubs as vampires, and almost all of them run the back rooms."

Darius was shaking his head. "I know the demons you're talking about. I saw them there, but those are lesser demons. They feed off living magic, but never take more than they can digest at one time. They're relatively harmless. This woman I was with wasn't one of those. I don't know why I didn't recognize her for what she was the minute I saw her, except that maybe my ability to sense the magical auras in others is as dysfunctional as the rest of my magic." He was rambling, but now looked at Lexi, wanting to make sure she caught the full impact of his next words. "She was a succubus."

"A succubus—in the Crypt?" Lexi asked, sounding incredulous. "I thought all the incubi and succubi were destroyed ages ago."

"They were," Darius said. "Or at least I thought they were. This one must have survived somehow."

"Is she the Big Bad that you're supposed to be fighting?"

"No. I remember Adrian saying that the ancient demon was male. While most demons can shift their sex, the incubi and succubi are gender specific and can't change."

Lexi gasped. "You're lucky she didn't kill you—isn't that what they do? Kill their partners? Why didn't you get out of there the moment you realized what she was?"

Because that was when he'd climaxed and Sekhmet's

spell had gone into effect, he thought derisively. But his being killed by a succubus wasn't nearly as important as his other discovery that night. "Because she said that she thought the back of the neck was a better place for the pentacle tattoo than on the cheek."

She gave him a confused look. "No offense, but so what?"

"Don't you see? She was talking about Tain. He must be there, at the club—and I have to rescue him."

Chapter Eight

Settled into a cab racing back to the city, Lexi turned her attention to Darius. The mere sight of him drove her nuts. One minute he was about to kiss her, and the next, he was immobilized by the sight of another woman walking by. One minute they're making love, and the next, he's fallen asleep. She was starting to detect a pattern here, and it all pointed to the same conclusion: Darius found her boring.

The thought was depressing, so she turned her attention to the matter at hand. "Adrian is convinced that Tain has turned rogue," she said. "What makes you so sure he's in need of rescuing?"

"Tain finds joy in every aspect of life," Darius said. "I refuse to believe that he now wishes to destroy it."

"Centuries of torture would affect a man's mind," she reminded him.

"Not Tain's," Darius said adamantly.

Lexi saw no point in arguing with him. "We should call Adrian and Amber and tell them you missed the flight," she said.

"Fine. Do that, but don't say anything about Tain."

She tried not to take offense at his abruptness, knowing that despite what he said, he must be troubled with doubts regarding his youngest brother.

After her call to Seattle, Lexi punched in Mai's number, hoping her friend might have gained some info for her article that they could use. But, strangely, there was no answer on Mai's cell phone. Lexi shrugged it off and disconnected.

Thirty minutes later, they were standing outside the front door of the Crypt. In daytime, the place looked innocent enough, but she knew that looks could be deceiving.

Just for the hell of it, she tried the door, but as expected, it was locked. "Now what?" she asked. "Technically, breaking and entering is against the law."

He looked down at her. "You think I care about your laws?"

She glared at him. "Being arrested wouldn't exactly do wonders for my career—and a stay in jail with some of the skips I brought in wouldn't do wonders for my health. Besides, there's a security system. If we try to break down the door, we'll have half the police force here before you can say 'bad idea.' "

"You worry too much," he told her, sounding much too calm. "I'll have it open in no time."

"Yeah?" she snarled. "Do you have a battering ram tattooed on your dick?"

His eyes momentarily widened in shock, but then he smiled and casually reached inside his duster and touched his back. There was a telltale shimmer of magic, and when he pulled his hand out, he was holding a small gold key. "More like a key tattooed to my ass—well, slightly north of my ass if you want to get technical."

He held it up, and she saw that it looked like an old-fashioned skeleton key, with a long, cylindrical barrel and a couple of teeth at the end.

"That's not going to work," she pointed out.

"Have a little faith." When he held the key to the doorknob, it shimmered and changed its shape until it resembled a modern-day key. To her further amazement, it slid easily into the deadbolt, and when Darius turned it, she heard the sound of the lock sliding back, and the light on the security system flashed green.

Totally amazed, she shook her head as Darius returned the key to his back. Then, glancing up and down the street to make sure there was still no one about, she pushed open the door. Inside, the place was empty, and the silence echoed eerily.

"Any idea what we're looking for?" she asked him, letting her eyes shift to wolf form, so she could see into the darkest shadows as she moved through the room.

"I'm thinking they're probably keeping Tain underground, or maybe in a parallel dimension linked to this building. What we need to find is the door or portal leading to it."

Lexi looked around and saw several doors leading to the restrooms, the sex rooms and the offices. "These doors all look pretty ordinary," she said. "How will we know we've found the right one?"

"It's not going to be any of these," Darius told her. "The doorway will most likely have a spell on it to keep it hidden." He glanced at her. "How are you at detecting spells?"

She gave him a dour look. "Maybe we should call Heather."

He shook his head and tapped his chest. The air above the Fury tattoo began to shimmer, and slowly the demon dragon emerged. This time, instead of becoming the size of a pony, Fury remained fist-sized and hovered quietly in the air.

"I'm looking for the mark of demon spell. Can you help me?" Darius asked.

Lexi saw Fury blink both eyes once, and then he zipped about the room faster than either she or Darius could have walked on their own. On his second circuit, he stopped before one of the red panels of drapes. Darius and Lexi quickly went to see what he might have found.

"There's a door here," Darius told her after they both looked.

"I don't see anything," she said.

"Trust me, it's there." He reached beneath his duster, and when his hand re-emerged, he was holding the skeleton key. He slowly waved it before the panel, and each time it passed over a specific spot, Lexi thought she saw the key shimmer, but it never changed its shape.

"It's here," Darius said. "But the spell is too strong for my impaired magic." He turned to her. "I wonder . . . if you were to generate one of your magical balls of fire, maybe I could tap into your energy."

Lexi was curious to see if it would work and immediately summoned her magic, creating a small fireball in her palm. Unsure how Darius planned to tap into her magic, she was surprised when he held the key near her. She immediately felt the magic in her hand being pulled toward the key. As the pull grew more powerful, the shape of the fireball distorted, stretching and twisting until the tip of the elongated sphere touched the key. Then the key sucked up the fireball and Lexi was left holding nothing but air. The key, however, was now glowing brightly.

Darius held it over the area where it had shimmered earlier, and this time, the key's form shifted, growing smoother, rounder, longer.

Lexi stared at it in surprise. "Did your key just turn into a wand?"

"Don't the witches and wizards in the modern century use wands anymore?"

Lexi frowned. "Actually, I don't know. I've not seen any. I thought they were mostly used as theatrical props."

"Well, this one is quite real." The key had completed its transformation, and Darius stood back. He sharply pointed the wand at the area of the panel where the key had shimmered. A flash of light shot out of the end of the wand and exploded against the panel in a shower of red, green and white sparks.

Lexi stared at the spot, positive nothing had happened, and then . . . "I'll be damned," she muttered as the panel of drapes vanished and in its place stood a door.

"Thank you, Fury," Darius said, and with a quick dip of his head, Fury flew to Darius, stopping to hover in front of the tattoo-free portion of his chest. Then the air began to shimmer, and when it stopped, Fury was a tattoo once more.

"Shall we?" Darius asked, grabbing the doorknob and opening the door.

Inside, they found a nice cherrywood desk, floor-to-ceiling bookcases filled with books and mementoes, and a credenza with a decanter filled with a bloodred liquid and glasses sitting on top. It was entirely too corporate-looking for a vampire-owned nightclub, in Lexi's opinion. Except for the artwork. The two graphic vampire-human orgy scenes were exactly what she'd expected.

"What are we looking for?" she asked Darius, who was studying the pictures. At her question, he turned, and she thought she detected the barest hint of a smile on his face, but, fortunately, he didn't make any suggestive remarks.

"I don't really know," he told her. "Anything that might tell us more about the demons holding Tain."

Lexi looked around the desk as it occurred to her that there was no computer. No one did business these days without one, and it didn't make sense that they would carry a laptop back and forth each day. As well hidden as the office was, there would be no need. They couldn't have anticipated someone having access to an Immortal's magic key.

The more she thought about it, the more the office looked fake, like this was yet another illusion.

She took another look at the layout of the furniture in the room. The two floor-to-ceiling bookcases flanking the credenza were piled high with books of varying sizes, stacks of papers and folded newspapers, most covered with dust.

The entire left wall was one large bookcase. The shelves of it were neatly lined with leather-bound book collections, and there was little dust on these books.

"How many demons do you know who read Tolstoy?" Lexi asked.

Darius looked at her and then at the bookcase she'd been studying. He moved to stand just before the wall and raised his hands, trailing them over the shelves and books. Then she heard a click and the bookcase split in two, with the top half rising up into the ceiling while the lower half disappeared into a space that had conveniently opened in the floor.

Lexi was left looking at six small screen monitors, one larger one, a panel of dials, switches and a central keyboard.

"Nice trick," Lexi said, impressed.

"Any idea what this is—or how it works?"

Lexi pulled the desk chair over and sat down. "An idea is about all I've got. I'm guessing that each of these screens is linked to a camera and depending on where these cameras are located, this is either a security system or an entertainment system."

She ran her hand across the panel, making note of each one. When she found the power switch, she turned it on. Immediately the six smaller screens flickered to life. "Entertainment system," Lexi said when the images cleared and she found herself looking into four different private sex rooms and two views of the group sex room.

She looked around the control panel and noticed a second power switch, so she pressed it and soon saw a sequence of boot-up commands flickering across the larger screen. She'd found the computer.

"Surprise, surprise," she said derisively a minute later. "They're mostly video files stored here." She randomly selected one and played it.

An image of a private room filled the computer screen, and she watched as a male vampire and a human female walked in. It was with a kind of stunned fascination that Lexi watched the vampire undress the woman and carry her to the bed. Soon he had her beneath him on the bed and they were vigorously getting it on. There was no sound, for which Lexi was grateful. It was bad enough to watch without the accompanying animal-like, rutting noises.

"Mother Goddess," Darius swore as he stood behind Lexi and watched the screen.

Feeling extremely self-conscious, Lexi closed the video file and selected another. This one showed two same-sex couples performing. Lexi closed it and opened another. This time, she got footage from the main bar area. She was about to close it when a familiar face appeared on the screen—Mai.

Lexi quickly checked the date of the video—it was from the night before. She turned back to the video and saw that Mai was no longer alone. Lexi zoomed in on the image, hoping to get a better look at the man she was with. He seemed to be in his mid-thirties, had short blond hair and was very clean-cut, different from the type Mai usually chose. Lexi fast-forwarded the video and saw Mai and the man disappear into a back room. Thirty minutes later, they reappeared together, walked to the front door of the bar and left.

Lost in thought, Lexi let the video run. She wondered if the reason Mai wasn't answering her phone had anything to do with the blond. He'd been very attractive.

The reappearance of the man on screen caught her attention. This time, he was alone and he walked through the bar straight to the back rooms.

When he came back out, he was accompanied by a petite woman with bright pink hair. Beside her, Lexi heard Darius gasp. "That's her," he said. "That's the succubus."

The couple on the monitor seemed barely able to keep their hands off each other as they walked through the bar. When they reached the front door, they stopped to talk to the bouncer. Lexi watched the bouncer pull out a card and pen from his pocket and hand it to the man, who scribbled something down before handing both back. The bouncer in turn took the card and tacked it to the wall, next to a series of other cards tacked there.

Then the blond man walked out the door with the succubus on his arm.

Lexi let the video play, but there was nothing more to see. Closing the file, she happened to notice the time on the computer.

"It's going to be getting dark soon," she told Darius. "We don't want to be here when the vampires start waking up."

He nodded. "Let's go."

She stopped the video, closed the files and turned off both the security and computer systems. Then Darius was able to locate the mechanism to return the bookcases to their previous position and they left the office. When Lexi turned to look back at the door, it was gone, replaced once again by the hanging panel of drapes.

They walked through the club and as they reached the door, Lexi saw the board where the bouncer had tacked the card. She found the one posted in the video and took it down.

"If the succubus is as dangerous as you say, maybe

we should pay this Howard Parks a visit," she suggested.

"Good idea," Darius said. "Let's go."

They left the club, taking care to lock the door behind them. As they headed down the sidewalk, Lexi pulled out her cell phone and called Mai's apartment again. There was still no answer. She tried Mai's office and cell phone in turn, with the same luck. Lexi was starting to get concerned now. This wouldn't be the first time her wood-nymph friend had gotten into trouble during an investigation.

Five years ago, Mai had infiltrated the inner circle of a major con-artist ring. But she had let herself get too involved with the thugs running the show. The only reason she was still alive was because she'd been arrested on minor charges for involvement in one of the scams before the ringleader had a chance to discover what she was up to and kill her.

Already into her next project, Mai had been too distracted to remember her court date and ended up in Lexi's in-box as the skip of the day. And they'd been friends ever since. Lexi just hoped Mai's luck was still holding out.

Darius was silent for much of the ride to Howard Parks's apartment. Lexi thought they were going there to question the man about the succubus. Darius just hoped Parks was still alive. For the succubus to leave the nightclub, she must have felt very confident about her safety. The demon lord's power and influence was even greater than Darius had first thought.

When they reached the apartment building, Darius found the front door locked.

"We can't get in without the access code," Lexi told him.

He started to reach for his key, but she put out a hand to stop him. "I don't think that will work this time." Instead, she turned to the panel of buttons beside the door and ran her finger down the list of names beside each button. When she stopped, she was pointing at the name "Parks."

She pressed the button and then looked at him. "Maybe he'll let us in."

They waited for a full minute, but nothing happened. "If not"—she continued pressing the rest of the buttons—"there's a chance someone else is home and expecting company.

To Darius's surprise, he heard a slight buzzing noise followed by the sound of the front door unlocking. Lexi grabbed it before it could lock again, and the two went in. They took the elevator to the fourth floor and Darius followed Lexi down the hall.

"This is the address on the card," Lexi told him, stopping in front of one of the doors. She looked at him. "You know that this guy might not know anything."

Darius nodded. "Let's see what he has to say anyway."

She knocked on the door and waited a full two minutes before knocking again. After the third time, Darius pulled out his key.

Inside, it seemed like an ordinary apartment—clean but lived in. Everything was turned off, like the owner had left for the day.

"Doesn't look like he's home," Darius said. Lexi didn't respond, and when he turned to look at her, she had a peculiar expression on her face. "Lexi?"

"I don't know," she said slowly. "Something doesn't

smell right." Without another word, she walked to the back of the apartment and disappeared into one of the three rooms.

Darius followed more slowly. He was noticing the trail of men's clothes that started in the living room and continued down the hallway. They lay in heaps, like someone had taken them off in a hurry and forgotten them. In an otherwise tidy apartment, he knew what it meant. Parks hadn't been *able* to pick up his clothes after sex with the succubus.

"Found him," Lexi hollered a second later, and Darius didn't need her to tell him Parks was dead.

In the back bedroom, he saw Lexi standing beside the bed, looking down at a very still form. "If I didn't know better, I would say he died of old age."

Moving to stand beside her, Darius looked down at the body. Howard Parks, whom he'd guessed to be thirty-four or thirty-five from his image on the video, now looked ancient. His face had aged, the skin withered. His blond hair had lost its luster and appeared gray. Even the hands, resting on top of the blankets, looked frail and worn.

"I've never seen a demon do this," Lexi said softly.

"Not a demon," he corrected. "A succubus. They're a thousand times worse than the demons you're used to seeing. They don't just feed off living magic. They suck their victims dry, leaving behind this dry, withered shell. It's why the Mother Goddess destroyed them all those years ago."

"All except this one," Lexi pointed out.

"Yeah. All except this one."

"Damn it," Lexi suddenly swore. "I've got to get out of here." She was already heading for the door.

"Wait, where are you going?"

She stopped and stared at him, for the first time truly understanding how he felt about his brother Tain. "My best friend was with this guy last night. I don't fully understand what's going on, but I'm afraid Mai is somehow mixed up in it. I've got to find her—now."

Chapter Nine

Lexi left Darius to further study Howard Parks's apartment and caught a cab to Mai's building.

The doorman greeted her by name as she entered, but Lexi had no time for pleasantries. She had a hard time holding still during the elevator ride. When she reached Mai's apartment on the tenth floor, she knocked and listened closely.

Knocking again, she waited. When Mai still didn't appear at the door, Lexi used the key her friend had given her.

"Mai, you home?" she hollered as she opened the door, not wanting to surprise Mai if she was in the bedroom entertaining a guest.

A quick inspection of the apartment showed that it was empty. There were signs that Mai had been there, however. The dress Lexi had seen her wearing in the video was lying on the bedroom floor beside the closet. There were dirty dishes in the kitchen sink, and an unfinished glass of soda was still on the table. The ice had long since melted, but when Lexi shook the glass, the soda still fizzed. Mai had been there sometime in the last couple of hours, which went a long way toward easing Lexi's worries.

She walked over to the kitchen counter, looking for a notepad so she could leave Mai a message to call her. Noticing Mai's calendar lying open, she turned it toward her and read the one appointment Mai had entered for the day—and it left her feeling cold. *9:00 p.m., The Crypt, Domino Costume Party—Party room in back.*

By 8:45 p.m. Lexi had turned down several offers to have sex. She was standing in the back of the Crypt, near the registration desk for the party room, so she supposed it was natural that men would assume she was looking for action.

Not for the first time since they parted that afternoon, Lexi wished Darius were at her side. As frustrating as he could be sometimes, at least he was someone she could confide in—someone she could trust. They hadn't made plans to meet up again, but she figured he'd be back at the apartment when she got home.

Home is looking better and better, Lexi thought as she waited in line for the domino party. She had hoped to find Mai before it started. After running home from Mai's place to change clothes and make a quick call to Heather, she'd immediately returned to the Crypt, but she still hadn't spotted her friend.

Lexi was beginning to grow anxious. She just wanted to find Mai and get the hell out of there. The longer she stayed, the greater the chance she'd actually have to participate.

She glanced at her watch and saw it was 9:00. The

party hostess was gesturing to her. Did she really want to go through with this?

The image of Howard Parks's withered face flashed before her, and she knew there was no decision to make. She pushed away from the wall and followed the hostess into the back.

There, she was shown into a dressing room, instructed to remove her clothes and don the black hooded robe hanging there. She was handed a shiny white domino mask and told not to leave the dressing room unless she was wearing that mask. It was not to be removed under any circumstance for the duration of the party.

Once she was in costume, Lexi turned to examine her appearance in the mirror. It was startling. The mask covered most of her face so that she was completely unrecognizable. With the cloak and hood on, it was difficult to tell if she was male or female. Distinguishing Mai from the rest of the guests would be next to impossible. But right now, this was the best option she had.

When Lexi left the dressing room, she was shown into the large group-sex room. Though she'd never been there before, it looked just as it had on the video. It was a large open room with area rugs laid out in two rows, so that the room seemed divided in half. On each rug there was either a collection of pillows or an overstuffed bench that reminded Lexi of a narrow twin-bed mattress.

Hidden behind the mask, Lexi felt more comfortable moving into the room. Other guests were arriving, and Lexi noted that while some guests wore the white domino masks, others wore black ones. She hoped this was how she could tell the men from the women.

Lexi walked about the room, taking a closer look at each figure, trying to decide which of the white-masked people might be Mai. She was distracted from her search when a black-masked figure walked up to her and let his hand trail down her arm.

"Have I got a treat for you, pet," he said in a self-assured tone that grated on her nerves. Before she could think of anything to say, he opened the front of his gown, proudly displaying his erection.

"Impressive," she said. But was it real? She silently spoke the incantation Heather had given her and generated enough of her magic to give the incantation strength. Immediately the man's aura shifted to black, and Lexi knew she was facing a demon. "Not interested," she said and moved on before he could stop her.

She invoked the incantation again and immediately saw that while most of the females in the room were human, most of the males weren't. There were only a couple of men whose aura showed the white of a living-magic creature. Lexi made her way toward them. If she were going to have sex with anyone tonight, it was not going to be with something of death magic. These times were too dangerous. But if she didn't find Mai soon, she had to get a partner, or they'd make her leave.

Spotting a tall, cloaked figure with a white aura, she made her way toward him. She was almost to him when she noticed another figure in a white mask moving his way. Before Lexi could get close enough to draw his attention, the other figure opened the front of her cloak, exposing her charms.

Almost immediately, several other males rushed to her from across the room. The male who had been the intended target merely walked past them—and away from Lexi.

By now, couples and small groups were forming. Lexi saw that the other living-magic creature in the room had taken a partner, which left her with the choice of a demon or the tall man. Though the demon was closer, Lexi hurried after the tall man, catching up to him just before he reached another woman. Lexi grabbed the back of his cloak and gave it a tug, to get his attention. When he turned around, she gave him a slow, seductive smile.

He reached out to brush the back of his fingers against the lock of hair escaping from her hood. His hand dropped from there to run lightly across her breasts. Her nipples immediately stiffened. She blushed, embarrassed to have such a reaction to a complete stranger, especially when he seemed to notice.

It's just because of the full moon, she told herself, though it was difficult to form the thought as the man was now palming both breasts through her robe. She felt a tightening between her legs and struggled to remember why she was there in the first place: to find Mai.

He kissed her then, and the hunger rose. The wolf in her demanded that she mate with this male, that she alleviate the need growing inside her. Her senses turned lupine, and suddenly everything in the dim room seemed more intense. The music being piped in rang clean and clear, distinct from the gasps and moans coming from the couples all around them. And the smell of sex was everywhere.

Lexi felt moisture pool between her legs, and when the man opened her robe and pushed the fabric aside, she welcomed the cool breeze against her overheated skin. When he ran his hands across her, his roughened palms created a delicious friction that left her shivering.

Individual actions were lost as her entire being was focused on the sensations he aroused. She was barely conscious of having moved to lie on one of the beds. When the man climbed on top of her, she didn't care that he still wore his robe—she only cared that his erection was merely pressing against her while she wanted it inside her.

She rubbed herself against him until he lowered his mouth to the nape of her neck and gently sucked at the skin, pulling a reaction from deep within her belly. She responded by reaching down between them to take his pulsing member in her hand and, closing her eyes, guided him to her where—thank the goddess—he finally took the hint.

She felt the rounded end of his shaft probing the opening between her legs as he used her moisture to coat the head of his penis. Her body stretched to accommodate him as he pushed into her, and she had the fleeting thought that this was the second time in less than a week that she'd been with a man who filled her so completely. Then the thought was gone and she was consumed with a hunger so fierce, she thought it might devour her whole if she couldn't satisfy it. She contracted her inner muscles around him, squeezing with enough pressure that his hiss of breath brushed against her neck.

Opening her eyes, she saw that the man's robe had fallen open. A rush of white-hot desire shot through her, and she didn't even try to suppress the urge to let her hand travel across the expanse of his chest, pushing his robe back.

Lost in the tactile sensation of all that male virility, she didn't at first notice the textured pattern of colors across his chest. When she did, she had to blink several times to make sense of them. Then, to her horror, she realized she was looking at a golden serpent in the shape of a figure eight tattooed over his heart and a smiling dragon tattooed on the opposite side.

"Darius?" she croaked, pushing at his chest until he stopped. "Mother Goddess—Darius, is that you?"

He blinked down at her several times as if waking up from a dream and forcibly swallowed. "Yeah, it's me."

"What are you doing here?"

He sort of shook himself and then glanced down to where their bodies were joined. "I would have thought that was obvious." He moved his hips, and it was enough to drag a gasp from her. She couldn't help moving her own hips in response.

"Mighty Re," he swore, "give me strength." He pulled off his mask first and then hers. "I thought I could . . ." He swallowed again. "I was wrong. You feel too good. I . . ."

He looked off into the room, like he wasn't sure what to do. Then his head jerked up a little further and she heard him mutter, "There she is." Then he was unceremoniously scrambling off her. "Lexi, I . . ." He looked across the room once more. "I'll explain later—I have to go."

She hadn't even had a chance to bring her knees back together before he was running away, leaving her more humiliated and angry than she'd ever been before.

Whipping her robe about her, she got off the couch and raced from the room, pushing through the crowd. She was barely conscious of being out in the cool night air. With her head down, she had only one goal—to go home—but she'd only taken a couple of steps when she ran straight into a warm, hard male body. She gasped an apology and tried to make a quick escape, but the arms holding her wouldn't let her go.

"Whoa, Lexi. It's me."

Startled to hear Ricco's voice, she looked up. "What are you doing here?"

His smile turned to a frown. "I'm looking for some missing members of my gang, but more important—are you all right? You're crying."

She shook her head, unable to find the words, but when she tried to move past him, he wouldn't let her. "Did someone hurt you? Because if they did—"

"No, it's nothing." She wiped at her eyes and tried to offer him a reassuring smile, but couldn't. Thanks to the full moon and recent events, her emotions were raw and her hormones were, apparently, beyond her control. Tears of hurt and anger started coursing down her face.

"Here, now," Ricco said, leading her away from the club and around the corner, where he pulled her into his arms and held her. It felt so nice to be comforted that, before she knew it, the tears were really flowing, but she couldn't bring herself to tell him why. That would have been too embarrassing.

After a few minutes, she'd stopped crying and felt more in control. "It's my fault. I should know better than to go into a party like that so close to the full moon. How could I possibly have thought I could stay detached?"

At that moment, Lexi heard Darius calling her name.

She must have tensed, because Ricco glanced down at her. "Is that the guy who hurt you?"

"Yeah, but I don't feel like talking to him right now."

"Well, I'd like a few words with him."

Alarmed, Lexi grabbed Ricco's arm before he could walk off. "No, Ricco. Please don't. It'll just make the whole thing more . . . humiliating."

Ricco studied her face, and for a second she thought he might argue with her. Then he nodded. "Listen, you should probably shift and go home," he said softly.

"But my clothes—"

"Have already been left behind."

Confused, she looked down and saw that she was still wearing the black cloak. There was no way she was going back inside for her clothes, but, "My wallet."

"I'll get it for you."

"What about the Vlads? They're not going to let the leader of the Bloods just waltz into their club."

He smiled and fingered the fabric of her robe. "With luck, they won't even know I'm there—and it'll give me the perfect opportunity to see who's in there."

"All right, but be careful. And thank you."

"No problem," Ricco said, leaning forward to place a kiss on her cheek. "You know I'm always here for you."

"I know." She smiled and then shrugged off the cloak and handed it to him. His gaze ran over her in a very male way, making her feel feminine and attractive. It helped lift her spirits a little after being rejected—yet again—by Darius.

"Be careful," she warned him. "I don't want you to get hurt."

"Ow," he said with a frown. "As you just pointed out, I

am First Fang of one of the most powerful vampire gangs in New York City. There are some people who consider me quite dangerous."

She gave him an apologetic smile. "You know what I mean."

Then, with a wave of her hand, she changed into wolf form and headed home, letting the night swallow her as she ran.

Darius hurried around the corner of the building just in time to see Lexi morph into a wolf and race off. He swore silently and ran after her, afraid that if she got away, he'd never see her again. He'd only taken a couple of steps when a hand closed around his throat.

The man Lexi had been talking with had moved with alarming speed. Darius grabbed his dagger and was about to plunge it into the man's heart when he spoke.

"I should kill you for hurting her," the man growled.

Darius hesitated. Though this man was a vampire, he seemed sincere in wanting to protect Lexi. Darius couldn't kill him for that.

He slapped his dagger back on his arm and with a quick twist, broke the vampire's hold on him. In the brief moment of the vampire's stunned hesitation, Darius punched him in the stomach, causing him to double over. But the vampire quickly came up, his fists moving so fast they were a blur.

Darius took a blow to the jaw that snapped his head back. White dots of light burst behind his eyelids, but it didn't slow him down. He anticipated the vampire's next move and dodged out of the way; delivering a massive kidney blow of his own. "Stop. I don't want to hurt you," he said. "Especially since you seem to be a friend of Lexi's."

"Save your breath," the vampire said. "Lexi doesn't want to see you again—ever. I'm going to make sure her wish comes true."

Darius understood that kind of protectiveness. "I'm not going to hurt her," he tried to explain.

"Too late."

That caught him off guard. "Are you sure?" he asked, blocking the vampire's punch to his jaw. "That I hurt her, I mean."

The vampire stopped fighting long enough to answer. "She was crying. I've known Lexi a long time, and do you know when I last saw her cry?" When Darius shook his head, he continued. "A year ago, when her sister died. Do you know how long before that? Never. Lexi's just not the crying type. So congratulations."

Now Darius felt even guiltier. "That's why I want to talk to her—so I can explain . . . things."

The vampire crossed his arms, making a formidable barrier. "She told me she doesn't want to see you again."

Darius studied the man, admiring his loyalty and willingness to fight for what he believed in. Those were the kind of traits one wanted in an ally, not in one's opponent. "I don't suppose you'd consider walking away from this?"

The vampire shook his head, and Darius couldn't blame him. If the shoe had been on the other foot, he would have done the same thing—which made fighting this vampire that much more painful.

They squared off, and Darius waited to see what the vampire would do. They moved around in a slow circle, each mirroring the moves of the other. When the vampire rushed him, Darius stepped to one side and gave him enough of a shove that his forward momentum carried him into the wall of a building. His head hit with a sickening thud, but he didn't go down. Instead, he turned and glared at Darius, his expression full of dark promise.

This time, the vampire's approach was more cautious. Darius considered pulling his golden cord to restrain the man, but using his tattooed weapons seemed an unfair advantage against such a worthy opponent. He let the vampire get close and took another punch to the head in order to catch the vampire off balance.

As the vampire's hand connected with his jaw, Darius snatched the vampire's arm and twisted it. The vampire fell to his knees, but he didn't make a sound or cry out. Darius knew the hold had to hurt, and he was impressed. After a second, he released the vampire, shoving him forward while he took several steps back to get out of the way.

"I think it's only fair to warn you that I'm an Immortal," Darius stated calmly. "Killing me could prove to be . . . difficult."

The vampire's gaze ran over him critically. "My mother and her witch friends used to sit around telling stories about the legendary Immortals. That's all they were, though. Legends to comfort old women in the night."

Darius dodged another jab to the head, caught the vampire's fist on the third attempt and held it in his hand as he slowly squeezed. He saw the vampire's eyes register the pain and stopped just short of breaking the bones in his hand. "Does that feel like a legend to you?"

The vampire smiled. "If you're real, then that's all the

more reason to defeat you. A mere taste of your ancient blood will make me stronger. Imagine what more blood can do. Since you're immortal, I won't have to worry about drinking too much."

"Don't make me stake you," Darius growled, growing weary of the fight. He brushed back his duster and pulled the broadsword from his back. He held it in front of him as if it weighed nothing and waited for the vampire to decide if he wanted to continue.

"How'd you do that?"

Darius saw the shadow of doubt behind the vampire's eyes. "I told you," he sighed. "I'm an Immortal."

"Aren't you supposed to have a mark or something?"

Darius lifted his hair and turned to show his pentacle tattoo, careful to keep an eye on the vampire to make sure he wasn't attacked while his back was turned.

"Well, I'll be damned."

Turning back, Darius lowered his hair, resheathed the broadsword, and was about to suggest a truce when the vampire's fist connected with his jaw in a lightning-fast punch. "You'd think someone who's been around as long as you have would have learned some fucking manners when it comes to women."

The blow sent Darius flying back a good three feet. He wasn't hurt as much as he was irritated. He pulled himself off the ground into a crouch and then leapt through the air at the vampire, knocking him down. Before the vampire could react, Darius grabbed his dagger off his arm and placed the blade against the vampire's throat just above where his hand held the vampire pinned to the ground.

"The only reason you're not dead is because I don't want to ruin all my chances with Lexi by killing her friend, which you seem to be." Darius gripped the vampire's throat a little tighter. "Don't make me change my mind."

For several long minutes, the two stared at one another. Then the vampire nodded as best he could. Slowly and with his dagger held ready, Darius took his hand from the vampire's throat, and both men got to their feet. "Truce?" Darius asked.

"Truce," the vampire croaked, rubbing his throat.

"What's your name?" Darius put away his dagger and held out his hand.

The vampire stared at it and then took it. "Ricco. And you?"

"Darius."

"Now what?" Ricco asked.

"Now, I suggest we . . ." Darius paused, feeling a stirring at the back of his neck. When he glanced around, he saw that a good eighteen vampires had appeared out of seemingly nowhere and surrounded them. He thought for a moment that Ricco had somehow summoned reinforcements, but then he heard the vampire's barely audible oath.

"Well, well. If it isn't Ricco. What's the First Fang of the Bloods doing in the Vlads' territory?" one of the newcomers asked.

Ricco pulled himself up a little straighter. "You used to be a Blood, too, Carlos. What happened?"

The other vampire shrugged. "I found a worthier cause to fight for. Me."

"That was a mistake," Ricco said. "The Vlads don't care about you."

"I disagree." Without taking his eyes from Ricco, Carlos raised his hand, and the vampires in the circle attacked.

Darius immediately slapped a hand to his arm. "Here." He tossed his dagger to Ricco, who caught it easily. Then, pulling his broadsword from his back, he turned so he and Ricco were standing back to back.

It soon proved impossible for all eighteen vampires to attack at once, so the assault continued in smaller groups of four and five vampires. It was easier for Darius and Ricco to fight them this way, especially since they were armed, but for every one that went down, another vampire stepped in to take his place. It made for a long, never-ending battle.

How long they fought, Darius had no idea, but with a number of vampires lying dead at their feet, he could hear the sound of Ricco's heavy breathing. Unlike himself, the vampire wasn't used to such fierce, sustained fighting. Darius knew Ricco wouldn't last much longer and stepped up his own efforts, trying to kill as many as he could.

He'd disposed of his fourth vampire when he and Ricco became separated. He tried to work his way toward Ricco, but three more vampires joined the two he was fighting and he was rooted in place as he fought. Over and over, he swung his broadsword; his arm muscles were growing wearier with the effort until they burned. Strange—he'd fought much longer battles than this and had never tired.

"Put down your sword or I'll cut out Ricco's heart with your dagger," Carlos shouted. Darius took a few last swings at the vampires around him, but they stepped back until they were beyond his range and he was left standing there, panting, trying to hold his sword aloft.

He saw Carlos standing beside Ricco, held prisoner between two vampires. The look Ricco gave Darius was not one of pleading, but of apology. "Let him go," Darius demanded.

"Lower your weapon," Carlos countered, drawing the blade across Ricco's throat so that a thin bead of blood appeared. Darius immediately let the broadsword fall to the ground. He didn't need the weapon to defeat the vampires; he needed time.

"Okay," he said, taking a step away from his sword. "I did as you asked. Now let Ricco go."

Carlos laughed. "I don't think so."

Darius wasn't surprised by the refusal. Time to call for assistance. He was about to lower his hand to touch Fury when suddenly both his arms were grabbed from behind. Darius fought with all that was in him, but six vampires were holding him and he couldn't break free.

Carlos strolled forward, an evil smile spread across his face. "Noble effort," he said mockingly. "Now it's time to die."

Chapter Ten

With a nod from Carlos, the vampires holding him grabbed Darius's head and twisted it to one side with such force he thought his neck would snap. Immediately Carlos bent forward to sink his fangs into Darius's throat.

"I'd be careful if I were you," Ricco shouted. "Can't you feel it? He's not human. Who knows what his blood will do to you."

Before his teeth could graze skin, Carlos straightened. "What do you mean?"

"You saw the way those weapons came off his skin. You can feel his energy. I don't know what it is, man, but I wouldn't just go sucking his neck without checking first."

Carlos's eyes narrowed, and he regarded Darius warily. "Fine. You check him out. We won't miss you none if you die."

Carlos gestured to the two vampires holding Ricco to bring him closer to Darius, and briefly their gazes met. Seconds later, Darius felt the pain as fangs pierced his throat. He heard the swallowing noises as Ricco drank, and he forced himself to remain calm. He knew he could survive the loss of blood, but the more he lost, the weaker he became.

Then Ricco pulled away. There was a new light in his eyes when he looked at Darius.

"Why have you stopped?" Carlos shouted, stepping close to Ricco. "You will continue to drink until I say—"

In a sudden move, Ricco threw off his two captors as if they weighed nothing and turned on Carlos. "You should have stayed in the Bloods." Before the other vampire knew what was happening, Ricco's hand shot out, punched a hole in Carlos's chest and came back holding the vampire's heart.

There was only enough time for surprise to register on Carlos's face before he fell to the ground, dead.

Immediately his skin began to shrivel and dry on the bone.

The other vampires stared in horror, and Darius used the opportunity to pull free of them. Slapping a hand to his chest, he loosed Fury, who roared so ferociously as he exploded to life that the remaining vampires screamed in terror and fled.

Darius and Ricco were alone in the alley, with only the rotting corpses of Carlos and the other vampires. While Darius waited for the demon's return, he bent over and retrieved his dagger. After wiping off the blade, he slapped it back on his arm.

Ricco, who had come to stand beside him, took a step back as Fury reappeared. "That was . . . impressive," he said, watching Fury transform back into a tattoo.

Darius smiled. "As impressive as you putting your fist through Carlos's chest? That was some show of strength, even for a vampire."

"I have you to thank for that. If I hadn't believed you before about being an Immortal, I do now after drinking your blood. Holy shit, what a high. I can't remember when I've felt that good—and when I think how close I was to dying . . . well, I owe you—for saving my life."

"Why don't we call it even?" Darius suggested.

"Agreed."

They started walking, but Darius stopped Ricco when he headed toward the Crypt. "Are you sure you want to go in there? Especially after what just almost happened."

Ricco picked a black cloak up off the ground. "I promised Lexi I'd get her clothes and wallet."

Darius patted his duster. "I've got her wallet, which I'll give back to her as soon as I see her, and you know she'd rather buy new clothes than have you go in there." He thought for a second that Ricco might argue—insist that *he* be the one to take Lexi's things back—but then he nodded.

The two started walking again, this time in the opposite direction from the Crypt.

"So why are you here?" Darius asked, wondering what had brought the leader of one vampire gang into the territory of another. He had to have known it was dangerous.

Ricco eyed him, like he wasn't sure how much he wanted to say, but then he made up his mind. "For the last five years, there have been two major vampire gangs in New York City—the Vlads and the Bloods. The size of these gangs has always remained fairly constant, because once you start exceeding a certain size, it's hard to retain control of your members and it's hard to feed them all. New York has strict state laws on how many humans we convert and how many gang members we let in." He glanced at Darius to see if he understood.

"Go on."

"Well, about four months ago, I started noticing that the size of my gang was decreasing. Some were said to have pledged allegiance to the Vlads, but I didn't believe it. When you join a gang, typically you swear your allegiance on penalty of death—staked-through-the-heart-and-turned-to-dust death. Others just disappeared, and no one ever saw or heard from them again. I'm pretty sure they've been turned to dust." He rubbed his head. "It all seems to be related to the Crypt—which, of course, is run by the Vlads."

"So you decided to come check it out. See if you noticed any familiar faces in the crowd?"

Ricco nodded. "Yeah. Something like that."

"You had to know that as soon as you arrived, you'd be recognized and they'd send out a welcoming party—like they did."

"I'd reached the point where I didn't care. I wanted answers. Now I'm thinking the problem is bigger than just one gang stealing members from a rival gang."

"It might be," Darius said.

Ricco gave him a sharp look. "You sound like maybe you know something about all this."

Darius shrugged. "It may be nothing."

"Then again, it might be something."

Darius thought it was probably a bad idea to tell a death-magic creature that the King Demon of death magic was trying to take over the world. Still, something in him decided to take a chance—and so he told Ricco as much as he knew about it. When he finished, he waited for the vampire's reaction.

"That would explain a few things," Ricco said, surprising Darius. "As it happens, I know that the Vlads have a new leader," he continued. "The old leader, O'Rourke, is still around, but apparently taking orders from someone else. I'd wondered about that whole situation. Normally, the only way a new leader comes into power is by killing the current one. A demon intent on taking over the world would want to keep the local leaders in place and work through them."

Darius watched him closely. "So how come this demon didn't approach you?"

"Who says he didn't?" At Darius's surprised look, Ricco nodded. "Yeah, the guy came to see me, but I wasn't thrilled with the idea of working for a demon, no matter what he promised in return. He said I could keep running the show, but under his direction. In return, I'd have more wealth and power than I could ask for. Said he was going to try to convert all of New York City into vampires. I thought he was joking. I told him that not everyone wanted to become a vampire, and even if they did, how was he planning to feed them all? He told me not to worry about it—but it's my job to worry about things like that. I told him no deal, and to be honest, I was relieved when he walked away and left me alone."

"How long ago was that?"

"Just over four months ago."

"And that's when your members started disappearing," Darius concluded.

"That's right."

"Did this demon ever give you his name?" Darius asked.

"Sure. Called himself Amadja."

Amadja. It was a name from out of the past. Son of

Apep, the serpent god; Darius had faced him as recently as five hundred years ago, when Amadja had dared to attack Sekhmet. Their battle had been fierce and bitter, but in the end, Darius had vanquished him. Unfortunately, Amadja hadn't died; he'd simply disappeared.

They'd reached the end of the block, and Ricco gestured to the right.

"I don't suppose you ever saw a tall, redheaded male with Amadja, did you?" Darius asked.

Ricco didn't even have to think about it. "No. He always came alone. At the time, I thought it was ballsy of him to show up at my club, making demands like he was without backup. After what you've told me, I guess he didn't need backup."

Darius agreed. "You're lucky there was another gang in town for him to turn to. He probably figured that once the other gang grew in power, yours would eventually go away—or be destroyed."

"Yeah. That's a cheery thought. So—do you have a place to stay tonight?"

Darius had considered going to Lexi's, but there was a good chance she wouldn't let him in. "No."

"You're welcome to crash at my club if you want. We're almost there."

Darius thought about his other options, realized he had none, and nodded. "Thanks. I appreciate it."

O'Rourke was in a foul mood, standing in the waiting room of the local police station waiting for the leprechaun to be set free. Errands like this were beneath him. As leader of the Vlads, he shouldn't be running errands at all. As leader of the Vlads . . .

His thoughts trailed off. Since the appearance of

Amadja almost four months ago, O'Rourke had done very little leading and much too much following. The instant that demon had swept into his place with his followers, they had taken over both his club and his gang.

Of course, he'd tried to order them out, but Amadja had been very . . . persuasive . . . when he'd gotten O'Rourke alone.

The door leading into the waiting room opened, snapping O'Rourke out of his musings. He looked over to see the small form of Paddy Darby walking out. He looked tired and worn, and there was a fresh cut above his eye.

"About time you got here," Paddy snarled as soon as he saw O'Rourke standing there.

"Mind your tongue if you don't want to go back," O'Rourke warned him sullenly. If it had been up to him, he would have left the little shit in there, but for some reason, Amadja wanted him out. "Come on," he ordered him, leading the way out of the station. "Amadja wants to see you."

He was gratified to see Darby nearly stumble at that announcement.

"Why?"

"How the fuck should I know?" O'Rourke growled. It was the essence of his problem: Amadja didn't tell him what was going on. He told that redheaded freak everything, but he couldn't be bothered to keep O'Rourke, First Fang of the Vlads, informed.

"Maybe he just wants to know if everything's ready for the initiation," Darby suggested hopefully.

"Or maybe he wants to know why every time he turns around, you're back in jail?" O'Rourke countered. "And by the way, the cost of bailing you out—again—is coming out of your commission."

They'd reached the sidewalk, and O'Rourke raised his hand to hail a cab. The sooner they were back at the club, the better he'd feel.

"No more, my pet," Amadja cooed in the sultry voice of his female persona, Aja. Tain, his arms braced against the wall, his magnificent body raw and bleeding where strips of flesh had been peeled off, stood before her, shaking from pain and anticipation.

Aja tossed the knife aside, and it disappeared into thin air. She ran the palms of her hands down the sides of her nude body, relishing the attributes of her current form: the fullness of her breasts, the inward curve of her waist and the gentle flare of her hips.

She moved, close enough to Tain that his body heat warmed her, and she gently brushed aside the tendrils of red hair that had matted against his head. She brought her lips close to his ear and whispered, "No one loves you more than I do, Tain." Then she placed a light kiss against his cheek.

Still he did not speak; did not beg for mercy or for release. He stood there obediently, waiting for her to decide his fate—whether it be further torture or redemption.

Already his body was healing in the rapid way of the Immortals, though centuries of this ritual had left his skin rippled with scar tissue. For Aja, the sight of it quickened her pulse and made her burn with need. Living beneath the vampire club, constantly feeding off the sexual energies from above, left her hungry all the time.

"Turn around, Tain," she whispered, smiling at the way he hesitated. "Turn around, so that I might pleasure you—just as I caused you pain earlier."

Slowly he turned, his wounds making movement painful. As soon as he faced her, Aja's attention was drawn to his engorged member, jutting outward. Even after all these years, she found him impressive.

Lowering herself before him, she wrapped her lips around him and took him deep into her mouth. Though he tried not to, his groan welled up from deep down inside him and escaped. From the corner of her eye, she saw his hands clench into fists, but otherwise he held perfectly still while she caressed the long length of him with her tongue.

A fine trembling began in his legs as she brought him closer and closer to his release. When he was almost there, she stopped and, holding perfectly still, watched as his ardor faded. She didn't want him coming too soon.

Once his trembling stopped, she began again, forming a moist, warm sheath around him with her tongue and sliding her mouth up and down his length in an ever-increasing rhythm.

The trembling in his legs started anew, this time racking his entire body. When he'd had enough, Tain uttered a primal roar and, lifting Aja into the air, turned so her back was braced against the wall. Then, in a single lunge, he buried himself in her and took control of their lovemaking.

Over and over, he drove himself into her with a fierce intensity. She rode him relentlessly, milking him for everything he could give until he could give no more. And then, together, they climaxed.

For several long moments, they leaned against the wall, wrapped in each other's arms, too spent to move. Aja had never once in seven hundred years found their lovemaking anything less than spectacular, and it sometimes left the demon wondering who was in control of whom in their relationship.

Finally, she felt the prickle of others coming down the hallway.

"We have company, love," she whispered to Tain, rousing him. He released her legs and let them slide to the floor. She laid her hand against his cheek in a gentle caress and gave him a smile.

Then she walked away, crossing the room to her desk. As she did, she waved her hand and changed back into her male persona, clothing them both at the same time. By the time the knock on the door sounded seconds later, Amadja and Tain were ready.

"Come in," Tain said, opening the door and standing aside so the leprechaun and O'Rourke could enter. They both glanced at the Immortal, the leprechaun with feigned nonchalance and the vampire with barely concealed hostility.

"Won't you have a seat," Amadja said to Paddy Darby, gesturing to the chair in front of the large desk where he now sat. He was glad to see that O'Rourke didn't seem to expect to be asked to sit down but went to stand off to the side, where he was available if needed.

"How are you tonight, Paddy?" Amadja asked politely.

"Very good, thank you," Paddy answered.

"So." Amadja let the pause lengthen. "I understand that you've been in jail again. After I expressly asked you to take measures to ensure you avoid catching the attention of the authorities."

"I—I'm sorry, Your Eminence," Paddy stammered. "I forgot my court date, and they sent a bounty hunter after me."

Amadja rolled his eyes. "Are you telling me you

couldn't escape a bounty hunter? Paddy, I thought I was paying you to avoid such entanglements."

"Of course I could have escaped the bounty hunter," Paddy defended himself. "But she wasn't alone."

Tain gave a snort of disdain. "Even *you* should have been able to outrun two humans."

Paddy glanced at Tain before giving Amadja a worried look. "But that's just it, you see. It wasn't two humans. The woman was a werewolf, and the man . . ." he paused; "I don't know what he was. He was covered in tattoos, and when he touched them, they came to life. There was one in partic—"

"Darius," Tain muttered, looking at Amadja.

"Let's make sure." Amadja turned to O'Rourke. "I want to see the security tapes from two nights ago. You know the one I mean?" The vampire nodded. "Fine. We'll be up in a minute to look at it."

O'Rourke hurried out of the room, and Amadja turned his attention back to the little man watching him so intently. "We'll get back to that shortly. In the meantime, I trust everything is ready for the initiation?"

Paddy nodded but said nothing.

"What is it? You seem worried."

"I wonder if, maybe, we should"—he glanced uncertainly at Tain, as if seeking support—"slow down."

"And why would we do that?" Amadja asked patiently, though he was in fact losing his temper.

"I don't know how many more converts I can provide. There just aren't that many people who want to . . . become a vampire," Paddy said.

"I thought we discussed this. It's not a matter of taking those who ask; it's a matter of taking those who won't be missed."

"But the authorities—"

"Are not your concern." Why couldn't these creatures just do as they were told and let him worry about the consequences? "The only thing you need worry about," Amadja continued, "is providing me with what I've asked for. In return, I will provide you with a new pot of gold, as I promised. Isn't that what you wanted? A pot of gold to replace the one you lost? I know you can't return home to see your family until you have it—so I would think the sooner, the better. Right?"

Paddy nodded miserably, though Amadja couldn't care less whether or not the little man was happy. He wasn't the one who'd given the man a drinking problem that resulted in his losing everything he had in the world.

A buzzer sounded on Amadja's desk. "They are ready for us upstairs," he announced, getting up from his desk. "Paddy, I'd like you to take a look at a video and tell me if the man who helped capture you is in it."

Paddy scooted off his chair and walked through the door that Tain held open for them. It didn't take long to walk through the underground passages to the doorway that took the trio into the club.

It was well after midnight, but the club was still filled with patrons. No one noticed them, however, as they made their way across the room, through the crowd and over to a door that had mysteriously appeared where a red panel of drapes had been.

Amadja, Tain and Paddy walked through the door and into the main office. O'Rourke was sitting at a control panel with six small screens and one larger one. At that moment, all six screens were showing scenes of couples having sex. Amadja ignored them, however, and focused his attention on the large screen where the frozen image of a tattooed man was displayed.

He gestured for Paddy to take a look, and wasn't surprised when the leprechaun's eyes lit up in recognition. "That's him. He's the one who took me in."

Amadja turned to exchange looks with Tain. Darius was interfering with their plans, whether he knew it or not.

"And that's her."

Amadja gave Paddy a startled look. "Who?"

"Her." Paddy pointed to the dark-haired woman on the dance floor with Darius. "That's the bounty hunter he was with."

Tain took a step closer. "Are you positive?"

"Yes." Paddy squinted and leaned closer to the screen for another look. "Yes, that's her."

So, the Immortal had found a confederate, Amadja thought. He wondered just how close the two of them had become. He turned to O'Rourke. "Study that tape. I want to know if they came together, and who they talked to while they were here."

O'Rourke nodded and hit the play button on the video.

"Do you know who he is?" Paddy asked.

No one answered.

"You may go now Paddy," Amadja said. "But do us both a favor and when you're not at work—stay close."

Paddy nodded, then escaped as quickly as he could. Just as the door closed behind him, O'Rourke called out. "Hey, boss. I think you might want to see this."

Amadja walked over to the monitor and watched the screen as O'Rourke moved the image in reverse. He watched as the dark-haired bounty hunter walked in the door with a much shorter but equally attractive woman by her side.

"Do you know who that is?" O'Rourke asked, though

it was clear that *he* knew the answer, so Amadja simply waited. "Mai Groves, the reporter. She's been here a lot lately."

"Are you sure?" Amadja asked.

"Yeah. I make it a point to know who comes into my club—especially reporters."

Amadja shot him a withering look for his insolence, but stepped forward to take a better look at the screen. "If she and this bounty hunter are friends, then she might be worth getting to know a little better."

"I'll do it," Tain offered, a little too eagerly it seemed.

Amadja felt a twinge of jealousy, but he quickly suppressed it. Tain was right. Having someone on the inside would be best, but he didn't think Tain would be the best choice. "I believe *I'll* deal with this one," he said firmly.

Tain looked disappointed, but Amadja didn't care and started walking toward the door.

"Where are you going?" Tain asked.

"No time like the present," he replied and then walked out the door.

Chapter Eleven

The evening had been a resounding success, Mai thought as she sat in the back of a cab the next morning, studying her reflection in a mirror. She noticed the bags under her eyes were getting darker. If she didn't start getting some sleep soon, she was going to look a lot older than she actually was. However, sometimes one had to make short-term sacrifices for long-term gains. At least, she hoped it was a short-term sacrifice. Going to the bars night after night and having sex with strangers was . . . okay, it was exciting and exhilarating, but it wasn't very satisfying.

There were times when what she really wanted was someone to settle down with. Finding Mr. Right, however, was a bit problematic. Although, there'd been that one man she'd met late last night. He certainly had potential.

At that moment, her cell phone rang. Looking at the caller ID, she recognized Lexi's number.

"Morning," she answered cheerfully.

"Where the hell have you been?" Lexi reprimanded her. "I've been worried sick about you."

Used to her friend's monthly mood swings, Mai didn't take offense. "I've been working on this new story."

"Are you all right?" Lexi asked, sounding concerned.

"Of course."

"Mai, are you telling me the truth?"

Mai sighed. "All right. If you must know, I'm a little tired, and I feel like I might be coming down with something."

"You need to take better care of yourself."

"It so happens that I'm on my way to see a doctor now. A Dr. Patrick."

"Listen. I found out something important about those back rooms at the Crypt."

Mai's interest was immediately aroused. "Do tell," she encouraged.

"There's a succubus working them. A real energy-sucking succubus," Lexi continued.

"No kidding?" Mai asked, hardly able to believe it. "Wow."

She heard Lexi's growl on the other end. "Mai, this *thing* is dangerous. It kills people. I think you should stay away from the Crypt."

"Not to worry," Mai said brightly. "A succubus is female, right? You know I don't do women."

"Mai," Lexi warned, "I want your promise."

Past experience told Mai that there was no point in arguing with Lexi when she was like this. In a couple of days, after the moon had passed, she'd be back to her normal, reasonable self. "All right, hon. I won't mess with the succubus. Will that make you happy?"

"Yes." She heard Lexi's sigh of relief and felt guilty for lying to her. She hoped Lexi would understand.

"Look, I'm at the doctor's office, so I need to let you go. I'll talk to you tonight, all right?" She disconnected the call before Lexi could object, paid the cab fare and got out.

The building wasn't exactly what she'd expected a physician's office to look like, but then she didn't really know what to expect. He'd been recommended by someone she'd met at the Crypt when she mentioned feeling run-down.

The wood nymph in her hoped he was young, gorgeous and single. With that thought in mind, she went into the building and located his office.

He didn't seem busy, but she still spent a good thirty minutes sitting in the waiting room filling out paperwork. There were a lot of questions on family medical history that Mai thought were a supreme waste of time. Instead of answering, she simply marked down she'd been orphaned at an early age. After finishing, she was shown into the exam room where she peeled off her clothes and put on the ugly paper gown that never closed properly. Then she sat down to await the arrival of the doctor.

When the doctor walked in a few minutes later, she couldn't help feeling disappointed. It wasn't that he was ugly. She simply hadn't expected him to be so . . . short.

Despite several cups of coffee and sleeping in, Lexi was tired and in a foul mood when she walked into the offices of Blackwell Bail Bonds. Not even her conversation with Mai had left her feeling cheerful, though at least she knew that Mai was alive, which helped.

"Morning, Marge," she greeted the older woman as she went to her in-box and the files sitting there. "Looks like another busy day."

The busier she was today, the better. She still couldn't believe what Darius had done to her the night before. Every time she thought about it, she wanted to curl up and hide. Let the Big Bad demon take control of the world. Why should she care? As long as the demon was in charge, business was booming. At the rate they were going, she'd be able to set enough money aside to retire early.

Lexi worked diligently all day and successfully brought in four of her six cases. None was a hardened criminal trying to evade the law. They were simply misguided lawbreakers who saw the error of their decision to not show up at court as soon as Lexi pointed it out to them.

By the end of the day, she had worked off enough of her built-up moon-induced energy so that she was feeling less edgy than she had been that morning.

As far as distracting her from thoughts of Darius, well, she'd only thought of him one or two—*thousand*—times.

Looking at her watch, Lexi saw that it was late afternoon. On any other day, she would have packed it in and gone home, but not today. She was afraid of what—or who—might be waiting at her apartment for her, so instead, she pulled out her notes and studied the specifics of her next case file.

His name was Martin Ironwood, and he was another first-time offender charged with disturbing the peace. Absolutely nothing in his profile suggested he was the type to run. When Lexi arrived at his brownstone home, a pleasant-looking woman in her late twenties answered the door.

"Can . . . can I help you?" She looked nervous, and it

was obvious from her red eyes that she'd been crying—a lot.

Lexi pulled out her bail enforcement license and flashed it. "I'm Lexi Corvin, with Blackwell Bail Bonds. I'm looking for Martin Ironwood—is he here?"

The woman's lower lip trembled. "No. I don't know where he is. Two nights ago, he called a car service to come pick him up, and I haven't seen or heard from him since."

Lexi studied her face. She didn't think the woman was trying to cover for her husband; she honestly didn't know where he was. "Has he done this before? Disappeared for a couple of days without telling you where he went?"

"No, never. We've only been married two years, and up until last week, he was so good about calling me all the time—you know? To say hello and see how my day was going. And the few times he was running late, he called to let me know that, too."

"Did you have a fight?" Sometimes couples ran into problems once the honeymoon was over and real life began. "Or maybe something happened at work?"

"I don't know. He works for a marketing firm, and last week they got a new client from out of town who'd heard about our vampire bars. Martin had to show him around, even though he didn't want to go. He wanted me to go with him, but since I'm pregnant, we decided that wasn't a good idea." She sighed. "I don't know what happened at that place—he wouldn't tell me—but after that night, he was different. He stopped calling me all the time. He started working late—really late." She took a shuddering breath. "And he was so tired. I thought he might be getting sick and begged him to stay home. He just laughed and said he felt great." She paused. "He finally agreed to see a doctor, but I think he just told me that to shut me up."

"What makes you say that?"

Her features grew hard. "How many doctors do you know who schedule routine exams at night?"

Lexi had to admit that, on the surface, it seemed suspicious. "So you think . . . ?"

"He was seeing another woman. It's the only explanation I can come up with that makes sense."

"Did you call the police and report him missing?" Lexi asked. "Or check the local hospitals?"

"Yes, of course," the woman said. "But they haven't been much help. They say there's no proof he didn't leave of his own free will."

"What about his job?"

She shook her head. "They haven't heard from him either. If he doesn't show up soon, they'll be forced to fire him."

Lexi took a deep breath. She felt sorry for the woman. "You said, on that last day, that he called a car service to come pick him up. Do you happen to remember the name of the company?"

"We always use Blue's Limos."

"Thank you." Lexi promised to let the wife know if she found her husband, then left. She wasn't looking forward to her next step. She pulled out her cell phone, called information for the Blue's Limos number and called it to request a car. When it arrived, she had the driver take her to their main office. As she feared, Blue's Limos was a small-time operation, but at least they kept a log of their calls.

The driver who had picked up Martin was currently

out on a call, so Lexi found a comfortable spot to wait for his return.

This was the glamorous life of the bail enforcement agent, she thought, hoping the driver planned to return sometime before tomorrow.

Darius stood against the wall between two panels of red drapes so his black outfit blended with the black section of wall. He was wearing clothes that Ricco had loaned him, since his duster and tattoos tended to stick out in a crowd.

As a precaution, however, he'd taken his dagger and cut slits running the length of the sleeves. If he got in a fight, he wanted easy access to his weapons.

He was lurking against the side of the room, watching the vampires and demons come and go, hoping to find the doorway that led to the underground passages he felt sure had to exist.

One section in particular interested him. He'd seen several exceptionally beautiful women approach the wall, only to suddenly disappear into the nearby crowd. Yet he couldn't recall the exact details. It was like one minute they were there, the next they weren't.

It had to be some form of illusionary magic that made onlookers believe one thing happened while something else entirely took place.

He waited for another group of demons to appear and watched closely.

There! This time, he saw clearly. They hadn't turned into the crowd, but rather, had disappeared through the wall.

He started across the room, walking casually in the

direction of the magic doorway. He was almost there when suddenly a powerful-looking vampire came through, accompanied by a beautiful woman with long dark hair.

Darius did a double take to make sure it wasn't Lexi. Something about them held his attention. When they walked over to the corner bar to get a drink, Darius slinked along behind them, blending into the crowd as best he could until he was close enough to overhear their conversation.

". . . things overseas I must attend to," the woman was saying.

"How long will you be gone?"

She gave a delicate laugh. "Not long enough for you to think you can take charge, if that's what you're thinking."

"Of course not," the vampire quickly denied, though he didn't sound sincere.

"I will be gone for the next two days. When I return, I will send for you. Bring Tain with you. We have things to discuss."

Tain! His brother was here, just as Darius had suspected all along. He watched the female walk off. He wasn't interested in her; it was the vampire who could lead him to Tain.

The vampire took his time finishing his drink, and when he finally left the bar, Darius was not far behind.

It was after dark when the driver who had picked up Martin Ironwood returned to the station.

"Do you remember where you took him that night?" Lexi asked after explaining the situation.

"Sure. I'll even take you there if you want."

"How far is it?" she asked once they were in his car.

"Not too far," he replied as he drove. "Up near Central Park. Popular place," he added.

"What do you mean?" she asked.

"Seems like I've dropped off a lot of fares there this week."

When they reached the old brick building, Lexi climbed out of the car and saw part of a sign hanging on the door that identified the building as some type of fellowship hall. The lights were on inside, but Lexi wasn't sure this was a place where she wanted to march up to the front door and knock.

After watching the car drive off, she looked around to make sure no one was about and then slipped around to the back of the building. There, she saw two back doors as well as four windows on the second story. Below each window was the fire escape—her ticket inside.

Looking around once more to make sure no one was watching, she hurried to the fire escape and pulled down the ladder. Quickly climbing it, she kept close to the side of the building so she wouldn't be seen by anyone standing inside.

She inched toward the first window and slowly leaned toward it until she could see inside. As far as she could tell, the room was empty. But when she tried to open the window, she found it locked.

Breaking it would make too much noise, so she walked to the next window. This time, she found the room occupied. Men and women wearing dark red ceremonial gowns were moving about. She quickly ducked out of sight before she was spotted.

Dropping to her hands and knees, she crawled under that window and on to the next. A peek inside showed the room to be empty, and when she tried to open the window, she felt it give. Looking through the window to the lock, she saw that it was the kind that latched, but both the window and the lock were old.

Pushing in on the lower pane so the two halves of the lock—one on the upper window pane and one on the lower—didn't touch, she pushed up on the window. Slowly it edged upward, and soon there was enough room for her to climb in.

Once inside, she opened the latch and closed the window, not wanting any cool breezes to attract attention, but also wanting to leave herself an option for a fast escape if she needed it.

She found herself in what looked like a small office. There was an old wooden desk with paperwork neatly stacked on it. The bookcases against the walls held as many knickknacks as books, and a musty odor of age clung to the furnishings.

She took a second to scan the papers on the desk and learned that she was in the Knights of Blood Fellowship Hall. Knights of Blood was a vampire organization trying to improve the image of vampires with their wannabe Knights of Columbus image and supposed charitable functions. To Lexi, it was almost as convincing as a used-car salesman endorsing buyer protection plans.

Why would Martin have come here?

A noise caught her attention, and she froze. Footsteps in the hall were coming her way. She looked about the room for a place to hide. She tiptoed to a closet and opened the door. It was filled with a huge, four-drawer filing cabinet.

The footsteps were drawing closer, so she hurried back to the door and barely managed to duck behind it as it opened. Holding very still, she watched a hooded, red-robed figure enter. It crossed to the desk, though fortunately didn't go around to the other side.

Lexi hardly dared to breathe. She considered ducking around the door, but without knowing what lay on the other side, it didn't seem a smart move. Maybe, if she was very quiet . . .

Then again, maybe not.

"Who are you?" the figure growled. "You don't belong here." He set the papers he was holding on the desk behind him. "Did you sneak in here to spy on us? Well, you picked a bad night to be curious."

He charged at her without giving her a chance to explain. Feet planted slightly apart, hands clenched into fists, she made two quick jabs to his head and followed with a roundhouse kick to his side. He doubled over, grunting in pain.

He didn't stay down long, though, and soon was coming at her again, arms stretched out before him.

Lexi feinted with her left fist and clocked him with her right. He fell back a step, shaking his head. She knew better than to give him a chance to collect his thoughts and immediately hit him with another roundhouse kick to his side and a jab to his head. Throwing back his hood, he came at her again, bloodlust turning his eyes a bright red that matched his robe.

Up until that moment, Lexi had been fighting to immobilize her opponent—maybe knock him unconscious. Now she knew it was going to come down to him or her. Lexi absolutely had no compunction about killing this vampire in order to save her own life.

She looked about for a weapon, wishing she had morphing tattoos like Darius did.

When the vampire came at her again, Lexi put all her strength into punching him. It didn't knock him unconscious, but he did fall back against the desk, clearly shaken. In that moment, Lexi found her weapon.

Grabbing the old wooden coatrack beside the door, she rested it against the floor and brought her foot down in the center of it, snapping it in two.

She had just straightened up when the vampire charged into her, driving her back against the wall. A wicked grin split his face and then vanished as Lexi shoved the coatrack deep into his chest.

He stepped back, shock etched across his face. He looked down at the piece of wood sticking out of his chest even as his body started to age and wither. He was dead before his skeleton collapsed to the ground.

Lexi felt a momentary remorse. She didn't like causing death—even to save her own life.

Stepping to the doorway, she stopped and listened. From below, she heard voices—a lot of voices.

Just what I need, she thought, *more vampires*. She wondered if she should give up trying to find Martin. She glanced back at the window, considering making an exit. Her gaze fell on the vampire. He'd been reduced to a pile of disintegrated bone beneath a red robe.

She quickly picked up the robe and shook out the dust. The piece of wood clattered to the floor, reminding her there was a gash in the robe. Still, it was better than nothing.

She pulled it on and tugged the front together, making sure the rip fell inside a fold. Then she pulled the hood over her head. She half considered carrying the piece of wood with her, but that would have been too obvious. Going back to the doorway, she took a bracing breath and stepped through.

She walked down the empty hall, glancing inside

each doorway as she passed. At the end, she found a stairway and took it to the first floor. When she reached the bottom, she almost lost her nerve. She was standing before two open double doors leading into a huge room filled with easily a hundred or more people dressed in red and white robes like the one she wore.

She had no idea what was going on—and she wasn't sure she wanted to know.

The room was set up with rows of chairs facing the front where there was a raised dais.

No one seemed to pay much attention to her as she slipped away. She just wanted to find Martin—if he was there—and leave.

She took a few minutes to explore the rest of the first floor, which was surprisingly empty. Finding nothing, she hurried back to the stairs and went down to the basement.

It was a finished basement and looked much like the second floor in that there was a hallway with doors opening on both sides. She went to each one and tried the knob. In most cases, the doors were open, and she found herself peering into very small offices piled with books and papers.

The fifth room, however, was different. This room reminded Lexi of a medical-school anatomy lab with rows of bodies stretched out on gurneys. The sight gave her an ominous feeling.

She had only to check the first body to know the truth of what she'd found: newly converted vampires—each bearing twin fang marks on their neck.

She walked up and down the rows, disturbed at the sheer number of people. There were young and old alike in the room, and it made her sick. Why would so many people choose this alternative to life?

She was halfway through the room when the face of one body caught her attention. She stopped and took a second, longer look. In death, Martin Ironwood looked much as he had in his file photo.

Lexi heaved a sigh. She'd found him. Now what? Carry him out?

Suddenly the hairs on the back of her neck prickled. Clenching her hand into a fist, she whirled around, swinging her fist with all her might at the huge vampire looming behind her.

There was enough power in her punch to knock a man silly—and it would have, she felt sure, if the man hadn't in one smooth move caught her fist with one hand and grabbed her wrist with the other. Before she had time to react, he twisted her arm and shoved her forward over Ironwood's body.

The speed and ease with which he immobilized her made a mockery of her abilities. When he leaned into her, she felt the size and mass of his body dwarfing her. She tried not to panic as he pulled back her hood.

"You're determined to get yourself killed, aren't you? I bet you gave your parents heart attacks growing up."

Lexi froze. "Darius?" He pulled her to her feet and released her, stepping away. She rubbed her arm and scowled at him. "You scared the shit out of me."

He pushed back his hood and smiled. "Serves you right. What the hell are you doing sneaking around down here?"

She gestured to Ironwood's body. "I'm working. That's my skip. What are *you* doing here?"

He frowned. "I was following a lead that I thought would take me to Tain." He shrugged. "It didn't. I was about to shake things up a bit when I saw you sneak down here."

"How'd you know it was me?"

His gaze heated. "I'd know your body anywhere."

His answer hinted at such intimacy, she felt flustered. "Wh-what do you mean you were going to shake things up? What's going on upstairs?"

He shook his head. "Lexi, Lexi. When are you going to learn to find out what's going on before you go rushing in? Upstairs, the vampires from the Crypt are initiating new members."

"So? That's not necessarily against the law—not if they have the proper Authorization of Conversion documents."

"I don't care if it's legal or not. With every converted member, the balance of magic shifts a little more to the side of death magic. I'm here to put a stop to it."

"How?"

He gave her an exasperated look. "It doesn't matter now. Put your hood on," he told her, pulling his own back over his head. "Let's see if I can get us both out of here undetected."

"I can't leave yet," she told him.

"Why not?"

"I'm not leaving my skip here."

Though she couldn't see Darius's face, she could imagine him rolling his eyes. She crossed her arms in an admittedly childish gesture, but it worked. She heard his sigh.

"Fine." He stepped beside her and lifted Ironwood to his shoulder as easily as if he were carrying a bag of potatoes. "Are you happy now?"

She hadn't expected him to help her, so she gave him a grateful smile and pulled her hood over her head. "Yes, thank you."

"Okay, let's go."

"What about these others?" she asked, looking at the rows of dead bodies.

"Want me to stake them?" he asked.

"No," she said quickly. "Let's just get out of here."

They left the room, and as they slowly climbed the stairs, she could hear voices joined in a ritual chanting. The faint coppery scent of blood floated on the air.

When they reached the top floor, the front door loomed less than a hundred feet in front of them. To reach it, they had to walk past the double doors of the large conference room, which were luckily closed.

Darius started forward, and Lexi hurried after him, keeping a lookout for vampires.

As they passed the conference room, Lexi couldn't resist stopping long enough to peer through the crack between the closed double doors.

At first, all she saw was a sea of red. Hundreds of robed vampires sat with their backs to her; their attention was focused on what was unfolding at the front of the room. Lexi shifted to get a better look.

A woman in a white robe stood quietly at the front as a vampire came up behind her. He placed his hands almost tenderly on her shoulders and then bent his head over her neck. As he sank his fangs into her neck, she never blinked, never even flinched.

Lexi saw blood seeping from the seal of his mouth, and again her lupine senses caught a whiff of the sweet metallic scent.

The woman's body began to tremble, but still the vampire drank. And drank.

There was a growing fervor in the room—a sense of anticipation. And then the woman's body went slack and she started to crumple. The vampire stopped drinking, and two others stepped forward to carry her away.

Lexi was still trying to digest everything she'd just witnessed when another white-robed figure stepped onto the dais from a line formed to the side. With their hoods off, Lexi could see their blank faces. None of them looked around or gave any indication that they knew what was happening to them. It was almost as if they'd been drugged.

She was debating whether she could do something to help when her gaze fell on the second person in line.

Mai.

Chapter Twelve

"Let's go," Darius prodded.

"I can't."

"Why the hell not?" His tone was sharp.

Lexi gestured to the room with her hand. "Mai is in there."

Darius pushed back his hood and frowned at her. "That's her choice."

"Mai would never choose to become a vampire," Lexi shot back with conviction. "I'm going in there."

"Oh, no, you're not." He joined her at the double doors and angled Martin's body so he could get close enough to peek through the crack. After a second, he turned around and shook his head. "There must be two hundred vampires in there. You'll get yourself *and* your friend killed."

"There must be a way," she reasoned.

"I'll do it."

"What?" She stared up at him in surprise.

He nodded. "You heard me. I'll go in there. I had

planned to before you arrived anyway." He set Ironwood on the floor. "Which one is she?"

"Second in line." She fought to keep the panic out of her voice.

He peeked through the crack again. "I see her." He pulled off his robe and let it fall to the floor. Then he slapped a hand against his arm and pulled off the dagger. "Stand over there and kill anything that gets close. Understand?" he asked, handing her the dagger.

She took it from him but didn't move. "I'm going with you."

"No, you're not." Their gazes locked in a battle of wills. "Now's not the time for heroics, Lexi," Darius added gently. "I'm immortal. Let me do this."

The last thing she wanted was to stand by on the sidelines, but getting killed wouldn't help Mai either. As much as she hated to admit it, her chances of storming into a room full of vampires and coming out alive were pretty slim. "Fine," she agreed. "But be careful."

Darius reached behind his back and brought forth a broadsword. Then, before she could figure out his plan, he kicked open the double doors and charged inside, shouting at the top of his lungs and swinging his sword.

There was a momentary stunned silence and then mass confusion as vampires snapped out of their shock and started rushing about. Half the vampires tried to escape, while others took advantage of the chaos to feed on the initiates.

Darius made it halfway across the room before he was forced to stop and deal with the vampires attacking him. Meanwhile, several initiates, who had finally awakened from their catatonic states, were screaming like banshees.

Lexi looked around for Mai, but there were so many people and vampires moving about, it was difficult to find her. She moved forward to get a better look.

Then suddenly she heard Mai scream. A vampire had grabbed Mai, and from the looks of it, had every intention of sucking her dry. Darius, under attack by at least a dozen vampires, had problems of his own.

Dropping the dagger, Lexi raced forward. Driven by raw fear for her friend, she leapt through the air and morphed into wolf form. She landed on all fours and barely broke stride, leaving a pile of torn clothes behind.

The scent of blood all around called to her predatory nature, and as she raced toward her friend, she ripped out the throat of any vampire that dared get in her way. When she reached Mai, the vampire had already sunk his teeth into her neck. Lexi launched herself at the pair, knocking them both to the ground. The impact was enough to separate them, and as the vampire tried to roll away, she attacked. He was dead within seconds.

She looked around and saw Mai standing close by, a horrified expression on her face. She had no idea if Mai would recognize her, but moved forward slowly. When she reached Mai, she pushed her head against Mai's hand.

Mai's fingers instinctively curled into Lexi's fur. "Lexi?" Lexi wagged her tail once to let Mai know it was she, but she didn't try to change back. The danger wasn't over yet. Grabbing Mai's robe with her teeth, she made a quick tug in the direction of the double doors.

As they crossed the room, Lexi ran interference, stopping anyone who got in their way. After seeing Mai safely to the door, she heard Darius's voice and looked back. He was standing in the middle of the room, surrounded by attacking vampires. As his blade flashed, vampires fell, piling up at his feet. Their corpses shriveled as the skin dried on their bones, and then even the bones dissolved until there was nothing left but white powder.

Lexi was about to go help him when she saw the last vampire fall. Darius looked around, his heaving chest glistening with sweat. She thought he'd never looked so magnificent and couldn't take her eyes off him. When his gaze met hers, a relieved smile replaced his furrowed brow. She felt such a rush of happiness that she started morphing to human form as he crossed the room to her.

As soon as he reached her, he pulled her into his arms. "Are you all right?"

"Never better," she assured him, her head buried in his chest.

"Then let's get out of here." He stepped back and looked around. Then he leaned over and picked up a robe, shook it out and handed it to her. At first she didn't understand, but then she felt the heat of his gaze and realized she wasn't wearing any clothes.

"Thank you," she said, letting him help her put it on.

He smiled at Mai, who stared up at him with unfeigned appreciation. "Are you all right?"

She nodded. "A bit confused," she admitted. "Thank you."

"No problem." Turning from them, he walked to Martin Ironwood's body and lifted him easily to his shoulder. He turned to Lexi. "Now can we go?"

He didn't wait for an answer, but headed for the door, leaving Lexi and Mai to trail after him.

"Oh, my God," Mai whispered, not sounding like

she'd almost been a victim of a horrible attack. "Where have you been keeping *him*?"

Lexi didn't like the obvious interest Darius was showing in Mai, and it was making her more than a little mad that her best friend would be coming on to a man who was clearly with her. That's what she got for having a wood nymph for a best friend—no male was off limits.

"Mai, this is Darius. He's . . . from out of town." Mai wasn't a Coven of Light witch and didn't know about the demon or the problems they were currently facing. Or did she? Lexi gave her a curious look. "What were you doing there?"

Mai, for once, looked distressed. "I have no idea. The last thing I remember is going to see the doctor."

Lexi remembered that Ironwood's wife had said he had gone to see a doctor as well, just before disappearing.

In the distance, Lexi heard sirens. "Let's get out of here."

"What about them?" Darius asked, referring to the initiates who were wandering around, dazed and confused.

"The police will take care of them," Lexi assured him. "Let's go. I want to get Martin to jail before he wakes up. He's going to be hard to deal with when he discovers he's a vampire."

The three left the building and walked down the street. They made an odd group. A giant Immortal with an unconscious vampire slung over his back, a wood nymph more interested in the Immortal than in her harrowing experience, and a sulky, hormonal werewolf currently fighting off fantasies of ripping out her friend's throat if she mewled one more time over Darius's "huge" muscles.

Lexi pulled out her cell phone and called the Department of Vampirism Hotline to report the attempted initiation. After she gave them the address, they promised to send people there to help the newly converted. Then Darius flagged down a cab to head home.

Lexi and Darius dropped Mai off at her apartment after making sure she was okay and securing her promise to stay in for the rest of the evening. She readily agreed and seemed eager to get to her computer, feeling certain she had the next day's lead story if she worked fast.

Darius and Lexi then took the cab to the police station. On the ride over, Darius, who sat in the middle of the back seat, couldn't help noticing the way Lexi kept glancing at Martin, who lay against the door on Darius's other side. The next time she checked on the vampire, she glanced up at Darius. He caught her eye and smiled. "Your friend seems nice."

That earned him a sharp look. "She's a wood nymph," Lexi said. "She likes sex—lots of it. You'd probably like her."

Darius chuckled. He could have told her he had no interest in her little friend, but he didn't.

There was a groan on the other side of him, and Lexi leaned across his lap to check on Martin. Always before, following battle, he'd burned off the excess adrenaline by having sex. The feel of her pressing against him was entirely too tempting, and he wondered just how far he could take things with Lexi before it was too late to stop.

Not that, after what happened the night before, she

would even let him get close. That hug earlier had been a battle-induced emotional moment.

"I think he's waking up," Lexi said, distracting Darius from his thoughts.

He glanced at Martin. "You may be right."

"When he does, he's going to be hungry."

"Probably."

She gave him a speculative look, clearly not liking the fact that he wasn't concerned. "Really hungry."

"Ravenous," he agreed.

She let out a huff. "Well, don't you think that might be a problem?"

He glanced at Martin, now beginning to open his eyes. "No."

"Darius," she continued, her voice now filled with urgency. "If we don't stop and get blood, he's going to—"

At that moment, Martin broke out of the death sleep he'd been in and sat upright, his eyes bloodred and his lips pulled back in a snarl, revealing bright, new fangs.

When he leapt across the seat at them, Lexi fell back. Darius put out one arm to shield her and, fisting his other hand, brought it up hard and fast. It connected soundly with Martin's jaw, making a sickening dull smacking noise, followed by the sound of Martin's head smashing against the window.

A second later, Martin slumped over, unconscious once more.

"Hey," the cabbie complained, as Martin's eyes rolled up into his head. "What's going on back there?"

"N-nothing," Lexi said, staring in awe at Darius, who enjoyed the look of incredulity on her face.

"Amazing," he thought he heard her say. "Are you hurt?"

"Nothing serious," he assured her, looking at a small cut on his hand that was already healing.

They arrived at the police station, and Lexi led the way in while Darius carried Martin.

The filing of the proper forms was waived until Lexi could get Martin behind bars. No one seemed to want to handle a vampire that might wake up at any moment. She ordered that bags of blood be made available as they carried Martin to the special cells designed for vampires. The bars were reinforced steel, and there were no windows to allow in sunshine.

"Lay him on the cot," Lexi told Darius just as the policeman she'd sent for blood arrived carrying two bags.

She handed them to Darius, who laid them beside Martin.

"Shut the door," he ordered her.

She looked at Martin and saw that his eyes were open. She immediately closed the door but didn't lock it in case Martin attacked and Darius needed a quick escape.

When Martin lurched up, Darius held out the bag of blood and Martin sank his teeth into it, spraying blood everywhere. He drank ravenously, finishing off the first bag so quickly that Lexi worried that two bags might not be enough. But Darius gave him the second bag and talked to him in a soothing voice. The second bag was three-fourths drained when Martin finally slowed down.

"Feeling better?" Darius asked when the bag was empty.

Martin looked lost, but he nodded.

"Good." Darius stood up, walked to the cell door and let himself out. The click of the bolt as it slid into place seemed to pierce Martin's daze. He looked around and finally seemed to notice his surroundings.

"Where am I?"

"Jail," Lexi told him. "I'm Lexi Corvin. I'm a bounty hunter. You failed to make your court appearance, so I was sent to bring you in." She paused. "There were . . . complications."

"What kind of complications?" He sounded anxious, and Lexi was trying to decide the best way to break the news to him.

"What's the last thing you remember?" she asked.

"I don't know." He went to wipe his mouth and stopped short when he saw the back of his hand. "Is this blood?" There was panic in his voice. Then he saw the empty blood bag still in his lap, and she knew he was putting the clues together. "Nooooo," he cried. "I'm not a vampire." He threw the bag as far away from him as he could and then rushed to the cell bars, gripping them. "Please. There's been some kind of mistake. I'm not a vampire. I can't be."

"I'm sorry," Lexi said as kindly as she could. "I think that two nights ago you were lured into an initiation scam. Probably drugged so you'd be more compliant."

Understandably, he seemed to have a hard time focusing his thoughts and kept rubbing his head. "I can't remember anything."

"I talked to your wife, Martin. She said you had taken a cab to go to a doctor's appointment and never came back. Sound familiar?"

He shook his head. Just then, one of the police detectives poked his head in the room and beckoned to Lexi.

"We've got guys over at the fellowship hall now, taking a look around," he told her when she joined him. "But they found these." He handed her a stack of papers. She saw they were official ACFs, Authorization of Conversion Forms. She looked up, a question in her eyes.

The detective nodded. "Yeah, they're all signed and legal."

She flipped through the papers and found both Ironwood's and Mai's ACFs. Even though it was Mai's signature, Lexi refused to believe that her friend had knowingly entered into such a thing. She took Martin's form to him and held it up. "Do you remember signing this?"

He looked at it, and a horrified expression crossed his face. "No, but . . . This can't be possible," he protested. "I would never . . ." He shook his head, and a single blood-tear slipped from his eye and traveled down his cheek. "My wife. My life is ruined." He looked at Darius. "Kill me. Please. I don't want to live like this."

Darius seemed to consider his request and then, to Lexi's horror, he slapped a hand to his arm and brought forth his dagger. Before she could stop him, he'd opened the cell door, grabbed Martin by the scruff of his shirt and held the knife beneath his throat, letting the blade slice the skin enough for blood to well up.

"No, Darius, don't do it," she pleaded.

The police detective, who was still standing in the doorway, barged into the room, pulling his gun. "Put the weapon down or I'll shoot," he demanded.

Darius glanced at them both, his expression dark and fierce.

"Stay out of this—both of you. It is insightful of Martin to realize that he doesn't have what it takes to face his new life. His wife will understand. If the roles were reversed, he'd expect her to do the honorable thing and kill herself, rather than learn to control her blood-lust and return to a different, but still satisfying, life."

Lexi watched the man's expression change from defeat to hope. "No," Martin said, taking a breath and straightening. "I've changed my mind."

Darius withdrew his arm, but didn't put his knife away until after he'd stepped outside the cell.

Martin walked up to the bars, his expression grim. "I want to know who did this to me," he told Lexi. "I want to know who murdered me."

"You weren't the only victim of this initiation scam," the detective said, eyeing Darius warily, but holstering his weapon since Darius had put his dagger away. "Several of our recent missing persons were found tonight. Unfortunately, many of them, like you, had already been converted. We're looking into it, and when we find the ones who did it, they'll pay—provided they haven't paid already," he added with a side scowl at Darius.

Lexi looked pointedly at the bars of the cell between them before giving Martin her attention again. "I'm sorry I had to put you behind bars."

He shook his head. "It's probably just as well," he told her. "I'm going to need time to sort things out. Learn to control my appetite." He hesitated. "Would you mind calling my wife and telling her what happened? Tell her that I'll understand if she never wants to see me again, but that I'm sorry, and—I love her." He paused and took a deep breath. "I'd call her myself, but I'm not sure I can handle hearing her rejection."

"I'll call her and tell her what's going on," Lexi promised, though it wasn't a conversation she was looking forward to.

"What now?" she asked Darius as they left the vampire holding area.

"I've been thinking about those conversion papers. You said they're legitimate?"

She'd given the stack of ACFs back to the detective, but at Darius's question, she led him to the detective's desk so they could look at the papers again.

They'd only flipped through a couple of forms before Lexi noticed something she hadn't before. "Does it seem odd to you that the same physician signed all of these?"

She flipped through several more forms, but the name on them was the same. *Dr. D. Patrick*. Suddenly she knew why it seemed so familiar.

"Mai went to see a Dr. Patrick this morning," she said. "It has to be the same physician." She looked at Darius to see if he agreed, but he seemed lost in thought. "Darius?" He blinked, and then his gaze focused on her. "Yes, I agree. It makes sense that it's the same physician.

"Right. So we find the physician and get some answers."

Chapter Thirteen

Find the physician and get some answers. That was *exactly* what Darius intended to do.

He was fairly certain that Lexi hadn't made the connection yet between Dr. D. Patrick and Paddy Darby. Only someone familiar with leprechaun culture and traditions would know that the "little people" followed a quirky naming convention. Their birth name was the one they used for formal occasions—but with friends and other acquaintances, they switched the order of their names, so their surname became their first name.

He left the police station with Lexi and stood with her while she hailed a cab. When it arrived, he held the door open for her, but instead of climbing in after her, he remained standing outside.

She looked up at him, confused. "Are you coming? I want to run by Mai's place and make sure she's okay, but then I thought we could go back to my place. We could order a pizza, watch TV—or whatever."

He wanted to smile. After last night, he never thought she'd invite him home with her. There was nothing like mortal combat to bring people together, he thought sarcastically. "I can't."

"Why not?"

"There's someone I need to talk to."

"Oh." She set her jaw. "Fine." Her expression became closed and unreadable, though he had a pretty good idea what thoughts were going through her head. She thought that he preferred other company to hers.

He heaved a sigh. The last thing he wanted was to get into lengthy conversations in front of the cab driver about why he would or would not have sex with her. "It's not what you think," he told her.

She leaned over and placed her hand on the door handle. "It never is. See you around." With that, she pulled the door closed and the cab driver took off.

Darius knew he was going to have to explain everything to her soon, before they reached a point of no return. Unfortunately, time was of the essence. The other night, when he'd been at Ricco's club, the vampire had introduced him to a friend of his—a young female leprechaun by the name of Alise Merriweather.

Hailing a cab, he instructed the driver to take him to the Blood Club. With any luck, Alise would be there tonight and he could ask her if she knew Paddy Darby. Then, if it wasn't too late, Darius intended to pay the leprechaun a little visit.

After stopping at her place to change clothes, Lexi was once again in the back of the cab feeling sullen and depressed. Was she crazy? Darius clearly wasn't interested in her—at least not sexually. How many times had he already made that quite clear? So why had she even hinted that they could have sex? Oh, yeah—because of the full moon, that's why. She was feeling as randy as a dog in heat. Oh, wait, she actually was in heat.

Several minutes later, she was standing at Mai's apartment door. She didn't knock right away, suddenly wondering if she was doing the right thing. After all, Mai was probably more exhausted than she was. Despite Mai's claim that she would be up the rest of the night working, she had probably fallen asleep.

Lexi knocked on the door anyway and waited. A few minutes later, she heard the sound of the chain being slid back and the deadbolt being thrown open.

"Is something wrong?" Mai asked as she opened the door, worry in her voice. Her hair looked mussed from sleeping, and her garnet silk nightshirt made the healing puncture marks and darkening bruises on her neck that much more noticeable.

"I'm sorry I woke you," Lexi said. "After everything that happened tonight, I wanted to make sure you were okay."

Mai waved away her concern as she stood back to let Lexi in. "I'm fine." She led the way through her living room to her kitchen. "You want something to drink? Maybe some coffee?"

Lexi thought about it, but shook her head. "No, thanks. I really just wanted to make sure you weren't suffering any side effects."

They sat down at the table, and Mai started rubbing the injured side of her neck. "Mostly, I'm fine," she began. "But there is one thing. It started about an hour ago and has me worried."

"What's that?" Lexi sat forward in her seat.

Mai's brow furrowed. "You're going to think it's sick," she warned. "But I have this craving for an extremely undercooked steak—bloodred in the center. The bloodier, the better."

"You're craving blood?" Lexi stared at her friend, hundreds of thoughts and concerns suddenly racing through her head. Had she gotten there too late when the vampire had attacked Mai? Had he somehow infused her with vampire-like tendencies without actually killing her?

Lexi was so deep in thought that at first she didn't recognize the small sound coming from Mai. When she did, she realized that Mai was giggling. Lexi rolled her eyes and pursed her lips. "That's not funny."

Mai continued to smile. "Yes, it is. I'm perfectly fine. But, hey, why aren't you with Darius? I certainly wouldn't be hanging out with you if I had a guy like that. I'd have him in bed, screwing him six ways to Sunday."

"Nice," Lexi said. "But for your information, he's not *my* guy."

"Really?" She raised an eyebrow. "Then you won't mind if I give him a try?"

"Knock yourself out," Lexi grumbled, because the truth was that she did care. Standing up, she went around to where Mai was sitting and gave her a hug. "Good night, Mai."

Mai returned her hug and then walked her to the door. "Just remember, if you need anything, I'm here."

Lexi smiled. "I should be telling you that."

It wasn't until some time later, in the back seat of another cab, that Lexi remembered she'd forgotten to ask about Dr. Patrick. Well, she'd do that tomorrow.

She stared out the window and found that she wanted to put her fist through it. Every time she thought about Darius turning her down and Mai wanting to make Darius her next sexual conquest, Lexi got angrier and angrier.

She was never going to get any sleep being wound as tight as she was. Leaning forward, she tapped the driver's shoulder. "I've changed my mind," she told him. "Can you take me to the Blood Club?"

She needed to siphon off some of the excess magic that was making her so edgy, and there was one proven way to do that—spend some quality time with Ricco.

After the cab dropped her off, Lexi walked through the crowded room, unaware of her surroundings. Her sole focus was on getting to the back rooms and finding Ricco. She was almost there when a hand snaked out and pulled her to a stop. Already fuming, she whirled around to confront the person who dared to lay a hand on her.

"Easy, pet." Ricco's velvety voice washed over her as he held his hands up to show he meant no offense.

Lexi looked up into the blue eyes twinkling down at her. Before she'd met Darius, she'd thought Ricco was the most attractive man she'd ever been with. Now, for the first time, she found herself thinking that he wasn't all that tall, and while he was definitely in good shape, his body lacked a certain muscular definition and his complexion was maybe too pale.

She stopped, horrified to realize she was comparing him to Darius. Feeling a bit off balance, she forced herself to relax and gave him a smile. "Hi, I was looking for you."

He smiled. "Everyone else in the club will be relieved to hear that," he teased, gesturing to her clothes. "Not that I mind if you come dressed in your kick-ass leathers and don't-fuck-with-me attitude." He smiled at her. "I lust for danger."

"The nice thing about you, Ricco, is that you lust—period."

"Only for you, pet. No other compares." She thought she saw him glance around before draping an arm around her shoulders and steering her toward the back rooms. "Now, please allow me to demonstrate just how well I lust."

She supposed it was a talent of his—to make every woman he was with feel special. At least Ricco wouldn't run away from her just when things were getting interesting.

They reached the back of the bar, and Ricco stopped at the hostess's desk to place an order for drinks. Then he continued to guide her to his private room.

When she walked in, she saw that the bed was made and the room was clean. Either she was his first tonight or the staff had been in to pick up the place and change the sheets after a previous session. She was inclined to believe the latter.

He closed the door and gestured to the bed. "Do you want to get right to my demonstration? Or would you like to tell me what has got you so worked up?"

She'd always liked his easy manner and the way he seemed to know just what she needed.

"There is something bothering me," she admitted. Suddenly feeling very vulnerable, she pressed on because she had to know the truth. "Am I boring to be with? I mean, sexually. When we're in the middle of—it—are you thinking of other women?"

Ricco stared at her in surprise. Then he placed a finger beneath her chin and tipped her head so he could look deep into her eyes. "You are many things in bed, but boring is not one of them."

"Are you sure?"

He smiled. "When I'm with a woman, I don't like to talk about how many women I've been with, but surely you have some inkling. Please believe me when I tell you that sex with you is some of the best I've had." He continued to hold her chin and leaned forward to kiss her. There was a time when it would have sent a bolt of desire rocketing through her, but not anymore.

As if he understood, he let the kiss end. "And I'm going to miss it."

"I'm sorry, Ricco. It's not you."

A sad look came to his face. "That's the problem. It's not me." He reached for her hand so he could lead her to the bed, to sit beside him. "Do you want to tell me who it is?" He paused. "It's the man from last night, isn't it? He's the one who has you tied in knots."

She shook her head. "It doesn't matter. He's not interested."

Ricco gave a kind of laugh. "Oh, I bet that's not true."

Lexi felt herself getting angry again, thinking about Darius. "Then he has a funny way of showing it—running after other women every time he has a chance to be with me." She shook her head. "No, he's not interested."

She stood up, suddenly not comfortable with their topic of conversation. "I'm sorry. I came here because I needed your help. The full moon is so close, and I haven't expended nearly enough of the energy this week. I'd hoped to do it tonight, but I'm not sure I'm in the mood anymore."

He nodded. "I understand."

Walking arm in arm, they left the back room.

"Do you want to dance before you go?" Ricco asked her as they skirted the dance floor.

"No," she said, leaning close to him so he could hear her over the noise in the room. "I think I just want to go home."

He nodded and, looking about the room, seemed in a quandary as to the best way to get through the crowd. She, on the other hand, had no compunction about pushing her way through.

She hadn't gone far before a couple stepped into their path. Lexi was about to automatically steer around them when she heard Ricco swear under his breath. It was drowned out by the sound of an all too familiar voice.

"Lexi."

She looked up, straight into Darius's face. A movement beside him caught her attention, and she saw a very attractive, very petite redhead tucked under his arm.

"I thought you were going home," he said.

She felt an unaccountable pain shoot through her at the sight of him with another woman and gave him an icy stare. "I changed my mind."

Darius gave Ricco a nearly lethal glare. "Is that right?" His voice was razor sharp.

Ricco pulled himself a little straighter, clearly not intimidated. "Yeah, it is. Have you got a problem with that?" His gaze pointedly touched on the redhead before going back to Darius, who gritted his teeth. There was a tense silence as the two men glared at each other.

The redhead stirred uncomfortably at the silence. "Maybe I should go," she suggested hesitantly, glancing once more at Ricco and Lexi before turning a questioning look on Darius.

As if he'd forgotten she was there, he peered down at her and opened his mouth to say something. Then, without uttering a word, he snapped it shut again.

Lexi got the impression that he didn't want the redhead to leave, but was, for some reason, reluctant to say so in front of her. Well, she would make it easy on him.

"No, that won't be necessary. We're leaving."

"If you'll excuse us," Ricco said, taking Lexi by the hand. He then pushed past them into the crowd, pulling Lexi after him.

Fortunately, Darius didn't try to stop them.

Once they were outside, he gestured to the doorman to hail a cab for her, then stood beside her while they waited in companionable silence. When the cab arrived, Ricco kissed Lexi good-bye. It wasn't the heated kiss of two lovers but an affectionate kiss between two old friends. Then she climbed into the back seat of the cab while Ricco leaned in and gave the driver directions and money to cover her fare.

"Remember," he said. "Any time you need me, you know where to find me."

"Thanks, Ricco." She didn't know what else to say. There was so much emotion, and no words to adequately convey it. Ricco, however, seemed to understand. With a final smile, he slammed the cab door shut and Lexi felt as if he'd just shut the door on a phase of her life; a comfortable, safe phase that she wasn't sure she wanted to end.

Chapter Fourteen

Darius cursed under his breath as he watched Lexi storm off.

"Your girlfriend looked pretty upset," Alise said kindly. "I hope you're not in too much trouble."

Me, too, Darius thought. But at least rescuing Alise from that thug had given him the information he'd been hoping for. "Don't worry. I'll explain things to her later. Right now, let's get you out of here safely." He cleared a path for her through the crowd, slowly fighting his way toward the back exit.

"I appreciate this," she said. "My ex can be a real jerk at times, and I just know he's standing by the front entrance waiting for me to leave."

"Maybe I should have a talk with him," Darius suggested, not for the first time.

"That would just make him mad. Don't worry. I'll be fine. He's not a bad guy, just misdirected. He won't hurt me, but I don't feel like getting into another fight with him tonight."

By now they'd reached the back door. Darius

pushed it open and went outside with the young woman. After he saw Alise safely into a cab, he was going back into the club to beat the crap out of Ricco. The image of the vampire standing with his arm around Lexi after they'd obviously come from the back rooms still burned in his mind.

"Ouch."

"Oh, sorry." Darius loosened his hold on Alise's hand as they walked along the street. The minute he saw a cab, he hurried to hail it and, moments later, watched Alise being driven away.

She'd told him as much as she could about Paddy Darby—that the leprechaun was a physician who'd accidentally maimed a child because he'd been drinking prior to performing surgery. He'd used his pot of gold to pay off the child's family so they wouldn't take him to court, thus retaining his medical license but losing face with the medical community. Without his pot of gold, he was considered an outcast among leprechauns and had lost contact with all his friends and family, including his wife and children. She'd also heard he'd recently fallen in with one of the local vampire gangs. Darius hadn't needed her to tell him which one.

Since the back exit to the club only opened from the inside, Darius walked around to the front entrance to reenter the club. He stopped just inside and scanned the crowd. He didn't see Ricco anywhere and assumed the vampire was once again in the back rooms, so he headed that way.

He was halfway across the room when a flash of pink caught his eye. He froze and tried to catch sight of it again, but without luck. He spent the next ten minutes wandering through the crowd of people, positive that he'd seen the succubus. When next he caught sight of spiky pink hair, it was on a male vampire.

Giving up, he continued on to the back rooms, where he stood at the front of the hallway looking at the row of closed doors. He figured he had two options, and, while kicking down each door held a certain appeal, it was bound to attract more attention than Darius wanted. The other option—listening at each door—made him feel like a sick freak, so instead, he stood at the end of the hall and fumed.

Just then, a door opened. The first thing Darius noticed was the very feminine, sandaled foot that appeared. His gaze was instantly drawn up along a slender, shapely calf and thigh. When his gaze hit the bottom of the short skirt, it jumped up to the outline of full breasts barely contained beneath a shiny black camisole that exposed a generous amount of cleavage.

He looked at her face. The crystal blue eyes staring at him with such obvious interest were made even bluer by the short, spiky, neon pink hair. *Daphne*.

"I've been looking for you, Darius," she said, moving toward him seductively.

He knew he should attack and destroy her. At the very least, he should walk away, but he could do neither. In fact, he couldn't move.

A small, still-functioning part of his mind told him she must be using some kind of glamour. Normally, such magic had no effect on him, but without his Immortal life essence completely restored, his powers were not at full strength.

She closed the distance between them and brushed the back of her fingertips down the side of his cheek as she gazed into his face. A thrill of excitement skittered along his nerves. His pulse started to race. When she leaned into him, his entire body came alive.

Even as his brain reminded him that her function was to seduce and kill men, his subconscious took control of his actions. He slipped his hands around her waist and lowered his head.

The taste of her lips intoxicated him—though there was something missing. There was no emotion, no fire. He fought to tear his mouth away from hers and finally succeeded.

"Don't fight it," she cooed. "We were meant to be together." She took his hand and gave it a gentle tug to get him to move. Like an automaton, he followed her into the room she'd just exited and found it was already occupied by her last unfortunate partner.

The man's dead eyes stared blankly at the ceiling; his lifeless nude body lay sprawled across the bed. The succubus waved her hand, and a blast of energy lifted the man and tossed him aside. Darius barely noticed.

Every ounce of effort in him was fighting the demon's influence. He knew what was at stake; he had to stop her.

She stood before him and slipped the straps of her camisole off her shoulders, one at a time. Darius couldn't look away as the silky fabric slid to her waist, baring full, luscious breasts that beckoned him. He heard her throaty laugh as she cupped herself and ran her thumbs across distended nipples.

She was gorgeous—but she wasn't Lexi. That above all else gave him the strength to take a step back.

"What's this?" Daphne asked, somewhat startled. "Do you think you can resist me? Silly man." She stepped toward him, reaching out.

Darius fought through the fog of her glamour and

compulsion. "What do you want?" he grunted, hating to expend precious effort just to speak, but he had to buy more time.

"You." She undid the fastening of her skirt and pushed it down her legs until it rested on the floor. Standing before him naked, she pushed the twin lobes of her breasts together, distracting him again. "Or rather, your life force."

"You don't look like you need it," he noted, mesmerized by her body.

She smiled and gave a soft laugh, rubbing her breasts against his chest. "Oh, it's not for me."

"Amadja."

She stopped her seductive assault long enough to look surprised. "You know Amadja? Interesting. Yes, I guess the magic is for him—indirectly." She smiled. "But enough about Amadja and his . . . pets." She raised herself on her toes and wrapped her arms around his neck. "I want to focus all my attention on you."

Her lips captured his in a tantalizing kiss as she started to suck his energy from him. Her hands were already working with the fastening of his pants. He knew that if she could force him to succumb to sex, she'd drain his life force more quickly.

He needed something to repulse the succubus long enough to break her hold on him. Voices floated to him through the open door. Salvation was close if he could only summon it.

He focused every thought on Lexi, knowing it would dampen the ardor he felt for the succubus. Then, with a mighty effort, he broke the kiss and shouted, "Ricco!"

The succubus looked at him in confusion. Out in the hall, Darius heard footsteps.

"What's going on here?" Ricco demanded from the doorway. "Darius?"

"Touch her," Darius croaked, fighting the ardor as hard as he could.

"What?"

"Touch her!" Darius yelled.

Ricco stormed into the room. "Miss, I'm sorry, but—"

At his touch on her arm, the succubus screamed, cutting off Ricco's words. She jerked away and emitted a loud hiss. Then she ran from the room, and Darius felt the last of the glamour slowly fade.

"What the hell is going on?" Ricco demanded.

Darius lowered himself on the edge of the bed and rubbed his head. "That was a succubus. She's working for the demon lord."

"Why didn't you kill her?"

"It's not that easy," Darius muttered. "You'd appreciate her tactics. She uses glamour—like you."

"I've never had to resort to using glamour on my partners," Ricco said.

"Whatever."

"Why wasn't she able to use that glamour on me?" Ricco asked.

"Because you're a death-magic creature. The glamour only works on those with living magic. The stronger the magic she can suck, the more powerful her glamour becomes." Darius was starting to feel better and smiled. "Sucking on *your* life force would be like sucking on the tailpipe of a cab."

"Thanks for the analogy. You all right?"

Darius nodded and stood. "Yeah. Thanks to you."

"What are you doing back here anyway? I thought you left with Alise."

Darius fought the urge to put his fist in Ricco's jaw.

"Actually, I came back here to beat the shit out of you, but since you saved my life, I guess that's out. I still want to know what you and Lexi were doing in the back room, though."

"Believe it or not, we were talking."

"About?"

"You."

Darius studied the vampire's face, but decided Ricco was telling the truth. "What did she say?"

Ricco shook his head. "If she wants to tell you, she will. Right now, though, tell me about this succubus."

For the next hour, Darius and Ricco talked. There was no doubt in either of their minds that having both the demon lord and the succubus in town was dangerous. Having them working together was even more so.

"She said something about Amadja's pets," Darius said. "And earlier, I heard Paddy Darby singing about the hounds of hell."

"It could be a coincidence," Ricco pointed out.

"Yeah, it could, but let's say for the sake of argument that it's not. Let's say that the hounds of hell are the same pets the succubus was talking about. If she's siphoning off living magic to feed them, then they have to be demons."

"It makes sense that Amadja would have demons working with him," Ricco summarized.

Darius nodded. "In addition to a growing number of vampires." He paused, thinking. "There's a lot more to that club than what we see from the bar. I need to find a way behind the scenes to see what's really going on. I'm afraid the demon lord has amassed greater forces than we know about—and that could prove deadly for our side."

It was well after midnight when Darius left Ricco's

club. He wandered aimlessly until, without even realizing it, he ended up at Lexi's apartment.

Now he needed to decide if he was going to stay or leave. Without conscious thought, he reached beneath his duster and pulled off his key tattoo. He held it to the lock, and soon it changed its shape.

He told himself that he was sneaking into her apartment because he didn't want to wake her, but maybe the truth was that he needed to see her and knew that if he knocked, she'd refuse to open the door.

He inserted the key, unlocked the door and pushed it open. As soon as he stepped inside, a scorching fireball hit him square in the chest, leaving him momentarily stunned. Before he could recover, a force rammed into him and knocked him to the ground.

Reacting on instinct, Darius grabbed his attacker and flipped their positions so he was on top. The glow of a newly forming fireball provided enough light for Darius to see Lexi's angry face. He grabbed her wrists and pinned her to the floor before she had time to hurl her magic. "Lexi, it's okay. It's me, Darius."

"I know who it is," she snarled. "What right do you have to break into my apartment?"

"You invited me," he reminded her.

"That was before you went off to be with your little redhead."

"Is that jealousy I hear?"

She struggled to free her hands. "Don't flatter yourself."

"I was only with Alise because I needed information."

"I'm sure you were very persuasive," she spit out.

He heaved a sigh. "We talked. That's all."

She glared at him. "Did you forget that I saw you going into the back rooms?"

"What you saw us doing was going out the back way," he told her.

"Do you think I'm totally stupid?" she snapped. "You two couldn't have been any cozier if you were Siamese twins."

"Come on, Lexi. You saw her. The woman is barely taller than my waist. She wanted to sneak out the back because there was someone at the front of the bar she didn't want seeing her. But she couldn't get through the crowd without every available male thinking she was an easy target. I was just making sure she got out safely." He waited a second.

"And you expect me to believe that."

"Yes," he said, starting to get a little mad himself. "It's the truth. And I know you won't ask, but for the record, we didn't have sex." His gaze locked with hers. "We. Didn't. Have. Sex," he said again, slowly.

The fireball that had been blazing ominously in the palm of her hand slowly dissipated. Now that she was no longer trying to attack him, he became more aware of their positions. He was straddling her hips, practically lying on top of her in order to pin her hands to the floor. Arousal shot through him, and his gaze shifted from those gray eyes staring up at him to the dusky rose lips he so badly wanted to kiss.

"We didn't have sex either," she said softly. "Ricco and I."

"I know."

She was clearly surprised. "You do?"

He leaned down a little closer to her. "Yeah. Ricco and I had a little—talk—after you left. He told me you just talked."

She looked so vulnerable staring up at him that he

continued his downward descent, intent on tasting those lips once more, even though he knew he shouldn't. He felt the rise and fall of her chest as her breathing grew more rapid.

He was nearly there; could almost taste her sweetness.

"Please don't," she begged, her voice breaking with emotion. "I can't do this again."

The effect of her pleading was like being doused with ice water. She sounded so distraught.

He wanted to tell her that he'd never hurt her, but Ricco's words from the other night floated through his head. *Too late.*

Reluctantly he got to his feet and then helped her up. There was a moment of awkward silence while he tried not to stare. She was dressed in a loose shirt and pants that clung to every delicate curve.

"You can stay here tonight if you want," she said, breaking into his thoughts. "But you get to sleep on the couch."

Since he'd expected her to kick him out, he was surprised. "Thank you."

She gave him a look like she didn't entirely trust him. "Follow me."

She walked down the hall, and once they reached her bedroom, she opened the closet and pulled out a pillow. She turned to hand it to him and almost hit him in the chest with it because he was crowding her—intentionally. He couldn't help himself; he liked being near her.

He saw the way her breath hitched at the contact, and it made his own pulse quicken to know that she was as attracted to him as he was to her. He looked into her eyes, holding her mesmerized; willing her to feel the intensity and sincerity of his feelings for her.

He leaned close to her again, pleased to see that she didn't shy away from him. Her lips parted, and he felt her warm breath fan his face when she sighed. He reached behind her, took a blanket off the shelf, and then, with great willpower, stepped back. "This should be enough. Thanks."

He left her standing there and went back into the living room. He tossed the pillow on the couch, lay down and covered himself as best he could with the blanket. It wasn't quite long enough to cover his tall frame, but it didn't matter. It wasn't like he was going to get much sleep anyway.

Chapter Fifteen

It was late the next morning when Lexi finally woke up. After dressing, she mentally steeled herself to face Darius, but needn't have bothered. The blanket he'd used was on the couch, neatly folded beneath the pillow, and Darius was nowhere to be found.

Lexi couldn't help the crushing disappointment that swept over her. She was a fool. Principles be damned. She should've gone with instinct, ripped his clothes off and shown him what he'd been missing. She sighed. He knew what he was missing, and he didn't want it. Yet there were those moments when they were together. A touch. A heated look. A suggestive smile. Was that real? Or simply the imagination of a desperate woman?

But even that wasn't the truth. Granted, she was in desperate need of sex, but if that was all it was, she'd had plenty of opportunity to take care of it with Ricco. What she felt for Darius was different. Even a little frightening, because she'd only know him a short time. How did someone become so important so quickly?

The answer was something she didn't want to examine too closely.

She went into the kitchen to make breakfast, determined to forget about Darius. She had other, more important, things to worry about. Work, for instance.

Luckily, there were several cases waiting for her when she finally made it into the office, and she wasted no time in tackling them. She worked straight through the day and, instead of going home for dinner, picked something up and took it back to the office to eat while tackling stacks of paperwork.

It was nearly 8:00 p.m. when she caught a cab ride home. She rested her head against the back seat, eyes closed. All she wanted to do was soak in a hot tub—no looking for the demon or Darius, and definitely no clubbing. In fact, if Mai called asking her to go, she'd tell her—

Lexi eyes shot open. Now that Mai knew about the succubus, she wouldn't be foolish enough to go back—would she?

Lexi got an uneasy feeling. When had Mai ever exercised caution when there was a potentially award-winning article to be written?

As the cab drew to a stop outside her apartment building, she found the thought too frightening to ignore. Feeling the driver's eyes on her as he waited for her to get out, she leaned forward.

"I'm sorry," she told him. "I've changed my mind. I need you to take me to a different address." For the second time in less than twenty-four hours, she had a driver take her to Mai's apartment instead.

"Where the hell do you think you're going?" she asked minutes later when Mai answered the door wearing a sparkling gold party dress and heels.

There were dark circles under her eyes and she looked tired, but she gave Lexi a dazzling smile. "Out."

Lexi walked in, closing the door after her. She followed Mai into her bedroom. "I see that. After your brush with death last night, do you think that's wise?"

Mai waved her concern away. "I'm fine," she assured her, picking up an earring to put on. "In fact, I feel great." She stopped in the process of applying lip gloss. "Hey, why don't you come with me? You'll have a great time."

It was the last thing Lexi felt like doing tonight, but, given Mai's propensity for trouble, she wondered if maybe she should go with her. "Where are you going?"

Mai, now finished with her makeup, wandered out to the living room where her purse lay on the couch. She picked it up and riffled through the contents, leaving Lexi with the impression that she was purposely ignoring the question.

"Mai," Lexi said in a stern voice. "Where are you going tonight?"

Mai, who had been looking through her purse, closed it and let her hands fall to her sides with a sigh. "The Crypt."

"What?" Lexi was shocked. "How can you even think about going back there after they almost converted you into a vampire? Plus, there's the succubus. Mai, there's bad stuff going on at that club."

"Exactly," Mai said excitedly. "Lexi, the public needs to be informed, and it's my job to tell them."

"Even if it means your death?"

"I can't shy away from exposing the truth because of what *might* happen. Besides, I think you're exaggerating."

"Oh, excuse me," Lexi said sarcastically. "Wasn't that you who almost died last night?"

Mai sighed again. "But I didn't die, and now I have an obligation to expose them. Now, are you going with me?"

Lexi crossed her arms and stared defiantly at her friend. If she had to stop Mai by force, she would. "No."

"Okay, then. I'll see you later." Mai waved her hand and was gone.

Lexi swore. She'd forgotten that Mai's magic allowed her to teleport like that.

Left standing alone, Lexi didn't know what to do. She could go after her friend, but then what? Mai had just proved how easy it was for her to get away.

Lexi used her key to lock Mai's front door and left. There had to be another way to keep Mai from getting in trouble, but it would be easier to shut down the club than to convince Mai to leave.

That was when it hit her. She would call in an anonymous tip to the police branch of the Department of Vampirism and report an illegal mass conversion taking place at the club. Such an event would be equivalent to mass killing. After last night's disaster, the police would shut down the club in a heartbeat.

She caught a cab and had the driver drop her off about a block from the club where she found a pay phone and placed the call. Then she ducked behind a trash Dumpster, where she took off her clothes and shifted to wolf form. No one would pay much attention to a stray dog.

She only had to wait about ten minutes before she heard the sirens. It wouldn't be long now.

Inside the Crypt, Darius sat at the bar nursing his drink. He was scanning the crowd, looking for Paddy Darby, when a commotion to his left caught his attention. He turned and saw the crowd part for a little gray-haired man who climbed up on a bar stool.

He seemed unsteady in his movements, and Darius knew the leprechaun had been doing some heavy drinking that evening.

Darius stood and moved along the bar until he reached the empty stool beside the little man. "Hello, Paddy," he said, sitting down.

The leprechaun looked up, startled. "What are you doing here? You can't take me in. My court date isn't for another week."

"Relax. I'm not really a bounty hunter. I was just helping out a friend," Darius added when Paddy looked confused.

That seemed to make the little man less worried, and he called to the bartender. "You there—how about a drink over here?" Paddy turned his attention back to Darius. "You want a drink?"

"No, but I'd like some answers."

"Can I get a glass of whiskey over here?" Paddy shouted impatiently at the bartender, who seemed to be ignoring him. He sighed and turned back to Darius. "What kind of answers?"

"Like what's your name doing all over a bunch of ACFs found at last night's vampire initiation ceremony, Dr. D. Patrick?"

The leprechaun sighed. "I help people die," he said. "I'm the Dr. Kevorkian of the vampire world. Just because you don't approve doesn't mean what I do is illegal. I assure you that my medical credentials are quite legitimate, and the signatures on those forms were put there by the initiates themselves."

Darius was starting to think that there was more to Paddy Darby than he'd first assumed. About to press him further about his participation in the conversions, he was stopped by the sound of a shrill whistle. People suddenly started shouting and running for the door.

"What's going on?" he asked Paddy, who was using the opportunity to lean over the counter and help himself to a full bottle of whiskey while the bartender was distracted.

"It's a raid," he said casually. "They're trying to outrun the I.S."

Darius wasn't sure he wanted to ask. "What's the I.S.?"

Paddy glanced at him in surprise. "Where are you from anyway?" Before Darius could answer him, Paddy's eyes shifted to something behind Darius's shoulder. "That," he said, gesturing with the whiskey bottle, "is the I.S. Immobilization Spell." He tipped the bottle back and took several healthy swallows. "They're all crazy." He gestured to the people scrambling to get out. "No one ever outruns the I.S."

Darius turned to see what Paddy had been pointing to and saw a shimmering wave of light passing over the room. Each person it touched froze instantly. Darius didn't even have a chance to consider outrunning it before the beam touched him and left his body in a state of paralysis.

The noise of chaos in the room slowly subsided as more patrons were touched by the spell until, finally, silence reigned. After several long minutes, he heard voices talking behind him.

"Did you find anything in the back?" one asked.

"Just the usual," a second answered. "No initiation taking place here."

"Damn it," the first voice swore. "It must have been a crank. Still, after that incident at the KOB, better safe than sorry. Let's take everyone back until we can sort things out."

"The van's here," a third voice announced.

"Then let's get started," the first replied.

Though he couldn't move his head, to a limited extent Darius could still see what was going on around him. Men in uniforms moved into his field of vision and, one by one, picked up an immobilized patron and walked off with them. When it was Darius's turn, he tried to move, but whatever magic they were using still held him in its grip.

He was carried outside and placed, standing up, in the back of a van. When it was full, the doors were closed and the van took off.

It didn't take long to make the trip to the police station, where he was placed in a large cell with others. They stood like so many statues, and then, as soon as the doors were closed and locked, the spell wore off and they could move about.

Immediately several men started yelling for their lawyers. Darius noticed that Paddy simply walked over to one of the benches and sat down.

Darius went to sit beside him. "Now what?" he asked.

Paddy gave him a surprised look. "You really don't know?"

Darius shook his head. "I'm not from around here," he said simply.

Paddy studied him through blurry eyes. "You might as well sit back and relax. The police will have to talk to everyone in order to decide who they want to detain and who should be released."

"How long will that take?" It occurred to Darius that if he could get to the club while everyone was still being questioned, he'd have time to start exploring what lay beyond that magically protected door he'd discovered.

Paddy shrugged. "I don't know. A couple of hours, at least—unless you know someone who can get you out early."

"Like?"

"Like a lawyer, or what about your girlfriend? She's in the business, right?"

Darius wasn't about to tell him that he'd be lucky if Lexi ever talked to him again. "Yeah, but I don't want to bother her."

Paddy gave him a look that clearly said he thought Darius was crazy, but he only shrugged. "Suit yourself."

The little man leaned his head against the back wall and closed his eyes. Darius let him sit for a minute before asking him a question that had been bothering him since he first started talking to him in the bar. "What happened to your accent?"

Paddy opened a single eye to stare at him for a long moment. At first, Darius thought it was because he either didn't understand the question or didn't want to answer it, but then he realized it was because the little man was starting to feel the full effects of having guzzled all that whiskey just before being brought in.

"The accent?" Darius reminded him.

"Never had it," he admitted, his words growing a bit slurred. He teetered precariously on the edge of the cot until Darius was afraid he might fall off. "Born and raised here in New York City."

Darius gave him a curious look. "Then why—"

"Because people expect to hear it, don't they? They see a leprechaun and expect him to talk like he just stepped off the boat from Ireland."

Darius supposed Paddy was right. They fell silent, and

Darius's gaze traveled over the other men in the cell. They were an assortment of vampires, humans and possibly even werewolves, though he wasn't positive. Definitely not the type one wanted to get chummy with.

As he continued to study them, he slowly became aware of a soft humming coming from beside him.

"Oh, the end is nigh, me bonny lass, so here's a kiss good-bye. We'll not fare well when they loose the hounds of hell, so lift the tankard high, love, and drink until ye die."

"Hey, wee man," one of the men across the way shouted. "Shut the fuck up."

Darius looked over and saw three inmates glaring at Paddy, who fell quiet beside him.

"On second thought," the man continued, "why don't I come over there and show you what you can do with your mouth?" He stood up. "I bet you're the perfect height for it—you won't even have to get on your knees."

The man and his buddies gave roars of laughter while Paddy shifted nervously on his seat.

"Leave him alone," Darius said, standing up.

The man gave him a condescending smile. "I'm sorry, did you say something?"

"You heard me," Darius said as the two buddies stood to join their friend. "Leave him alone."

"Or what?"

Darius didn't have a chance to reply before the three attacked. Since none of them had weapons, it didn't even occur to him to lift one of his tattoos. He blocked the first man's punch, slammed his fist into the man's stomach and heard the satisfying sound of hissing air.

"Is that all you've got?" Darius taunted.

The other two rushed him, and he smiled. He hadn't trained for seven hundred years for nothing.

He went to work, fists flying, and soon the two lay in a heap on the floor. Darius turned to find the first man holding Paddy against the wall, his hand gripping the leprechaun's throat. Already, Paddy's face was turning a dark red as the man's hand tightened.

Darius moved with lightning-fast speed, grabbed the man by his shoulder and turned him enough that Darius could drive his fist into his face. It was enough to snap his head to the side, and he fell to the ground, unconscious.

Darius turned to address the rest of his cellmates with a hard look. "Is there anyone else who wants to make sport with the leprechaun? No?" He nodded and sat down on the bench. "Someone get this scum out of my sight," he muttered, scowling at the man's unconscious form. Several men stepped forward and pulled the body to the other side of the cell. They dropped him beside the bodies of his two friends.

Suddenly tired, Darius leaned forward, resting his elbows on his knees.

"Thank you," Paddy said beside him.

"No problem," Darius said without bothering to lift his head. He heard the little man walk off, and a second later, he felt something cool against the back of his neck just before it started stinging.

"You're bleeding," Paddy said when Darius tried to lift his head. "Let me take a look at the cut."

Darius put his head down, gathered his hair in one hand and pulled it out of the way. Paddy had to stand on the bench in order to see.

"Is it bad?" Darius asked, hearing the leprechaun's quick intake of breath.

"This pentacle tattoo—where'd you get it?"

Darius considered how best to answer. "It's a family mark," he said.

Paddy stared at it a little longer. "I know someone with this same mark on them. Only it's not on his neck. It's on his cheek."

Darius tried not to show his excitement. "You've met my brother Tain?"

Caution flashed across Paddy's eyes. "He's your brother?"

Darius nodded.

"What about Amadja?" Paddy asked. "Do you know him?"

"He's an old acquaintance," Darius said.

"How come I haven't seen you around the club before?" Paddy asked warily.

"Because I've been away, tending to other business," Darius replied. "I only got back the other day, and before I let Amadja drag me into his schemes, I wanted to spend a little time with a certain bounty hunter. You can understand that." He gave the leprechaun a wink and waited to see if the little man bought his story.

Apparently he did, so Darius pressed his advantage. "Why does a leprechaun physician get mixed up with demons?"

Paddy sighed. "Money." Darius felt more of an explanation was coming, so he didn't say anything. "About six years ago, I got drunk before an operation and I accidentally maimed a patient. A child." So far, the story meshed with what Darius had heard from Alise.

"I lost everything" Paddy continued. "That's when I fell in with the vampires. Vampire gangs pay for new members, and I needed the money. Someone wants to become a vampire? I don't care. I'll sign their conversion forms. The money was good—better than I was getting paid from my regular practice, so I started focusing on just the conversions." He looked away, and Darius knew that what the little man wasn't telling him was that he'd focused a little *too* much on finding new converts—to the point of occasionally converting patients who didn't want to be converted.

"Eventually, the Bloods found out what I was doing and refused to take any more, so I started working exclusively with the Vlads. Then Amadja came to see me and told me that he would replace my pot of gold if I sent him five hundred converts in a year's time. It was a lot, but it was doable. Then, a couple of weeks ago, he tells me I have to find the five hundred in four weeks." Paddy looked at Darius in frustration. "It's impossible, but you know Amadja. You can't cross him."

"So that's what the initiation ceremony last night was all about? Meeting the quota for converts?"

"You know about that?"

Darius nodded.

Paddy shook his head. "Then you know what a disaster it was. Now I have to find replacements. How can I possibly find that many people and get them converted by the full moon?"

"Why the full moon?" Darius asked.

"Because that's when he's going to open Satan's Gate."

Darius could only stare at Paddy in amazement. He'd forgotten all about Satan's Gate. How long ago was it that Re and Eosphoros, the "dawn-bringer," fought? Eosphoros, later known as Lucifer, had unleashed his 666 shade demons on the world in an effort to destroy all human life. Many had died before Re had succeeded in luring the shade demons into a secret dimension, where he'd locked them away for all eternity.

But if what Paddy said was true, then Amadja had found them and was planning to release his "hounds of hell" once more on an unsuspecting world. He was about to ask the little man more when several policemen walked in.

"When I call your name, line up at the cell door," one of them instructed.

He started calling out names and, one by one, men from the cell went to stand by the door. Paddy was one of them. They were led off and didn't return. About twenty minutes later, the police came back for another group.

Darius began thinking about his escape. He considered using his key, but he wasn't about to fight the entire New York City police force to get out of jail when he knew it was just a matter of time before he was released.

Finally, he was led to another room where police questioned him about why he'd been in the bar. He assured them that he'd been there for a drink only, and after hours of no doubt hearing the same story, they believed him.

"Okay, Darius with no last name. Do you have anyone who can come down to the station and vouch for you?" one of them asked when they were done with their questions.

Darius gave him a bored look. "Can't you just let me go?"

"Normally, yes, but since you don't have any ID on you, we're going to have to run your prints through the system first. That could take a while."

Darius was afraid "a while" might turn out to be a

very long time. "You can try calling Lexi Corvin," he said. "Her number is with the things you took from me."

The officer nodded. "I know Lexi. You're a friend of hers?"

The exact nature of their relationship was not something Darius cared to go into with a stranger, so he nodded and watched the officer leave.

He returned a short while later with an amused expression on his face. "The good news is that she knows you. The bad news is that she's not coming for you. You two have a fight?" The officer laughed. "You might as well get comfortable, friend. I'll start running your prints through the system."

Darius couldn't say he was surprised. He'd lived enough years with Sekhmet to know that hell truly hath no fury like a woman scorned.

Chapter Sixteen

Lexi walked into the office the next morning feeling drained and tired. She'd had no idea Darius was in the bar when she'd made the call to the police, so when Mike from the station had called asking if she could vouch for him and pick him up, she'd been stunned.

Unfortunately, she had just returned from the police station with Mai, who was already talking about going back to the Crypt that night. There was no way Lexi could afford to leave her, and she hoped Darius would understand.

Dealing with Mai had been a nightmare. Lexi had spent the whole night trying to convince her how dangerous the Crypt was. In the end, she was afraid her cautions had fallen on deaf ears. Mai was likely to return to the Crypt at her first opportunity, and Lexi simply could not spend every waking minute making sure she didn't. Hence her reason for going into the office a little earlier than normal.

Marge eyed her when she walked in. "You're not looking so hot," she said bluntly. "And don't tell me it's that time of month, because I've known you for three years and 'that' time of month has never been this hard on you."

"This month is the exception," Lexi muttered, nodding toward the back. "Is TJ in?"

"Yeah, he's in."

"Is he alone?"

Marge shrugged and went back to working on the computer. "Would it matter?"

Lexi realized Marge was right. "No."

"Before you go back there," Marge hollered after her, "are you working today?"

Lexi didn't even break stride. "No."

"Today is some skip's lucky day," she heard Marge mumble.

Lexi walked past her own office to TJ's. His door was closed, and she was about to just walk in, but at the last minute changed her mind. She was, after all, about to ask him for a favor.

She knocked and waited for him to growl, "Come in," before opening the door.

TJ was sitting at his desk, scowling fiercely at his computer.

"And I thought I was in a bad mood," she observed.

He clicked something on the screen and then sat back in his chair to give her his full attention. "Damn paperwork," he grumbled. "It's bad enough we have to fill out so many forms at the police station, but then for Jonathan to pile all these others on top . . . it's enough to make you want to quit."

Lexi hated the paperwork too, and they shared a sympathetic moment. Then they both smiled. "You love the job as much as I do," she said. "We both know we'll never quit."

He smiled and ran his fingers through his hair. "What brings you here so early?" he asked. Outside, Lexi could hear cars driving along the street. The garbage truck was making its weekly circuit, and the banging of a Dumpster lid was a loud staccato in the otherwise relatively quiet morning.

"I need a way to keep track of someone without them knowing it," she said simply, getting straight to the point. "Something nonmagical. I thought maybe you might know of something I could use."

"A personal tracking system?" He nodded. "Sure, I might have something you can use. How close can you get to the subject?"

"As close as I need to—she's a friend."

His expression turned grim. "You know that if she finds out you put a trace on her, she'll probably get pretty mad."

Better mad than dead, Lexi thought. "I'm willing to risk it." She figured putting a tracer on Mai was the only way to keep her safe at this point.

Seeing that Lexi wasn't going to change her mind, TJ picked up the set of keys on his desk, selected one and opened the lower file drawer.

He pulled out three necklaces, a pair of earrings, a pin and a small plastic bag filled with flat metal discs no bigger than the end of a pencil eraser. Then he pulled out a small handheld receiver. "You have a couple of choices," he said, laying everything out before her. "Each piece of jewelry has a transmitter, which works great if she wears one of them."

Lexi tried to remember if she'd ever noticed Mai wearing the same jewelry two days in a row. She couldn't remember. "What about these?" She pointed to the bag of discs.

"These you can slip into pockets, or use the adhesive back and stick them on clothing."

She couldn't decide which would be better, and, seeing her dilemma, he came to her rescue. "Tell you what—take them all. Use what you want and then bring me what's left when you're done."

"Thanks. Are they all synced to the same receiver?"

"Yes." He picked it up and turned it on. After adjusting a couple of buttons, he handed it to her. She saw a grid for the lower west side of Hell's Kitchen. There was a blinking dot of light on the spot where their office was located.

She looked up at TJ, and he smiled. "Watch." He took one of the small flat discs from the plastic bag and wadded it up in a piece of paper. Then he went over to open the window. The sound of the garbage truck grew louder. TJ waited, and when it lumbered by, he tossed the ball of paper out the window.

Lexi's eyes were glued to the screen of the receiver where a small dot of light started moving along the line that represented their street. She continued to watch as it turned the corner and continued down the next street.

She looked up at TJ and smiled. "Very cool."

He laughed. "I thought you'd like it." He gathered up the jewelry and remaining discs and placed them into a velvet bag, which he held out to her. "Here you go."

"You're sure?" Lexi wanted to double check. "I know this stuff is expensive."

"I won't refuse any contribution you want to make," he said suggestively. Lexi just rolled her eyes, and he laughed. "Seriously," he continued, "I have a friend who's an electronics engineer. He likes to tinker with new things. He gives me a lot of these. The receiver is another matter. Break or lose it, you just bought it, and don't ask how much it costs, because neither one of us can afford it."

Lexi wasn't so sure she wanted to take the chance and started to hand the stuff back to him.

"No, keep it. Just don't let anything happen to it."

She thanked him, took the stuff and headed home. She was exhausted, but worse than that, she was in pain. The buildup in sexual energy had become a continuous ache.

When she walked into her apartment twenty minutes later, she was surprised to see Darius there, making himself at home.

"How'd you get in here?" she growled at him, trying to harden herself against the sudden excitement of seeing him.

He gave her a lazy smile. "I have a key, remember?"

"But I had wards guarding the apartment. How'd you get past those?"

"Those wards only work to keep out the things you want kept out. They obviously don't apply to me," he said with a smile.

She rolled her eyes and, doing her best to ignore him, carried the bag of electronics to the kitchen table.

"Where have you been?" he asked, getting up from the couch to follow her.

"I've been with TJ," she replied automatically, her attention focused on getting out the necklaces so she could decide which to give to Mai.

"All night?"

"What?" she asked distractedly.

"Your bed hasn't been slept in."

She held up the first necklace, searching for the transmitter. "That's right."

"I see."

It was his tone that finally made her realize he'd drawn the wrong conclusion. She was tempted not to set him straight, but seeing his closed expression made her change her mind. "I was with Mai all night. She was determined to go back to the Crypt after I picked her up from jail." She paused and looked at him. "I'm sorry I left you there. I was afraid to leave Mai alone."

He raised an eyebrow. "So you didn't leave me there because you're mad at me?"

"No."

That seemed to lighten his mood, but then he frowned. "Who's TJ?"

She picked up a different necklace to study. "He's the other bounty hunter in my office. I needed to talk to him about tracking devices, so I went in early."

Darius gestured to the array of jewelry laid out on the table beside the receiver. "What's all this?"

"Micro-transmitters and a GPS receiver." At his confused expression, she went on. "It's the stuff I got from TJ."

"What's it for?"

"I'm hoping it will help me keep tabs on Mai without her knowing it. That way, if she goes to the Crypt again, I'll know it. Then I might be able to stop her before she gets herself into trouble." Of course, she couldn't call in a raid each time, she thought. She'd have to think of other tactics.

"Are they magic?" Darius asked, coming over to take a closer look.

"No. Technology. Here's how they work." She went through the same demonstration TJ had given her, and the look on Darius's face afterwards made her smile. He seemed truly awed.

"It's fascinating." He picked up the receiver and looked at the screen. "What happens if one of the transmitters goes beyond the area shown here?"

"There are ways to adjust the view to show as much or as little of the city as you want—up to a limit. After that, you lose the signal."

She stood next to him, leaning over so he could see the screen as she zoomed the view in and out. She tried hard to ignore the warmth of his muscled arm, and when he took the receiver from her, she couldn't help remembering how those strong hands had felt against her naked skin.

She suddenly realized that she'd stopped talking, and, feeling the heat of his gaze on her, she looked up and her breath caught in her throat.

Seeing the way she looked at him, Darius wanted so badly to pull her into his arms, but knew he shouldn't. "I ran into Paddy Darby while I was in the Crypt," he said, stepping away from her. "We ended up in jail together and had an interesting conversation."

"Really?" she asked, almost too casually. "What about?"

"About how he's Dr. D. Patrick."

"What?"

He had her undivided attention now, so he told her about Paddy's involvement with the initiation ceremonies and the demon.

"I just can't believe it," Lexi said when he was done. "We have to tell the police. I know a lot of those people didn't ask to be converted, so he's responsible for murder."

"We'll have to deal with that later. There's more. Do you remember how we heard him singing that song in the bar? Well, the hounds of hell are real. They're shade demons believed to be locked away. If Amadja releases them . . ." He shook his head. "Now I know what the succubus meant about needing to feed Amadja's pets."

Lexi's eyes widened at the mention of the succubus. "When did you talk to her?"

He quickly told her about his encounter with the succubus, though he did his best to skirt over the seduction parts. Somehow, he didn't think Lexi would appreciate hearing that.

"And that's not all," he hurried on, hoping he was giving her too much information at once for her to focus too long on Daphne. "Paddy saw my tattoo and as much as admitted he'd seen the same one on Tain. So I know Tain is there—it's just a matter of finding him."

Lexi took a step toward him and laid her hand on his arm. "I know you're worried about your brother, but you can't go after him yourself. Not with the succubus out there. Talk to Adrian first—please."

"Okay," he agreed, somewhat reluctantly. "Let's call him."

She picked up the phone and dialed Adrian's number, and soon Darius was talking to him.

"I think you should come to Seattle as soon as possible," Adrian said, unsurprisingly, after Darius explained everything. "They know you're there, which means your life is in danger."

"But I know who this demon is," Darius argued. "I can bind him and destroy him."

"Don't you think we thought of that?" Adrian asked. "Amadja isn't his real name any more than the name I knew him by. The only sure way to destroy him is to combine our powers."

"Tain is here," Darius said.

"You saw him?"

"No, but I know he's here. If I can get to him—"

"Don't even think of trying to rescue him," Adrian said. "Trust me, he's not the same—he's crazy."

"So we turn our backs on him?"

He heard Adrian's sigh. "I don't like it any more than you do. Come to Seattle and we'll figure out what to do."

They talked a few minutes more before Darius hung up the phone. He looked over at Lexi, who was studying him closely. "He wants me to fly to Seattle."

"I think you should go," she said. "I'll get you another ticket."

Darius felt a stab of disappointment. "Careful," he said, keeping his tone light. "I might think you want to get rid of me."

"It's not that," she said. "I don't want anything bad to happen to you."

"Ah, so you *do* care." He'd been keeping his tone light and teasing, but there was nothing playful in the way he looked at her.

"I don't know why I should." He heard the hurt in her voice. "I obviously repulse you."

"What?" He was stunned. "Nothing could be further from the truth."

"Then why is it that every time we start to have sex, you stop?"

He saw the pain and hurt in her eyes and knew he had to tell her the truth. "When I was summoned to the dream dimension, Whitley warned me about two things. The first was about my life force—which I told you about. The other thing he warned me about was . . . embarrassing, if you must know the truth."

"Go on," she encouraged when he hesitated.

He took a breath. "Sekhmet was afraid I'd enjoy myself too much while I was here, so she quickly cast a spell as I was being pulled to Earth. But only pieces of the spell touched me, and it got twisted." He looked at her, praying she'd understand. "The gist of the spell is that if I climax while having sex, I'll forget everything, including—"

"—who you are," she finished for him. Then her eyes shot sparks. "You were with that woman that first night, weren't you? The one with the pink hair. You climaxed with her, and that's why you lost your memory."

"You make it sound like I was cheating on you," Darius countered, getting a little heated himself. "As I recall, you weren't interested in having sex with me at the time. Furthermore, I wasn't with a *woman*. She was a demon. And not just any demon—a succubus. She sucks the life out of you and leaves you for dead. Although now that I think of it, maybe that's just women in general." He was beyond frustrated and making matters worse, but he couldn't seem to stop. Then he heard a small chuckle and turned to see Lexi smiling at him.

"If you are planning to spend any time with me at all, I think it's only fair to warn you that I get a little bitchy around the full moon."

"Lexi," he sighed, all the fight leaving him. He closed the distance between them and cupped her cheek with his hand as he gazed deep into her eyes. "I never meant to hurt you." He dipped his head and captured her lips with his. The hunger that shot through him was intensely primal, and when she wrapped her arms around his waist, he kissed her like he might never get the chance again.

Finally, they broke apart, both a little breathless.

"Much as I want to stay, I should probably go now," he said. "But when this is over, I'm coming back to finish what we started. That's a promise."

"I'll be here," she told him. "However long it takes, but please be careful."

"I will." And then, before he could change his mind, he walked out the door.

After Darius left, Lexi couldn't help wondering if he had really told her the truth this time. His explanation about being jinxed by a partial spell, while possible, was a little hard to believe.

Not sure what to make of it, she forced her attention to more urgent matters. She went to the kitchen table where the necklaces were spread out and found the one she thought Mai would like. She put it into the velvet pouch, put the bag with disc transmitters in her pocket, along with the receiver, and left.

When she got to Mai's apartment, she found her friend busy working on her story.

"How's it coming?" Lexi asked. "Any chance you'll let me read it?"

Mai scowled at her. "You know the rule—not until it's finished."

"So—do you have plans for tonight?" Lexi asked, not bothering to be subtle.

"As a matter of fact, I do," Mai replied. "But don't worry. I'm not going to the Crypt. I have a friend coming over—a male friend."

At Lexi's surprised look, Mai smiled. "Before you ask, he's not anyone you know. Just a guy I met, but he's drop-dead gorgeous, and so considerate and fun to be with."

"Oh, Mai. I'm so happy for you." But Lexi couldn't

prevent the cynic in her from wondering exactly where Mai might have met this man. Who was he? What was his background?

"Stop it," Mai said. "I see the expression on your face. Can't you just, for once, be happy that I found someone?"

Lexi felt guilty now. "Of course. I'm sorry. Yes, I'm delighted you've found someone. And I'm thrilled you're not going to the Crypt. So," she said with a smile. "Tell me more about this mystery man."

Mai merely shrugged. "There's nothing to tell. What's that you have?"

Lexi handed the velvet pouch to Mai, whose eyes lit up with childlike excitement. "What's the occasion?"

"I'll tell you in a second. First tell me if you like it."

Mai opened the pouch and pulled out the obsidian necklace. She held it up, and Lexi breathed a sigh of relief at the look on her friend's face.

"It's not my birthday," she said to Lexi, obviously fishing for the reason Lexi gave it to her.

Lexi took a breath. "I gave it to you for your protection."

"From what?"

Lexi looked around and then gestured to the couch. "Let's sit down, and I'll tell you what I know."

Mai listened as Lexi told her everything—about the demon lord trying to destroy the world, Calling the Immortals, the vampire conversion scheme, the succubus—even about finding Howard Parks dead. To her credit, Mai listened to all of it, asking only a couple hundred questions.

"I didn't tell you sooner because I didn't know all of it until just recently," Lexi finished.

"And the necklace?"

"Obsidian is a protective stone. It might not be the strongest magic, but it will help. Please wear it—for me. So I'll stop worrying about you constantly."

Mai reluctantly nodded and put the necklace on. "Happy?"

Lexi smiled. "Yes, thank you."

"So where are things between you and the Immortal?" she asked.

"They're . . . I don't know. They're confusing. He's gone to Seattle to be with Adrian until the other two brothers—Kalen and Hunter—show up."

"Kalen?" Mai repeated thoughtfully. "That's not a name you hear often."

"No, I suppose not," Lexi agreed, finding Mai's statement odd.

"You like him, don't you?"

"Kalen? Oh," Lexi said when Mai shot her a look. "Darius. Yeah, I suppose I do." She glanced at her watch and stood up, worried that if she didn't leave, Mai would bombard her with questions she wasn't ready to answer. Questions about how she really felt about Darius. "I need to go. Please wear the necklace for me and be careful. I'll call you later tonight."

"I promise," Mai said, following her to the door.

It was getting dark when Lexi left Mai's apartment and caught a cab. She thought about Darius, sitting alone at the airport, waiting for his flight. He must be—

She stopped in mid-thought and frowned. How was he planning to fly to Seattle without a ticket? Had Adrian bought him one? That had to be the case, because she certainly hadn't. She'd been distracted by his confession—and then later by his kiss.

She pulled the receiver from her pocket and turned it on. When she'd kissed Darius, she'd been holding one of the small discs in her hand. Without knowing why she'd done it at the time, she'd slipped the disc in his pocket when she'd wrapped her arms around him.

Now she turned the dials of the receiver to adjust the grid. Almost immediately she saw the light that belonged to Mai's necklace. She enlarged the geographic view and searched for another blinking light. Two appeared. One, she remembered, would be the garbage truck, while the other had to be Darius. Neither, she noticed with a frown, was at the airport.

She checked the location of each dot in turn and saw that one of them was in a part of town she wasn't familiar with. The other, however, was blinking at a location that was all too familiar—the Crypt. She didn't need two guesses to know whose dot that was.

Chapter Seventeen

Darius moved down the hallway of Amadja's underground dwelling, searching for Tain. Instead of going to the airport when he left Lexi, he'd gone straight to the club. Using his key, he'd sneaked inside and found the magically disguised door. In the end, getting in hadn't proved that difficult. He'd simply walked through the door.

He'd worried about being spotted, but soon discovered that none of the vampires or demons below ground seemed interested in him. He supposed it was because the only creatures down there were supposed to be down there.

Beyond the door had been a series of chambers he'd not yet been able to search. Beyond the chambers, a long tunnel stretched out before him like a long, untraveled road with no beginning and no end; dark and desolate, with only magical lanterns to light the way.

The end of the tunnel, when he finally reached it, split into three hallways. He explored each in turn, but only the last one was of any interest, with a set of huge double doors guarded by two vampires.

Too late to turn back unnoticed, he considered pulling his sword and dispatching them, but something made him hesitate. Instead, he strode toward them, and, to his surprise, they opened the doors at his approach and allowed him to enter the room beyond.

As soon as he stepped into it, Darius knew this was a room of some significance. It was a huge, relatively open area with a high domed ceiling. To the right was a dais on top of which sat a throne and a side chair. A heavy drape hung from the ceiling behind the dais, sectioning off a portion of the room. When Darius went to check it out, he saw that behind the curtain was a small, plush bedroom with thick area rugs and a luxurious bed piled high with pillows.

In the middle of the room, sunk in the floor, was a large rectangular pool. He moved to the edge and stared at the opalescent substance inside. On a hunch, he dipped his hand in and scooped some up. Even as he watched, it melted into his skin, and he felt the rush of energy that could only come from living magic.

He remembered what Daphne had said about collecting magic for Amadja. This pool of living magic was the culmination of all the life forces the succubus had collected to feed the shade demons. But where were the shade demons? Had they already been released?

Darius recalled Paddy talking about the full moon, and he wondered how that played into Amadja's plan.

Leaving the chamber with more questions than answers, Darius searched the other rooms at that end of the long tunnel. Each turned out to be a luxurious bedroom that could only have been used for sex.

Next he found a door that led out of the tunnel into

a damp room filled with pipes and electrical wiring. It seemed to be some type of huge underground utility room.

There were two "non-magical" doors, and Darius went to each in turn and opened it. One opened into a hallway with elevators. The other door, he discovered, led to a short set of stairs that ended at a pair of metal double doors. Darius used his key to open them, stepped through and found himself standing outside the building, on the sidewalk.

He looked up at the building he'd left and noticed the scalloped top that tapered to a spire. He'd seen this building before when he'd familiarized himself with the layout of the city and had been struck by its interesting architecture. It was the Chrysler Building.

Walking into the Crypt felt a lot like walking into the enemy's camp, Lexi thought. Every nerve in her body screamed at her to turn around and go home, but she squared her shoulders and kept walking, determined to find Darius.

She pushed her way through the crowd, ignoring the small groups of vampires standing around, eyeing her hungrily. She was careful not to meet their gazes, not wishing to accidentally encourage unwanted attention.

Fortunately, the evening was young and they weren't so hungry or desperate that they felt the need to press their attentions, and they allowed her to continue on her way.

Pushing past a group of inebriated humans, she worked her way farther into the room and looked around.

She stopped moving as her gaze touched on a particularly tall man, leaning against a wall. He was wearing regular clothes and would not have caught her attention except for the pentacle tattoo on his cheek. Tain. It had to be.

Several very attractive, scantily dressed women were vying for his attention, but he seemed oblivious to them. His gaze was fixed on an exotic-looking woman with long black hair across the room. She was talking to several vampire males who seemed to be trying to outdo each other in a bid for her attention.

Listening to the woman's delicate laughter, Lexi looked back at Tain and saw him frown. A minute later, he pushed away from the wall and stormed over to the woman. He placed his hand on her shoulder, whispered something in her ear, then walked off. She left the group of clearly disappointed males and followed him.

Lexi saw them meet up a short distance away, and together they walked toward a spot in the wall. Then suddenly they were gone.

At first, Lexi couldn't believe it. She looked around, thinking that her eyes must be playing tricks on her, but Tain and the woman were nowhere to be seen. Lexi turned her attention back to the wall and stared at it hard. For a moment, nothing happened, and then, as if she'd conjured it by sheer will, she saw a door appear in the wall and a woman stepped out.

Lexi blinked, and when she looked again, the wall was back, as if it had never changed. Yet the woman was still there. That was when Lexi realized she'd found the door leading to the underground part of the club that Darius had been searching for.

So where was he? Had he already found it?

She pulled out her receiver and checked the grid. Relative to her position, he was practically beneath her, which meant he had found it and was now below. Immediately her mind conjured horrible scenarios of Darius getting caught or being tortured.

She was moving even before she'd made up her mind to go through the door. When she reached it, she stopped and turned around, staring back into the crowded room. What was she doing? She had no idea what lay on the other side. It could be dangerous—it could be deadly.

Darius had gone in there, a small voice echoed.

Before she could talk herself out of it, she stepped backward.

It was like stepping through a field of static electricity, but once she passed through the door, the prickling sensation disappeared.

She stood in a hallway lit by lanterns. Demons walked past her without seeming to care that she was there. Well, she thought, she'd made it this far. She might as well see what else there was.

She picked a direction at random and started walking—not too fast, but not too slow. She wanted anyone who happened to notice her to think she knew where she was going.

As she walked along, she studied her surroundings. Every few feet, she came across a door, which presumably led into a room or another hallway. Lexi wasn't ready yet to try opening any of them. The walls were made from the same brick as the club, but it was hard to believe that this entire system of hallways had been built without magic. The area seemed too large and too well constructed.

Lost in thought, she was passing before one of the dark, open doorways when someone grabbed her arm and pulled her inside. Before she could scream, a hand clapped over her mouth and a warm, hard body pinned her against the wall.

"What the hell are you doing?" Darius hissed into her ear.

"Looking for you," she whispered back unfazed as soon as he took his hand from her mouth. "You were supposed to be going to the airport," she chastised him.

"I changed my mind," he said. "I know Tain is here."

"Yeah. I saw him—not ten minutes ago, upstairs."

"What?" Darius gripped her arms and practically shook her in his excitement. "Are you sure it was Tain?"

"Yes, yes," she assured him, trying to dampen his eagerness. "I'm sure. You said he had a pentacle tattoo on his cheek. I saw it."

"How did he look?"

Lexi bit her lip, wondering how to tell Darius that Tain had not looked like he was being held prisoner. "He looked . . . good," she said lamely.

"He might still be up there," Darius said, starting to turn.

Lexi held him back. "No. I followed him down here."

A door down the hall opened just then and three nude demons stumbled out, two females and a male. They appeared to be so drunk, it seemed a miracle that they could even walk, but they managed.

Safely hidden from view in the doorway, Darius watched the three head toward him and Lexi. He eased Lexi farther into the shadows of the doorway and turned to face her, knowing she would be completely hidden behind him. With luck, his dark clothes would help them blend so well into the shadows that the demons wouldn't notice them. But waiting for the trio to pass was torturous.

Standing so close to Lexi was a mistake—as he'd

known it would be. She smelled of wild forest and sweet spice. He found it intoxicating and pressed even closer to her, wanting to feel her body against his. He cupped her face with his hands and bent his head to kiss her.

She returned his kiss with an eagerness that both pleased and surprised him. It was almost impossible to keep his attention focused on the hallway beyond, and only very reluctantly did he finally break the kiss and step back from her.

He smiled down at her. "When you followed Tain through the door, did you see where he went?"

"No, I'm sorry," Lexi answered a little breathlessly. "The hall was empty by the time I made it through."

Darius stepped out of the doorway and looked to make sure the passage was clear. Seeing it was, he gestured to Lexi. They were approaching an intersection in the tunnel system when Darius heard the deep rumble of male voices coming from around the corner. One voice, in particular, stood out. "Amadja."

Darius didn't realize he'd spoken it out loud until he felt Lexi flinch. He looked around, knowing that the approaching group stood between them and the magically protected door into the bar. He looked the other way, hoping to discover a means of escape, but before them stretched the hallway, endless and open.

That left only one option. Darius pulled Lexi to the nearest doorway and tried the door. It was unlocked, and he pushed it open.

They stepped into what appeared to be yet another large bedroom. There was a king-size four-poster bed covered with a thick, fluffy black comforter. Ruby-red fabric hanging from beams between the posters encased the bed like a giant tent. The floor was a shiny black tile, and there was a small ebony wardrobe off to one side. An ebony tri-fold partition stretched across the opposite corner.

Darius stepped near the door, listening to the voices draw closer. He hoped the voices' owners would keep on walking, but when it seemed they were coming to this room, Darius grabbed Lexi's arm and pulled her behind the partition. They stood silently as the seconds ticked by.

When he heard the doorknob turn, Darius tensed. Arranging themselves as close together as possible, they were able to peek through the gap between the three parts of the partition.

As he watched, the door opened and in stepped Amadja, accompanied by O'Rourke, who Darius recognized from Ricco's description as the leader of the Vlads, and two lesser demons. There was a fifth person with them, but he was blocked from view.

". . . and the pool is not at full capacity," O'Rourke was saying.

Amadja nodded. "The arrival of another Immortal has forced me to move ahead with my plans sooner than I'd expected—but hopefully, by taking advantage of the full moon, the magic we have will be enough. Soon the hounds of hell will be mine to command."

Amadja smiled, but Darius thought O'Rourke looked worried. "Are you sure you can control them?"

Amadja waved his hand as if dismissing O'Rourke's concern. "They will bow to my superior power."

O'Rourke still didn't look convinced. "I know you've said they once terrorized the world, but they've been locked away a long time. If they're even still alive, they can't be very strong."

"We will feed them until they achieve their former power," Amadja assured him.

"But how? I don't understand."

"The collection pool," Amadja said as if it were obvious. "We will feed them the magic in the collection pool."

O'Rourke stared at him, aghast. "That much living magic will kill them."

"If we were only talking about one or two hundred demons," Amadja agreed. "But there will be six hundred and sixty-six demons feeding at once. We'll be lucky if there's enough magic in the pool to whet their appetite."

O'Rourke opened his mouth to say something, but Amadja waved him to silence. "I have important things to see to. Go check in with the other gang leaders around the country and make sure they are ready to do their part."

O'Rourke nodded and started to leave, but when he reached the door he hesitated.

"What is it?" Amadja asked irritably.

"What about the reporter? She could be trouble."

The demon gave a slow smile. "Don't worry about her. She's being taken care of."

Beside him, Darius felt Lexi stiffen. There could only be one reporter they were talking about—Mai. He laid a hand on her arm, warning her not to give them away by making a noise. It was still too dangerous.

Then the two other demons in the room moved and all thought failed him. There, standing in handcuffs, was Tain.

Darius was instantly filled with both fear and jubilation. Adrian's accusations that Tain had turned rogue were wrong. Seeing his brother's bare chest covered with scarred welts, Darius had no doubt that Tain was and always had been a prisoner.

It took almost everything in him to remain standing there, and he might not have succeeded if Lexi hadn't held him back.

Darius saw Amadja gesture, and the two demons holding Tain led him over to the far wall. There, the handcuffs were removed and each wrist was locked into a heavy metal cuff chained to the wall.

Across the room, Amadja opened the double doors of the wardrobe. From inside, a tray slid forward and he examined its contents.

"It is time," Amadja said solemnly. "Do you understand, Tain?"

Darius looked at his brother and saw that he had turned as much as the cuffs would allow in order to look over his shoulder at the demon. The look of complete and utter misery on his face was one Darius would never forget, no matter how long he lived. It was filled with utter hopelessness.

"Just get it over with," Tain muttered.

Darius felt Lexi tense beside him and quickly glanced at her to see what was wrong. Following the direction of her gaze, he felt his pulse quicken at the sight of Amadja holding up a gleaming silver scalpel.

Darius felt nauseated. Now he knew what had caused such extensive scarring on Tain's back, and it pained him to think how much Tain had endured over his long centuries of captivity.

A protective rage consumed him. How dare any creature treat his brother that way? Guilt followed quickly on the heels of the rage. He couldn't help but think that maybe, if he'd made the decision to leave

Ravenscroft earlier—before Sekhmet had made it impossible—he might have learned the truth about Tain's disappearance. He might have found him sooner.

A movement from Amadja pulled Darius from his thoughts. He watched the demon cross the room to his brother, who was trembling in anticipation of what was to come.

Darius glanced down at Lexi. Her gaze was filled with all the anger, sadness and rage he felt. He knew then that no matter what he did next, she would understand.

At the sound of a small gasp, Darius turned back to his brother and saw that in the moment he'd looked away, Amadja had sliced a perfect rectangular strip of skin off Tain's left shoulder. Blood flowed down his back and side. Even as Darius tried to make sense of such atrocity, Amadja lifted the scalpel to start again.

"You are unworthy, Tain," he said. "You failed in your duties as an Immortal. You disappointed your mother and your brothers until they had no choice but to abandon you. No one even came to look for you, Tain. No one cared."

Darius's temper exploded. He kicked down the partition, making a racket that momentarily stunned Amadja and his demon guards. Darius immediately slapped a hand to his arm and pulled off his dagger. Then, with a mighty war cry, he raced across the room.

Chapter Eighteen

His intended target was Amadja, but out of the corner of his eye, Darius saw that one of the guards had recovered from his shock and was charging him.

Before he could reach him, however, a bolt of fire shot across the room and the guard was engulfed in flames. Darius kept racing forward. Amadja simply stood there and smiled, goading him forward with one hand while the other held the scalpel like a street fighter might hold a switchblade. Darius was too angry to be cautious. When he drew within striking distance, he plunged his dagger into Amadja's chest.

At the same moment, pain ripped through him, and he stumbled back. Looking down, he saw the silver scalpel sticking out of his chest, just missing his heart but still within the twin circles of his life-force tattoo.

Though the pain was nearly blinding, Darius pulled the scalpel out and tossed it aside. Amadja also seemed to be having a hard time recovering from his injury, but he pulled himself upright. He raised his hand, and Darius had just enough time to realize what was coming and jump out of the way before a bolt of black energy struck the floor. It left a nasty, raw burned spot on the once shiny floor. Darius returned fire, pulling Re's fire bolts from his shoulder and hurling them.

One struck the demon lord, who howled in anger. He loosed another burst of black energy that singed Darius's arm as he dodged to get away. Despite the burning pain, Darius kept fighting.

Nearby, Lexi took on the guards. Darius could hardly spare her a glance and prayed she wouldn't come to harm.

As Amadja gathered his strength for another assault, Darius could feel himself weakening and knew he only had one shot to take down the demon.

He pulled his golden cord from around his waist and made a lasso of it. Just as Amadja attacked, Darius let the loop fly. It soared through the air and landed around Amadja's neck. Darius pulled the cord tight and held on, despite the way Amadja fought. The lasso kept the demon from morphing or using any other magic while it slowly cut off Amadja's air supply. Finally the demon lord slumped to the ground, unconscious.

For a second, Darius was tempted to pull his broadsword and cut off Amadja's head, but killing a demon—especially an old one such as Amadja—took more energy than Darius could command at the moment. Right now, it took all his effort just to stand up. The most Darius could hope for was that Amadja remained disabled long enough to give Darius time to free his brother and make their escape.

"You're hurt," Lexi said, rushing to him.

He looked down and saw the blood. "It's just a cut,"

he told her, though it was really starting to hurt and the bleeding wouldn't stop.

"I can help," she offered. "If you'll let me."

"How?"

She held up her fist, forefinger extended. A small ball of fire suddenly appeared and grew stronger. He guessed her intentions and nodded.

"It's going to hurt," she told him, glancing up to his face as she stepped toward him.

"I doubt it can hurt more than it already does. Just do it. We don't have much time." He knew his words were abrupt, but fortunately, she didn't seem to take offense. Instead, she guided the tiny ball of flame to his chest and then, giving him a second to prepare, placed her finger over the wound.

As the fire cauterized the wound, he gritted his teeth against the pain. He knew this was much better than bleeding to death—in this case, a very real possibility.

When Lexi took her finger away, the pain subsided ever so slightly. He looked down at the burned flesh, knowing it would heal in time. At least the bleeding had stopped.

He gave Lexi a grateful smile and hurried across the room to where his brother was chained.

"Darius?" Tain asked, obviously shocked to see him.

"It's me," Darius assured him. "Everything's going to be okay. I'm going to get you out of here."

Tain seemed surprised, but a small smile spread to his lips. "You're rescuing me?"

"Yes." Darius reached behind him and pulled off his key, which he held up to the first cuff. "I'll have you free in a moment."

"I'd forgotten you had that," Tain said, watching him work.

The first cuff opened, and Darius pulled Tain's hand free before going around to the other side. He spared a quick glance at Amadja to make sure he was still unconscious, noticing as he did the scars that covered his brother's back. New scars layered over old ones. The amount of suffering his brother had endured was unfathomable.

Darius forced his attention to opening the cuffs. As soon as both arms were free, he pulled Tain into his arms and held him close. "I never thought I'd see you again," he said, his voice gruff with emotion. "I'll get you out of here, and soon we'll all be together again—you, me, Adrian, Kalen and Hunter."

"They're here too?" Tain asked, clearly startled.

"No, not here. But we'll be with them soon."

Lexi's hand on his arm reminded Darius that now was neither the time nor place for this happy reunion. Amadja was slowly coming around.

"That's not all," Lexi said, gesturing to the door. "Company's coming."

Though he couldn't hear anything, Darius didn't question her. He knew her hearing was better than his. "Are you all right?" he asked her. "Can you walk?"

"I'm good," she said. "Let's go."

He turned to Tain. "Do you need help?"

He reached out a steadying hand, but to his surprise, Tain pulled away.

"What's the matter?" he asked, thinking Tain was hurt more seriously than he'd thought.

"I'm not going."

Darius couldn't believe he'd heard correctly. "We have to go. Reinforcements are coming. Soon we'll be outnumbered."

"I'm not going," Tain repeated. His insistence bothered Darius. It spoke of serious psychological injuries. Darius only hoped the Mother Goddess could heal him once Darius returned him to Ravenscroft.

At that moment, the door burst open, followed by a flash of energy. The shock wave crashed into Darius, Lexi and Tain, knocking them back as six demons raced in.

Darius was the first to recover. When he saw the demons gathering their magic for another assault, he stepped in front of Lexi and Tain, pulling his shield tattoo from his right shoulder and holding it before them. When the blast hit, the shield deflected the energy to other areas of the room, scorching the drapes around the bed and slamming the wardrobe against the wall.

As Darius feared, when the demons saw how ineffective their initial assault had been, they quickly split apart, intending to attack from all directions. It was time for him to go on the offensive.

The moment he lowered his shield, Lexi was beside him, conjuring a massive fireball. With the shield still in one hand, he pulled his broadsword with the other. Then, at his signal, Lexi hurled her fireball at the nearest demon while Darius stormed the others.

Darius took his sword to the next lesser demon, while Lexi blasted more fire at another.

Darius had hoped that Tain would join in the fight, but when he didn't, Darius worried that centuries of being held prisoner might have broken his spirit.

As he did in the old days, Darius focused on the battle before him until a cry of pain from Lexi tore his attention away. He turned and saw her clutching her stomach where his dagger, previously stuck in Amadja's chest, now protruded. Before his brain could register what had happened, her knees buckled and she sank to the floor.

A new, nearly paralyzing fear shot through him. She couldn't be dead. Darius whirled around, swinging his sword in a deadly arc laced with crackling energy. Each of the last four demons rushing him fell to the ground and disappeared in a flash of sulphur and brimstone.

He hurried to Lexi's side. She was on the floor, blood seeping from between her fingers as she pressed her hand against the wound. Her eyes were open, but he knew she was having trouble focusing, and her complexion was paling from the loss of blood. If she could only generate enough magic to cauterize her own wound . . .

The thought broke off as a low-level droning caught his attention. Darius turned around and saw Amadja, fully recovered, holding his hands out to the side, palms up. The air above them shimmered as he summoned his magic once more. When he met Darius's gaze, his eyes were glowing like hot coals.

The next few minutes unfolded in slow motion. Amadja pointed at Lexi and there was a brilliant flash of light. At the same instant, Darius threw himself on top of her, shielding her body from whatever magic Amadja had just unleashed.

If he'd been anyone else, the impact of his body would have driven the dagger through her, sealing her fate. But the dagger was his, and the instant it touched his skin, it morphed into the tattoo once more. Then he felt a blistering heat on his back as Amadja's magic burned him. He could smell the sickening stench of his own charred flesh and thanked the Goddess he'd gotten there before the bolt had struck Lexi.

When the blast subsided, he looked straight up into the face of Amadja, though the effort cost him dearly. Amadja looked triumphant, and Darius could understand why. Lexi was bleeding to death from her wounds, and he was injured almost to the point of being unable to move. As he prepared himself for Amadja's final attack, Tain suddenly stepped between them.

"Get out of the way, Tain," Amadja ordered. Darius had little time to wonder about his brother's change of heart because at that moment, Tain rushed Amadja.

Darius bent over Lexi, who was lying deathly still. He caressed the side of her face and felt her clammy, cool skin. "Come on, baby, stay with me," he encouraged when he saw her eyelids flutter.

He lifted her into his arms, wincing at the shooting pain radiating from the scalpel wound and the burns on his back. Cradling her against his chest, he turned to check on the fight. To his surprise, Tain was alone.

"Where's Amadja?" he asked, looking around. The door to the room stood open.

"He ran for reinforcements," Tain gasped, still breathing hard. "We need to leave before he returns."

Darius needed no further encouragement. He had to get Lexi out of there before she died. He pushed through the open doorway and glanced up and down the hall to make sure that Amadja and his demons weren't waiting for them. Seeing that the coast was clear, he headed for the door to the bar, Tain close on his heels. They were within sight of it when a figure stepped through. Daphne. Her sultry gaze drew Darius in, and though he tried to resist, he'd taken a step toward her before he even realized what he'd done.

Lexi shuddered in his arms, and he looked down. For a moment, the fog in his head lifted, and he remembered why he was there. He had to get Lexi to safety. She was his number-one concern, not the succubus coming toward him.

"Darius." The sound of his name from Daphne's lips was a siren's song, and every fiber in his being wanted to go to her. He had to fight the temptation.

Then, suddenly, Tain came to his rescue again, stepping in front of him. Immediately the temptation to go to the succubus faded as she focused on his brother. A new fear shot through Darius. He hadn't rescued his brother from Amadja only to have him fall victim to the succubus.

"Tain," he shouted. "Don't listen to her. Come with me."

"Go," Tain growled, a strange light in his eyes. "I can handle this."

"Tain." All the pain and helplessness Darius felt was in that single utterance. It must have pierced the glamour affecting Tain, because he turned to look back at Darius.

"I'll come back for you," Darius promised.

"I know."

Still Darius hesitated. He couldn't leave Tain behind. But as soon as the thought formed, it died. The succubus had reached Tain. Her arms were around his neck, and she was kissing him. If Darius tried to interfere, she would only siphon off the last of his energy as well and Lexi would surely die. Tain's sacrifice would be for nothing.

Hating to leave his brother, Darius turned and raced down the long hall that led to the collection pool. He was betting that Amadja wouldn't realize that Darius knew about the underground network of tunnels.

"Hang in there, baby," Darius kept saying softly as he

hurried along with Lexi in his arms. "Be strong. I'll get us out of here." He hoped when he did that she would have enough magic to change into wolf form. Whenever a shifter changed form, any damaged muscle, bone or tissue replaced itself in the new body. Given the extent of her injuries, shifting might be the only thing that could save her life at this point.

Darius was tired and in pain, but he shut out his own feelings as he hurried through the tunnel until he reached the other end.

Lexi's breathing had grown shallow, and he knew she needed to morph soon. He found the door he was looking for and stepped through. Once again, he was in the utility room beneath the Chrysler Building.

Sensing they were alone, he looked around the room to be sure. Then he carefully set Lexi on the floor and bent over her.

"Lexi, wake up, baby," he said, brushing the hairs from her face.

Her eyelids fluttered and slowly opened. "Darius . . ." she breathed, trying to focus on his face.

"How are you feeling?" he asked her.

"Like I'm dying," she said with a lame attempt at humor.

Darius was afraid she was, too. They were out of time. "I need for you to shift."

"Can't," she whispered. "No energy."

He made his voice stern. "Yes, you can, damn it—and you will. Now!"

His tone caught her by surprise, he could tell. There was fear when she looked up at him—not fear of him, he knew; fear of what might happen.

"The demon?" she asked.

"Gone for now, but he is sure to come back. We don't have a lot of time. You need to shift—it will heal your wound. It's the only way."

After an eternally long second, she nodded. "Help me out of my clothes—can't do it myself."

With no time to waste, he pulled his dagger from his stomach where it had attached itself and sliced open all her clothes. He was careful when he peeled them away from her wound, but some blood had dried around it and when he pulled, she cried out in pain.

"I'm sorry, Lexi. I know this hurts." He pulled the last of her clothes away. The wound gaped dark and ugly against the perfection of her body, and his anger at Amadja grew to mammoth proportions.

"What now?" he asked her when he was finished.

"Help me," she said. "Need more energy."

"What can I do?" He felt nearly helpless.

Lexi gave a strangled cry. "Full moon . . . wolf in heat . . . improvise."

He nodded, but hesitated. This felt too much like taking advantage of her, but he knew he had to do it. Lying next to her, he bent over and kissed her, hesitantly at first but then more deeply as his fears and emotions surfaced. He tried to convey to her how he felt—how much he cared for her, and his nearly desperate fear that she might leave him. In his kiss, he promised her what he couldn't promise her in words—that they had a future together. He was so into the moment that he didn't notice at first the hum of energy around them. When he did, he let the kiss end and lifted his head. Lexi smiled up at him.

He saw her take a couple of deep breaths, and then she closed her eyes and gripped his hand with a strength that belied her condition.

He felt the magic closing in on them, and, wanting to help it along, he placed his free hand across his heart. The life-force tattoo shimmered, and he felt what little magic he had left travel along his arm and into their clasped hands.

Her eyes turned first, growing a shade lighter and becoming elliptical in shape. Then everything happened at once. Her dark hair seemed to get longer and spread across her body, covering her. Her skeletal system reshaped itself, as did the bones of her face.

Darius had only enough time to wonder if the process hurt when it was done and he was leaning over a beautiful black wolf, holding its paw. Lexi's paw.

It was hard to imagine this beautiful creature was the woman he'd held in his arms moments before. She lifted her weary head and looked at him. Though she couldn't speak, he felt like he knew what she wanted.

He stooped over her and examined her stomach. "It's better, Lexi," he told her, hoping she could understand him. "It'll take a little time, but it's healing."

She seemed to understand because after a second, she struggled to her feet. Then she nudged him, and he smiled. Pushing himself to his feet, he gathered what was left of her clothes and led her to the stairs leading outside, watching to make sure she didn't have any trouble climbing them.

Using his key once more to open the metal doors, they exited into the cool night air.

Tain pulled the succubus more tightly against him and kissed her with a thoroughness only centuries of having sex can teach a man. He knew the instant she lost control of the situation, and he reveled in the experience of being in charge. Of being the dominant one.

Seconds later, he felt rather than heard Amadja approach, but he didn't hurry to end the kiss. He took his time. When he did release the succubus, she stared up at him with eyes wide with wonder and glazed with passion. This was not the first time he'd kissed her. They'd had sex frequently. Not because he liked her particularly, but because it seemed to annoy Aja.

He turned now to face the demon lord, wondering what guise he would take for this confrontation. As Tain had expected, it was Aja standing there, hands on her hips, eyes blazing in anger.

"If you know what's good for you, you'll let go of the succubus immediately." The look she gave Daphne fairly sizzled. Tain felt a stab of guilt for having used the succubus in such a way, but quickly shrugged it off. If he'd had more living magic in him, she would have sucked him dry without batting an eye. What did he care if, because of him, she was now the object of Aja's wrath?

"Do you want to tell me why you stopped me in there?" Aja continued. "I had them. I could have destroyed them both."

Tain smiled and moved closer, Daphne already forgotten as he slipped his arms around Aja's waist and pulled her close. "Let's go someplace private, shall we? After you hear my idea, you'll no doubt want to show your gratitude, and this time, I don't want an audience."

Even in New York City, a tall, half-naked man covered in tattoos with blood running down his chest and a rare black wolf by his side was a sight to see in the middle of the night. Darius ignored the stares. He just wanted to put some distance between him and the demons chasing them.

He felt something cold against his palm—Lexi nosing his hand—and realized that he'd stopped walking.

"I'm just a little tired," he told Lexi, who was looking up at him with a question in her lupine eyes. He looked around the street and saw what appeared to be an abandoned warehouse a block ahead.

He looked down at the wolf and saw that she had seen it too. It was like they both silently agreed that the warehouse was where they should stop to rest, and they moved off toward it.

"How about over here?" he suggested, pointing to one of the cleaner corners once they were inside. Lexi lumbered over to it and sank to the floor. Almost instantly, she fell asleep.

Darius sat beside her, propping his back against the wall. He'd thought she was asleep, but she raised her head and, seeing him seated close beside her, dragged herself the few inches needed to lay beside him. Then she laid her head in his lap.

Darius was at first unsure how to react. He'd never been close to a woman before. He'd had sex with plenty of them, but that was all it had ever been and he'd rarely spent time with a woman without there being sex involved.

Being with Lexi was different, though. He gave in to the temptation to run his fingers through her silky fur.

The world seemed better when he was touching her. It scared him to think how close he'd come to losing her. Closing his eyes, he saw again the way she'd fought by his side, hurling fire without hesitation. How many women did he know who would do that? He thought about the vampire initiation where she'd exhibited a fierce loyalty to her friend, and about her devotion to duty as a bounty hunter. Both were traits he respected and admired. It was easy to understand why he liked her so much.

But it went beyond that. When he was with her, his pulse raced and his body quickened with need. Clothed or nude, she was gorgeous, and he ached to make love to her . . .

Darius paused as he realized what he'd just thought. He ached to make love to her—not have sex with her. It was an important difference, and it left him with a life-changing revelation. He was in love with her.

Gazing down at her sleeping form, he was filled with warm satisfaction, a sense of wholeness. It was a feeling he held on to with fierce determination because tomorrow it could all end.

Chapter Nineteen

Lexi woke and, without moving, opened her eyes to look around. She wasn't in her room. In fact, she didn't know where she was. Her head was resting against something warm but hard, and everything seemed sharper and louder than usual. With a start, she realized she was in wolf form.

The memories of the night before came rushing back with painful clarity and a sense of urgency. Darius!

Raising her head, she looked around. He was there beside her, his back against the wall, his eyes still closed. She relaxed a little, until she noticed the angry, red striations radiating out from a wound that should have healed but clearly hadn't.

Pulling on her magic, which thankfully had been restored while she slept, she morphed to human form. Then she knelt beside Darius and laid her hand against his chest. It slowly rose and fell with each breath he took, but the skin was hot.

"Darius?" She laid her hand against his forehead, and it too felt hot. "Darius, wake up."

He came awake with a start, wild-eyed and instantly alert for danger, automatically reaching for his dagger before she had a chance to place her hand on his arm to quiet him. "It's okay. We're safe."

"Lexi?" He turned to her, blinking a couple of times like he was trying to bring her face into focus. "You're okay?"

She smiled at him and touched her stomach where the wound was completely healed. "All better. You, on the other hand, don't look so good."

He tried to wave his hand to dismiss her concern, but the effort proved too much. "I'll live," he said weakly.

"Right," she muttered, not convinced. She leaned closer to him, trying to get a better look at the wound. The scalpel had sliced through the top circle of the figure eight, just along the upper inside edge. "Is this your only injury?" she asked, needing to know the extent of the damage.

He was very careful about meeting her gaze when he answered her. "My back. Amadja burned it."

She nodded. "Okay. Let me take a look. Do you think you can lean forward?"

She could tell it hurt him, but he cooperated. She moved so she could see his back. "Nothing."

"Are you sure? It hurt a lot worse than the knife wound."

She looked again, feeling a little confused. "No, it's all clear. No scars or anything. I don't get it. Aren't you supposed to heal quickly?"

"Yes."

"So the wounds on your back healed the way they're supposed to, but this one didn't." She stared at the wound on his chest. "This is what he meant by your being vulnerable," she said at last.

"You mean Whitley?"

She nodded.

He leaned back against the wall, wincing with the effort. "Yeah, I think so."

"You need medical help," she said firmly, her mind already working out the logistics of getting him to a hospital.

"No. They won't understand about me being an Immortal, and once they do, they won't leave me alone. Not to mention that the whole world will know we're here."

She could hear the pain in his voice when he spoke and knew that he was suffering the way any human would have.

"If he'd struck you a little lower—"

"I'd probably be dead," he finished for her.

She shuddered at the thought. "There must be something we can do." She thought about it. "It looks infected." She reached out to touch the wound, but he put his hand up to block her. In doing so, he accidentally brushed his hand against his chest and the life-force tattoo moved. It shifted just enough that the edge of the upper circle dropped down below the top of the cut. Instantly the striation marks outside the circle faded and the cut began to heal.

"Darius, what would happen if you moved this tattoo?" she asked hesitantly. "Does it have to be over your heart?" She suddenly had the fear that the tattoo fed his life force directly into his heart, and if he moved it, he might die.

"Let's find out," he suggested.

"No." She put out a hand to stop him. "What if we're wrong?"

"If I start to have problems, take my hand and move it back."

She guessed that would work, though she thought it was risky. Feeling Darius's gaze on her, she nodded. "Okay."

She watched him place his hand over his tattoo and saw the shimmer of magic above the surface. Then, moving very slowly, he dragged the tattoo off to one side until the scalpel wound was completely outside the twin circles.

Almost immediately it started to heal. It took a full five minutes for all the angry red marks to fade from his skin, and another five before the cut was completely healed. She'd never seen anything like it. She looked up into his face and smiled. "That's pretty amazing. How are you feeling?"

"Like I might actually live," he said with a smile. Then he frowned. "How are *you* feeling? You gave me a real scare last night."

"I'm fine, thanks to you. You saved my life. Thank you."

He raised a hand and brushed his fingers down her cheek. "I should be thanking you for saving mine."

She smiled. Despite everything that had happened to them, she enjoyed being with him. Then the rest of the evening came rushing back, including Amadja's comment about Mai. "I have to get to a phone and check on Mai." She looked around, starting to feel a bit desperate.

"Slow down," Darius told her, standing up. "I'm sure Mai's okay. I doubt Amadja has had time to do anything. Let's go back to your place and consider our next move, all right?"

She nodded, and he pulled her to him. "I'm sorry," he said, slipping his arms around her. "I've tried to ignore the fact that you aren't wearing any clothes, and while I might be an Immortal, I'm still just a man—a man who finds you the most enticingly beautiful woman he's ever known." He touched his lips to hers, and she felt a rush of desire shoot through her. She wrapped her arms around his neck and kissed him back with unabashed enthusiasm. When he finally broke off the kiss and told her in a voice gone hoarse with need that they had to stop, she didn't feel rejected in the least.

"Let me morph and then we can leave," she told him.

"If that's what you want to do," he said. "Of course, I don't mind if you want to stay human."

She gave him a smile. "I don't think New York City's ready for me to walk down the street nude."

He smiled. "Their loss. But just so you know, I still have your clothes from last night—though they're a bit torn."

She felt a burst of joy and irritation. "You mean to tell me you've had clothes for me and you let me stay naked this entire time?"

The smile he gave her was sinful. "Baby, if it were up to me, you'd never wear clothes around me again."

It was late morning by the time they made it back to her apartment. The wards she'd placed were still intact. Nevertheless, Darius insisted on going in first, wanting to make sure Amadja hadn't set any traps for them. He found the apartment clean.

While Darius showered, Lexi called Mai's apartment. There was no answer, and Lexi's heart lurched. She dug out the GPS receiver from her pants pocket and turned it on. In no time, she had a grid of the city, and the blinking dot of light that was Mai's necklace showed that Mai—or at least the necklace—was near Times Square.

Lexi released the breath she was holding. Mai's office was near Times Square. Picking up the phone, Lexi called her there.

"Mai, are you all right?" she asked when she finally heard Mai's voice.

"If you consider getting the lead story of tomorrow's edition fine, then I'm great," she shouted excitedly.

Lexi smiled. Mai certainly sounded fine. "Listen, I want you to be careful."

"I'm always careful," Mai countered.

Lexi debated whether to tell her about what she'd heard Amadja say. "Listen, Mai. This demon we're after. He's dangerous, and now you're involved. He knows about you, so you have to be cautious."

There was silence on the other end, and then Mai spoke, her tone more serious than Lexi had ever heard it before. "It may not seem like I always take your warnings seriously, but when my best friend gives me a protection necklace that turns out to be a tracking device—yeah, I found the chip—then I know there's something serious going on."

"So you're taking precautions?"

"I'm carrying my thornalis."

Lexi frowned. "I've never heard of it. What is it?"

"It was invented by my people centuries ago, back when the wood nymphs were still at war with the trolls. It's about the size of a small squirt gun and shoots out tiny thorns. The thorns travel through the air at such a high velocity, they're like bullets. And the force of the air causes them to elongate until they are about four inches long. They are razor sharp, extremely painful, and if they hit a vital organ, I assure you, they are one-hundred-percent deadly."

It was Lexi's turn to fall silent. In all the years she'd known Mai, she'd never witnessed this lethal side of her. "And you know how to shoot it?" she asked hesitantly.

Mai laughed. "I was captain of the girls' thornalis team back in high school. So even though you don't need to worry about me, I know you still will, so tell you what: After I finish here at the office, I'm going straight home. All right?"

"All right." Feeling only slightly better, Lexi hung up the phone and went into the kitchen to make something to eat. She was starving and suspected Darius was hungry too.

As she was putting food on the table, he walked in wearing only his leather pants and shoes. She supposed she should try to buy him more clothes, but, damn, he looked nice in that outfit. Lexi smiled as they sat down at the table together.

They carefully avoided talking about Tain or the demon while they ate. Afterward, Lexi showered while Darius cleared away the dishes. When she returned to the kitchen, she noticed Darius's frown. She didn't have to be a mind reader to know what was bothering him. "I'm sorry about Tain," she said. She knew his brother's sacrifice must hurt. "I guess we all misjudged him."

"I have to go back for him." Darius looked into her face like he needed her to understand.

"I know. I'll go with you."

Darius shook his head. "No, you won't. I almost lost you once—I'm not taking that chance again. I'll go alone."

"Amadja is up to something," she reminded him.

"And while we have a rough idea of what he's up to—releasing those shade demons—we don't know when and we don't know where."

"It's going to happen tonight."

"How do you know?" she asked.

"When I was in jail, Paddy said he had until the full moon to convert all those vampires. That's tonight."

That was so much sooner than she expected, and Lexi had to let the news sink in. "Do we know where?"

"I've got a guess," Darius said, surprising her. He told her about the room he'd found under the Chrysler Building. He described the pool filled with living magic and the funny domed ceiling. "There were a thousand or more pinpricks of light," he said, "but in a line running up the center of the dome to the very top and then down again on the other side was a set of larger circles, with every seventh one larger than the others. Most of the circles leading up one side were lit."

Lexi thought about it. "It sounds like a lunar calendar," she said after a while.

Darius stared at her for the longest moment, and then he smiled and kissed her forehead. "That's exactly what it is. At the stroke of midnight, that light at the very center, representing the full moon, will light up."

"So what do we do now?" Lexi asked. Midnight was less than twelve hours away.

"I think I need to call Adrian. Maybe he'll know of something we can do."

While Darius waited, Lexi dialed the number. She listened to it ring with a growing sense of defeat. When the answering machine came on, she left a message for Adrian to call as soon as he could and hung up. "Now what?"

Darius took her hands. "We wait for him to call back."

"And if he doesn't?" Darius didn't answer her; he didn't have to. "You're going in anyway, aren't you?"

He gave her an apologetic look. "I have to."

"No, you don't." Her sense of dread grew. "Please don't go."

"A lot can happen between now and tonight, Lexi. Let's not get worked up about things too early. Let's just wait for Adrian's call."

She nodded, but couldn't relax enough to sit down. She didn't like sitting around doing nothing, and a quick glance at Darius showed he was having as much trouble as she was.

The situation was surreal, and she couldn't stop her imagination from running through all sorts of world-ending scenarios. A week ago, the Crypt had just been another vampire club—not the focal point for the world's destruction.

She tried to convince herself that Mai, feeling protected now that she was carrying a weapon, wouldn't still run off to the club tonight. Tonight, in particular.

Picking up the phone, she called Mai's office. The phone rang and rang. She hung up and tried Mai's apartment. There was no answer there either.

"Lexi," Darius said gently, coming up behind her. "What's the matter?"

"I'm worried about Mai," she admitted. "She won't answer."

She got out the tracking receiver and saw that Mai's signal was coming from her apartment. If she was home, why wouldn't she answer the phone? Unless she *couldn't* answer it. Once the thought was formed, Lexi couldn't let it go. "I need to go check on her."

She started walking toward the door, but stopped when she noticed Darius walking with her. "Where are you going?"

"With you, of course. You don't think I'm going to let you run all over town with Amadja out there trying to kill us."

Lexi laid her hand against his cheek, thinking how much she'd come to care for this man. "You have to stay here in case Adrian calls. Don't worry. I'm a bounty hunter. I'll be okay."

Darius clearly didn't like her leaving without him, but he slowly nodded. "When you find Mai, bring her back here." He kissed her forehead. "Because I won't rest easy until I know you're safe."

Lexi nodded. "All right. Do you need anything before I go?"

"Yes," he said with a smile. "But there's no time. I guess I'll have to settle for getting Ricco's phone number from you—if you have it."

She gave him a sharp look. "I didn't realize you and Ricco were friends."

"We have an understanding," he said. "But I'm fairly certain he's not the kind of death-magic creature who wants to see the world destroyed."

Lexi happened to agree with him there, so she wrote down Ricco's phone number, gave Darius quick instructions on how to operate the phone and then left.

Lexi felt like it took forever for the cab to get to Mai's apartment. As soon as she paid the driver, she dashed upstairs and knocked on the door. She was on pins and needles waiting for Mai to answer and had started to reach for her key when the door opened. Mai stood there looking perfectly fine. In fact, she looked better than fine. With her hair messed up, her eyes still dilated and her clothes askew, she looked like she'd just had sex.

"Mother Goddess," Lexi swore. "Do you have company?"

Mai looked embarrassed as she straightened her clothes. "As a matter of fact, I do." She giggled. "I'm so glad you told me about the Immortals," she said. "Isn't it exciting?"

"Isn't what exciting? Mai, what are you talking about?"

"You remember you told me that after the Calling spell, one of the Immortals appeared before you? But that they were still looking for the other two? Well, I found one."

Lexi was having a hard time keeping up with the conversation. It wasn't making sense. "You found one of the Immortals? Are you sure?"

Mai gave her a look. "Of course I'm sure. You told me about the tattoo, so I made sure I found it—though it wasn't difficult to find—right there on his cheek."

Warning bells in Lexi's head started ringing. "We should leave," she said, reaching for Mai's hand, but Mai eluded her grasp.

"Don't be silly. I can't leave. Besides, I want you to meet Kalen." She pulled Lexi into the living room, shutting the door behind them.

"Kalen?" Lexi repeated dumbly. Hadn't Darius told her that Kalen was in Scotland?

The door to Mai's bedroom opened, and Lexi watched as a tall, good-looking man stepped out. She recognized him instantly.

"That's not Kalen," she said, desperately trying to think of a way to get Mai out of there safely.

Before she could do a thing, he waved his hand and a bolt of black lightning shot out and hit Mai. Her body tensed in reaction and then toppled, unconscious, to the floor.

Lexi sprang into action, but just as she reached him, he slammed her with a bolt of the same black lightning.

Every fiber in her body screamed in pain. The intensity built until it became too difficult to stay conscious, and she welcomed the black void that swallowed her.

Chapter Twenty

It was after dark, and Darius still hadn't heard from Adrian. Worse yet, Lexi wasn't back and he was starting to move past worried into seriously concerned. When he heard a knock on the door, he rushed to open it, hoping to find Lexi on the other side.

"Heather," he said, surprised, when he opened the door and saw her standing there. She was wearing the same type of flowing dress she'd worn the day he and Lexi had gone to see her.

"Hello, Darius." She smiled. "I didn't realize you were still here. Is Lexi about?"

"No, she's not," he said, standing back so she could enter.

He closed the door behind her and stood awkwardly in the living room, too distracted to play the polite host.

Heather, apparently sensing his unease, smiled. "I hadn't heard from Lexi and wondered if your memory ever returned."

"Yes, it did. Thank you." His gaze shot to the clock on

Lexi's wall—it was five minutes later than the last time he looked. Where the hell was she?

"I've been working on a new spell for you," Heather said, unaware that he wasn't paying much attention. "I thought it might prove more helpful—at least until we can find out what caused the loss in the first place."

She held out a pouch and he took it from her. "Oh, thanks. I'll . . . be sure to use it."

"Is something wrong?" she finally asked, looking around. "You seem distracted. Has something happened to Lexi?"

Darius gave up trying to put on a front and sighed. "I don't know where Lexi is. She was supposed to be back hours ago, and I'm really worried about her."

Heather came up to him and put a comforting hand on his arm. "I can't help you if I don't know what's going on." In as few words as he could, he told Heather everything, half hoping she'd tell him he was worried for nothing. But, of course, that didn't happen.

"Would you know how to get in touch with Mai?" he asked her, wishing he'd thought to keep the tracking receiver with him.

"No," Heather said with the sound of an apology. "I've never met Mai. But if you know her last name, I could look her up," she said hopefully.

Darius scowled. "I don't know her last name."

Just then another knock sounded on the door and Darius hurried to answer it. Mai stumbled in. She would have collapsed to the floor if Darius hadn't caught her. Picking her up, he carried her to the couch, and laid her down.

With her pale complexion, the dark circles under her eyes and bruises on her body, she looked like she'd been beaten.

Darius knelt beside her, barely reining in his rage. "Mai, what happened? Who did this to you? Where's Lexi?"

Heather had joined him by Mai's side and was digging through her large purse. She pulled out a vial. "Where's the kitchen?" she asked.

Darius pointed, his attention focused on Mai.

"Make her as comfortable as you can," Heather said just before she disappeared.

Darius had no idea what to do, so he remained kneeling beside Mai, gently stroking her hair away from her face.

A minute later, Heather was back holding a glass filled with an amber liquid. "Help me get her to drink some of this," she said.

Darius gently raised Mai to a sitting position and supported her with his arm while Heather held the drink to her lips. "Drink this, honey," Heather whispered. "It will help you feel better. That's right," she added when Mai took several sips.

Soon Mai's eyelids fluttered open, and she took a shaky breath. She looked about wildly until her gaze rested on Darius. Then she reached for him, her expression wobbly with emotion. "I made it. I knew I had to find you."

"Mai, what happened?"

"I thought I'd found one of the Immortals," she said, surprising him. "He had the pentacle tattoo—on his cheek."

Tain? Had he escaped his captor? Darius wondered.

"He said his name was Kalen," Mai continued, giving Darius a start.

"Are you sure?" Why would Tain pretend to be Kalen?

Mai shook her head. "Lexi said it was wrong. She told me we had to leave, but I didn't listen." She took a breath. "I don't remember much after that. Kalen came out of the bedroom. There was a flash of black light, and then it was like a freight train hit me. I've never felt such pain before." She visibly trembled.

"And Lexi?" Darius asked.

"She's gone."

Darius felt his heart stop, and for a moment he couldn't breathe. "She's . . ." He stopped, finding it difficult to ask the question. "She's dead?"

"What?" Mai looked at him, horrified.

"You said she's gone," Darius said. "Gone how?"

"Missing," Mai clarified. "I don't know what happened to her. I was hoping she might be here—although I knew she wasn't. Lexi would never have left me there like that if she'd had a choice."

Darius gritted his teeth. At least he knew who had Lexi—Amadja. Only a demon could generate the black magic that had knocked Mai unconscious. And it made sense that he'd try this ploy. Amadja had interrupted the Calling, so he knew they were expecting other Immortals to appear. He knew Mai was a friend of Lexi's, and it wouldn't take a leap of logic to know that after last night, Lexi would want to check on her. Amadja had the ability to change his form, so he could easily disguise himself as Tain. But if Amadja wanted Lexi dead, he could have killed her and left her at the apartment for Darius to find. That must mean the demon had something else in mind. Something for which he expressly needed Lexi.

The only thing Darius could think of was that by taking Lexi, Amadja knew Darius would follow.

"I'm going after her," Darius told the women.

Heather put a hand on his arm. "You can't do that. You know it's a trap."

"I know, but I can't let them hurt Lexi."

Heather's lips thinned. "I don't want anything to happen to her either, but Adrian and the Coven need your help. Only by combining your power with ours can you hope to defeat this demon. If you go after him by yourself"—she paused—"you could be condemning the world to death."

Darius shrugged off her arm. "I know I should be considering the greater good and the whole future of the world. But if Lexi dies, I'm not sure I care what happens to the world."

Heather studied his face and then nodded. "All right. What can I do to help you?"

"Me too," Mai said, struggling to a sitting position.

"Nothing." He held up a hand to stop their protests. "Yet. What I need now is for you both to stay here. I'm expecting a call from my brother in Seattle. Heather, when he calls, can you please tell him what's going on?" He looked at them both. "Do either of you know Ricco?"

Mai gasped. "I do."

Darius was confused by her attitude. "What's the matter? Don't you like him?"

Mai looked worried. "I like him fine. I just didn't think you knew him—and if you did, I didn't think you'd like him. He and Lexi are—"

"Friends," Darius finished for her. "As of a couple of days ago, strictly platonic friends." Darius ignored the way Mai's face broke out in a smile. "I need you to wait for Ricco. He should be on his way before too much longer, now that the sun has set. Fill him in on what's going on and then ask him to meet me beneath the Chrysler Building."

At the women's perplexed expressions, he tried to explain how to find the meeting place as best he could, but all the while, in the back of his mind, the clock was ticking.

Darius's cab trip to the Chrysler Building passed in a blur. He was preoccupied with trying to remember all the bits and pieces he'd heard over the past couple of days and figure out what they meant. He knew the answer would play a critical role in saving Lexi's life.

He tried to get past his worry for her safety and think in terms of Amadja's greater purpose. Was the demon's entire plan to lure him into a trap to kill him? That would mean he knew about Darius's vulnerability. Maybe there *had* been demons present in the dream dimension when Whitley told him about the spell. He'd know the truth soon enough.

When the cab pulled to a stop, Darius got out. He'd borrowed money from Mai and now used it to pay the driver. Glancing up, he studied the building. The light of the full moon reflected off the scalloped pieces, making them glow brightly.

Tapping into his magic, he used his key to open the metal doors that led down into the utility room. Once he was through, he concentrated on the wall where he knew the magically concealed door lay. It took careful focus, but the edges of the door slowly appeared.

Grabbing his dagger, Darius slipped through the door.

On the other side, he found himself standing alone in the hallway. Cocking his head to one side, he paused to listen. Silence.

He proceeded directly to the chamber with the pool. He was fairly certain that Amadja would not have set any traps for him, but he still moved cautiously. He remembered the guards standing outside just before turning the corner, and he stopped. Moving slowly, he peeked around the corner and saw the guards still there.

It was impossible to know whether they would stand aside and allow him to pass as they had last time, or whether Amadja had ordered them to watch for him.

He took a breath and stepped out into the open. The minute they saw him, the guards squared off, answering at least one question. Darius gave them a slow, predatory smile and moved forward at a leisurely pace. The two guards exchanged quick looks. He could tell that the guard closest to him was looking forward to the fight, while the other one seemed hesitant, fearful.

Darius moved in, focusing his attack on the more aggressive guard. The vampire had probably been a bully in life, because he showed more attitude than talent. Soon Darius had reduced him to nothing more than a withering corpse.

Then he turned to the remaining guard. He'd clearly been young when he'd been converted and didn't look to be more than nineteen. Darius had no way of knowing how long ago that conversion had taken place, but the boy clearly did not want to fight.

"Get out of here," Darius told him. "Don't go back to the Crypt or the Vlads. Leave and don't come back for at least two days. After that, go to the Blood Club and tell Ricco that Darius sent you. Understand?"

The boy nodded. "If I find out that you disobey me, I'll hunt you down. When I find you—and I *will* find you—I'll finish what was started here tonight. Now go."

Darius watched him leave, then turned to face the door.

He briefly closed his eyes and sent a prayer to the Mother Goddess that Lexi was here and still alive. Then he opened the door. He half expected to find Amadja on the other side, sitting on his throne, waiting for him to appear. But the demon wasn't there.

In fact, at first glance, the room appeared to be empty. The light from the pool flickered and reflected off the walls, giving the room a peaceful feeling. Above, the large circle in the center of the domed ceiling was lit—as Lexi had predicted it would be for the full moon.

He noticed all this in an instant. His sole focus was on finding Lexi, and he couldn't believe she wasn't here.

He caught the faint jangling sound of chains coming from the shadowy opposite wall. Going around the pool, he approached cautiously.

As he drew closer, he saw not one but two figures chained to the wall. The first was Lexi, who seemed unconscious, and the other was . . .

"Darius, is that you?" Tain called, his voice sounding raspy, like he'd been shouting for help a long time.

Darius rushed forward. "Tain, I'm here."

Tain heaved a sigh of relief. "I knew you'd come." He tugged on his chains. "You have to get us out of these before Amadja comes back."

Darius did a quick visual check of Tain, saw that he seemed to be okay, and then turned his attention to Lexi. Laying his hand against the side of her head, he felt a rush of relief when she opened her eyes. It was quickly replaced by worry, however, when he noticed a shimmer of magic all around her.

"Damn," he swore. "What did they do to you?" Her eyes had partially shifted to wolf, and when he stepped closer to her, she dipped her head to his shoulder and inhaled deeply. Then her mouth was on his neck, tasting his skin as she breathed in his scent.

"Oh, you smell so good," she moaned.

Surprised at her behavior, he turned to look at her. That was when her mouth swooped down on his, and she kissed him with something akin to desperation.

He'd wanted her so badly for so long, it was impossible not to respond, but this was neither the place nor the time.

"Easy, baby. There will be plenty of time for that later."

"No," she insisted on a ragged breath. "Now. I need you now." She twisted in her chains, doing her best to rub up against him as he struggled to pull the key from his back. The task was made more difficult because of the way Lexi kept moving against him, distracting him.

"What's wrong with her?" he asked Tain, trying to keep the key over the lock long enough for it to change shape.

"Amadja gave her Demon Fire."

"That bastard," Darius swore. Demon Fire was the most powerful—and long-lasting—aphrodisiac in the magical world. Giving it to a werewolf in heat was just plain cruel. There was no need for it.

But it explained why she was in the state she was in—and why there was a field of energy surrounding her.

"What about you?" he asked Tain as the key finally began to change its shape. "Are you hurt? Did he—"

"No. He hasn't touched me since the last time I saw you."

"Thank the Goddess," Darius said. "I was worried about you. Thank you for stepping in when you did." He glanced over and saw Tain watching his every move. "I'll have you free in a second."

Darius ducked his head, trying to escape Lexi's mouth and managed to unlock one of her cuffs. The instant that hand was free, she was reaching for him, running it along his shoulders and neck.

When her hand stroked down his belly and still lower until she cupped him, his eyes nearly rolled back in his head. It demanded the utmost control to pull her hand away. "Lexi, honey. Not now," he croaked, trying to hold both of her hands with one of his while trapping her against his body by tucking her under one arm.

Unfortunately, now both his hands were occupied and there was not a limb left to operate the key.

"Where's Amadja?" he asked, having a hard time remembering why he was there at all.

"I don't know," Tain said. "But I know he'll be here tonight. He said he had plans for that one," nodding at Lexi.

Darius felt the pressure of needing to get them both out of there. "I'll probably have to carry her," he said. "Can you walk?"

"Yes. Just get me out of here." There was a shared sense of urgency to Tain's voice.

"I'm trying," Darius muttered, inserting the key into the cuff around Lexi's other wrist.

When it came undone, she threw herself into his arms. "Darius—oh, Goddess," she breathed. "Is that you?" She rubbed herself against him. "Oh," she moaned. "You feel so good."

"You, too, baby," he said, wrapping an arm around her waist and holding her close, hoping that in doing so, he'd stop her from grinding against him. It was very distracting, and he still had his brother to unlock.

"They gave me something," she whispered in his ear. "I feel like I'm about to go up in flames."

"I know. Hang in there. I have to get you and Tain out of here first. Then we can see to *all* your needs."

"Hurry," she breathed against his neck. Her breasts pressed against his chest, and he was in danger of forgetting where they were and why he shouldn't take her right there on the floor. He'd denied himself—and her—for so long; it was time he made up for it.

He looked down into her face, grateful that she was still alive. Her dreamy expression was too sexy to ignore, so he kissed her, briefly, or so he thought.

"Darius!" Tain's bark intruded.

"Right," he said quickly. He started to reach for Tain, but Lexi was wrapped around him to the point he couldn't maneuver. He gently but firmly shifted her until she hugged him from behind. Then he reached up and held the key in front of the lock of Tain's cuff.

It seemed to take forever for the key to change shape, and Lexi's moving against him made the waiting that much longer.

As soon as he could, he reached for the nearest cuff and unlocked it. Before he could move to the other side, though, Tain impatiently grabbed the key from him. "Give me that. I'll unlock myself. You see to her."

Darius pulled Lexi back into his arms, knowing he needed to get her out of the chamber and someplace safe quickly, before she burned up in her own unrequited passion. Even now, the magic was rising off her in nearly opaque sheets. Holding her this close, he felt the tingle of her magic crawling over him.

She nuzzled the side of his neck and whispered in his ear, "Don't trust him."

"What?" Surprised, Darius angled his head, trying to see her face. She looked up at him and then rolled her eyes toward Tain.

Darius didn't understand. He glanced at his brother, who had just managed to get the other cuff unlocked. With a victorious look on his face, he turned to Darius and smiled.

"Ready?" Darius asked.

"Yeah, but what about her?" He nodded toward Lexi. "She looks pretty much out of it. Want some help carrying her?" He stepped forward, and Lexi shied away, cowering against Darius. His arm stole around her protectively.

"No, I've got her," Darius said. "Let's go."

He started pulling Lexi across the room, making sure that Tain was staying up with them. They'd reached the edge of the pool when Lexi pulled to a stop.

"What is it—" He stopped speaking when he saw what had captured Lexi's attention. A filament of light hung in the air beside the pool. It hadn't been there before, but now, with the full moon lighting the center circle of the domed ceiling, it was visible.

It was a magical portal, a rip in space that connected two or more parallel dimensions. Darius wondered where this portal led. If it were made of living magic, perhaps they could escape through it without Amadja following.

Darius held his hand before the opening and felt the pleasant warmth of living magic. He decided to try and open it, but his first effort only caused the filament to shimmer. Whoever had created this portal had been powerful, and it would take more magic than Darius alone had to open it.

Pulling on Lexi's hand, he started for the door to the

chamber. "Let's go," he said. They had only taken a couple of steps when he realized Tain wasn't following. Instead, Tain was staring at something at the front of the room. Even before Darius turned to look, he knew what it was.

"Amadja."

Chapter Twenty-One

"Darius," the demon greeted him, stepping out of the shadows from behind his throne.

Tain rushed forward and grabbed Lexi from Darius's grip. "Keep her away from the pool," he shouted at Darius. "Don't let him get any more magic from her."

"Let go of me." Lexi tried to pull her arm free of Tain's grip. In that moment, Amadja raised his hand and shot a bolt of black magic across the room. It hit Tain in the chest, and he went flying back, hitting the floor with enough force to knock the air from him.

Enraged, Darius rushed forward and, dipping his hand in the pool, absorbed enough living magic that he could fire a burst of it from his hand and hit the demon in the chest.

It forced Amadja back a step. He recovered quickly and shot out another burst of magic. Darius pulled his shield just in time to keep the bolt from hitting him. Neither Tain nor Lexi were able to join the fight, so Darius was on his own.

He scooped up more magic from the pool, hoping it

would restore his lost powers. For several minutes, he and Amadja exchanged blasts, but Darius was tiring quickly. Even if his powers had been at full strength, he didn't think he could defeat the demon lord. If it were possible, Adrian would have done it already. The best they could hope for now was getting out alive.

Then Darius saw the focus of Amadja's attention shift. Tain and Lexi huddled off to the side, defenseless. Darius raced toward them, getting the shield up to protect them just as Amadja blasted them with black magic.

"We can't win," Tain moaned.

"We don't have to," Darius answered quietly. "I'll keep him distracted long enough for the two of you to escape. Once you're gone, get to Adrian. Lexi knows how. Tell him everything you can remember. Go."

Tain and Lexi both started shaking their heads.

"No," Lexi said. "I'm not leaving you—"

"She's right," Tain interrupted. "I won't leave you to face him alone."

Darius felt himself getting mad. "Now's not the time to argue, Tain. Take Lexi and get the hell out of here."

He stood, pulled Re's lightning bolts, and threw them at Amadja. "Go!" he shouted at the other two, while the demon dodged each fiery star.

Still sitting on the floor, Tain refused to move. Darius grabbed his arm and jerked him to his feet. "Damn it, Tain. You're going to get her killed."

He hauled Lexi up, noticing how hot her skin felt, and shoved them both in the direction of the door. Neither moved more than a few steps.

"I won't leave you," Tain insisted.

Darius saw the incoming black bolt of death magic and raised his shield to block it, nearly losing his balance when it hit him. There seemed no limit to

Amadja's power, while Darius's was seriously diminishing. Still, he pulled another weapon and hurled it, hoping to buy Tain and Lexi a few more seconds.

"Get her out of here," he ordered Tain, watching Lexi practically wilt before his eyes. "She needs help."

She was in full-blown heat, and her temperature was skyrocketing. She was literally burning up.

"But you can't fight him alone. He'll kill you," Tain argued.

"Don't you see?" Darius shouted back, keeping an eye on Amadja. "She's more important than anything." Without her, his life would mean nothing.

"I want to help," Lexi said weakly, coming to him. "Tell me what to do."

"No," he said.

She glanced at him, hunger burning in her eyes. "Darius, I can't take this much longer." She paused, and he could see her drawing on her inner strength. "If I'm going to die, at least let me die trying to beat this asshole."

It was exactly how he felt, so he couldn't very well deny her. "All right. You can—"

"Look out!"

At Tain's warning, Darius launched himself at Lexi, tackling her to the floor just as a black bolt of magic shot over her head. Hearing her groan, he shifted his weight, trying to see her face. "Are you hurt?"

"No," she said in a raspy voice. "Oh, Goddess, you feel so good." She ran her hands across his back and hips, emitting a small groan. When she looked up into his face, there was raw lust in the gaze that devoured his.

"Hang on, baby," he muttered, rolling off her. He got to his feet and pulled her up. When the next volley of death magic came, he held up his shield, and the magic bounced off. The shield was powered by Darius's magic, and wouldn't last long. "We have to end this—now," he said, turning to Tain.

"What about the portal?" Tain asked.

Darius shook his head. "I'm not sure I can get it open. Even if I could, we don't know where it leads. Who knows where we'd end up?"

Tain shook his head. "No. Not for us. For him." He nodded at Amadja, who was slowly walking toward them, a smug expression on his face.

"Put Amadja in the portal?" Darius gave the idea serious consideration. Once trapped inside a portal of living magic, Amadja wouldn't be able to escape on his own. They could keep him trapped there until reinforcements arrived. Yes—maybe it would work.

"But are we strong enough to force him inside?" Darius whispered. "Neither of our powers are what they used to be."

A bolt of black magic hit the shield again—a not-so-gentle reminder that Amadja wasn't giving up.

Tain was quiet, and Darius watched his gaze shift to Lexi. Yes, he thought. Right now, she was a veritable fount of living magic. Perhaps it would be enough.

"I'll draw him over," Tain offered, but Darius put a hand on his arm.

"No. I'll do it. You help Lexi open the portal." He turned to Lexi and saw her nod.

Then he lowered the shield and rushed Amadja. The demon hadn't expected such a direct attack and it caught him by surprise, giving Darius time to get in the first punch. Amadja fell back several steps from the blow and was slow to recover. It occurred to Darius that Amadja relied too much on his magic in fights and hadn't really learned the art of hand-to-hand combat.

Pressing his advantage, he circled around to the other side and hit Amadja again, repeatedly. The demon stumbled back toward Tain and Lexi, who had their hands on the portal and were using their combined magic to open it.

"That's for torturing my brother," Darius said, punching Amadja in the face. He pressed forward as the demon fell back. "That's for what you did to Lexi," he said, hitting him again as hard as he could.

Looking past Amadja's shoulder, Darius saw the portal opening wider and wider, blinding light spilling forth. He hit the demon several times in rapid succession, driving him back with each blow. Suddenly they were there, in front of the portal.

Too late, Amadja realized what they were up to and started to fight back. Darius didn't give him a chance. He hit the demon hard enough that he stumbled through the opening, where the living magic started to zap his strength.

"You won't win," he shouted at Darius.

"I think I already have," Darius said. "You can stay in here until we figure out what to do with you."

"No!" the demon screamed, struggling as Tain, Lexi and Darius used their combined power to slowly push the portal closed.

Suddenly, before their eyes, Amadja disappeared and a stunningly beautiful woman with long black hair stood in his place. "Tain," she pleaded in a pitiful voice. "Don't do this to me, Tain. I love you. I'm the only one who loves you."

Tain stopped pushing on the portal. "Aja?"

Darius grabbed Tain's shoulder. "It's a trick. Don't believe her." He turned to Lexi. "Keep pushing."

As they continued to work, Tain stared pitifully at the beautiful woman calling to him from the other side.

"It's an illusion, Tain," Darius shouted over the demon's cries. "Look away. Don't let him fool you."

But Tain wasn't listening. "I love her," he said. Then he shot angry eyes at Darius. "Do you even know what love is?"

Stunned at the vehemence in Tain's voice, Darius gave a final push on the portal and watched with satisfaction as it started to seal. They had won; the demon was trapped.

Then, to his horror, just before the portal completely closed, a hand reached out, grabbed Tain by the front of his shirt and jerked him through the small opening.

The portal sealed with a resounding hiss, leaving Darius and Lexi to stare at it in stunned silence.

Darius felt a sense of utter defeat. He had caught the demon, but once again had lost his brother.

For a long moment, Lexi couldn't move. Her heart was racing from whatever it was that Amadja had given her, the slightest breeze made her want to crawl out of her skin, she felt like she was burning up, and, despite the fact that the man she loved had just lost his brother, she wanted nothing more than to make mad love to him right there in front of the portal.

She silently chastised herself for her insensitivity and stared at the portal, expecting at any second it would open and both Amadja and Tain would come bursting forth.

Another minute went by and nothing happened.

"I'm sorry," she said to Darius, who had to have been

upset. "I'm . . ." A wave of pain hit her that was so intense her vision temporarily went black. She doubled over and prayed for it to subside.

Darius immediately wrapped his arm around her waist and held her. His touch was surprisingly gentle, and when the worst of the pain had passed, she tried to straighten, but couldn't. A ringing had started in her ears, and she knew that the end was near for her. She ran her hands up and down her arms, finding some relief in the tactile sensations, but still, fear and panic welled up inside her. She had to get out of here before it was too late.

She started for the door, but Darius stopped her. "Where are you going?"

She'd held herself together for this long but couldn't do it anymore. "I . . . I have to . . ." She waved a hand in the air. "You know."

He smiled and pulled her to him. "Yes, I do know." He dipped his mouth and kissed her with a thoroughness that set her blood to racing. As her skin heated in reaction, a small amount of magic was released into the air like a pearlescent cloud, rising until it hovered at the base of the domed ceiling.

After a long moment, Darius let the kiss end and pulled back his head to look at her. When she looked into his face, he smiled and dipped his head again. Before he could kiss her, she placed her hand across his mouth.

"No. I can't do this—not halfway." Her system couldn't handle getting to that level of excitement only to find no release.

He held her hand over his mouth and gently sucked her palm, sending a rush of heat to pool between her legs. "This time there's no stopping," he promised her.

"Really?" She could hardly believe it. "But what about the jinx? If you make love to me, won't you lose your memory? You'll forget everything."

The words hung in the air between them, and she knew he was thinking the same thing she was: that he wouldn't remember making love to her. He wouldn't even remember *her*.

That realization hurt more than the pain of the magic burning inside her.

She started to pull away, but he held her close. "There is nothing in this world that will *ever* make me forget you. This spell is temporary; it won't last."

She stared up at him, hardly daring to hope.

He caressed her face with his gaze. "I've never felt this way about anyone, Lexi. I love you."

Emotions overwhelmed her. He loved her. She was afraid to examine her own feelings too carefully for fear of what she might find. *Not love*, she declared hastily as memories of her sister's blind devotion to her husband came rushing back. She'd sworn on Bev's death that she'd never fall in love. Yet . . .

As if sensing her insecurity, Darius pulled her to him and kissed her with an urgency that mirrored her own. He kissed her until she finally lost the control she'd been holding on to so tenuously and kissed him back with a flood of emotions she couldn't have put into words.

They came together in a frenzied tangle of arms and legs as each tried to hold the other closer.

"Lexi," he breathed her name. "You taste so good. I want to make love to you all night long."

She gave a small moan. "Yes. Oh, yes."

His chuckle sounded deep in his chest as he swept

her up in his arms and started to carry her to the bed behind the dais.

"No, please," she protested. "I don't want our first time to be in *their* bed."

"Love, I don't care where our first time is, as long as there is a first time."

He lowered his arm supporting her legs and let her slide down the length of his body, still holding her close.

She started trembling, suddenly afraid that the relief she needed was coming too late. "I don't think I have time to go elsewhere," she gasped.

"Here works fine for me," he said, unbuttoning her blouse with deft fingers. Soon he'd removed all their clothing, and when he pulled her to him, she felt the hard, lean length of him pressed against her, and it drove her wild. She ran her hands up his muscled arms and across his broad shoulders. She buried her fingers in his long dark hair and pulled his head down to her so she could kiss him with fevered abandon.

Her breasts, heavy and swollen, were crushed against his chest. His erection pressed into her stomach, throbbing in tempo to her own heartbeat.

They both moved with a desperation born of long denial, and inside, she felt the magic building higher and higher.

He lifted her so she could wrap her legs around his hips, and then he drove himself into her. Her body stretched to accommodate him, and she was already in such a state of heightened need that her orgasm hit with such force, it ripped a scream from her very soul.

At that instant, a huge plume of magic rose up from her and floated to the ceiling where it merged with the rest of the magic floating there.

Before she could ride the wave of emotion, the need in her started building once more. Dismayed, she wondered how Darius would react, but she needn't have worried. It seemed he was just getting started.

Darius had waited a lifetime to find someone he cared about as much as he cared for Lexi—so he wasn't about to rush the experience of being with her.

He felt himself filling her; felt her feminine warmth wrapped around his length, hugging him close. With half a mind, he scanned the room, looking for a place to lie down, and decided that the floor would have to do.

Still buried deep inside her, he lowered them both until he lay flat and she was on top, straddling his hips. Once she started moving, he didn't even notice the cool hardness of the floor—only the heat that existed between them.

She leaned forward, her hands braced against his chest, her breasts hanging heavy in his face, enticing him. He laved first one dusky pink nipple and then the other with his tongue until both formed tight buds. Unable to resist the temptation, he pulled a nipple into his mouth and suckled.

He heard her quick intake of breath and felt her feminine muscles squeeze around his shaft. It was almost more than he could take, and he thrust his hips up, needing to be as deep inside her as he could get.

She was breathing rapidly now, and he knew she was close to another orgasm. He gave a gentle tug on her nipple with his mouth. She gasped, and came again. The quickening of her muscles around him almost sent him over the edge with an orgasm of his own.

He fought to control it, wanting to make this time together last as long as he possibly could. First, to make sure she released enough magic that her life was no longer in danger, and second, because he was afraid that, despite what he'd told her, Sekhmet's will would prove stronger than his and he would forget her.

Twice more she came, and each time only served to feed his own frenzy. Looking past her shoulder to the ceiling, he saw that a lot of the magic had been released and now circled above them like a pearlescent cloud.

His gaze shifted to her eyes, which were glazed over with passion. Her expression was one of complete satisfaction, and knowing that he'd put it there was one of his greatest triumphs.

As if she could read his thoughts, she smiled. It was all the encouragement he needed, and he rolled them over so he could be on top.

With one hand supporting his weight and the other under her hips to keep from grinding her into the floor, he drove himself into her repeatedly, his heart racing, the pressure inside him building.

As he neared the brink of his orgasm, he was filled with a sense of desperation unlike anything he'd ever felt before. It was pure, unadulterated fear—fear that in the next moment he was going to forget her. If he never saw her again, he wanted her to know that in this moment he'd loved her more deeply and more significantly than he would love anyone in the entire term of his existence—and he prayed that she would not hate him when she learned what he had done.

Please, Mother, he prayed to Sekhmet. *If you ever loved your son, you will not let me forget her.* It became a litany that he repeated with each stroke. *Please. Please. Please.*

The moment came, and he surged forward one last time. "I love you," he choked out just as his entire mind and body exploded. He rode the tidal wave, knowing that nothing he'd ever felt before could ever compare.

And then everything went blank.

"No," Lexi cried, seeing Darius shut his eyes. He winced like he was in pain, and she knew that the spell was at work. She was losing him.

She'd never felt so helpless in her life. He was slipping away, and there was nothing she could do. "I love you," she told him, her voice barely a whisper. "I love you." But her epiphany came too late. He wouldn't remember the words, would never know how she felt. Between one breath and the next, he'd forgotten her.

Chapter Twenty-two

Lexi watched Darius blinking his eyes like he was trying to clear his head. He looked around the room, but his gaze quickly returned to her. She could tell from his expression that he was both confused and startled to find himself lying on top of a woman as naked as he was.

"I sure as hell hope we know one another," he said with a smile. "Or this is going to be awkward." He paused, perhaps finally noticing that he was still buried deep inside her. "Too late."

"I can explain," she offered lamely. "But first, maybe you could . . . uh, you know . . . get off me."

"Is that wise?" he countered, sounding serious. "In cases involving head traumas, it's usually better not to make any sudden moves."

At first she thought he was serious and stared at him, dumbfounded. "You don't have a head trauma . . ." Then she noticed his suggestive smile and rolled her eyes. Shoving at his chest, she twisted her body to the side. "Get off."

He complied with a groan of protest, and she scrambled to her feet. She grabbed her clothes off the floor and dressed quickly.

When she was done, she turned back to see that he'd pulled on his black pants. "I imagine you have some questions," she began.

"I do."

She waited, not realizing how much she'd hoped that some small part of him would remember her. But his next three words shredded her heart to pieces. "Who are you?"

She swallowed the lump in her throat. *I'm the woman who loves you, the one you said you loved.* "My name is Lexi. We're . . . friends."

He raised an eyebrow. She had to admit the description was a little lame, but there wasn't time to explain the complexities of their relationship. Especially when she knew they had no future. He was, after all, an Immortal.

"You lost your memory because of a spell—when you have an orgasm, you forget everything."

He looked around. "Where are we?"

She sighed. "Beneath the Chrysler Building. I was being held prisoner down here by Amadja. Does his name sound familiar?" He shook his head, so she went on. "Your brother was a prisoner also."

"I have a brother?"

She glanced at the portal's opening, dangling above the collection pool. "Yes. He and the demon trying to kill us are trapped in a portal. There's no way to get your brother out without letting the demon loose. We'll have to get help."

Darius followed her gaze to the portal. "That portal?"

"Yes. It's more complicated than I'm presenting it," she explained.

Darius ran a hand through his hair. "This is all very confusing. I wish I could remember." He started pacing, and as she watched, she couldn't help feeling sympathetic. "You lost your memory once before and it came back," she told him. "Granted, it took some time, but it will happen. Patience is the key."

As he walked away from her, she studied his back. In her mind, she remembered the way his muscles felt beneath her fingertips when she'd traced the various tattoos . . .

"Wait a minute," she said suddenly, walking up to him. "That's not right."

He started to turn toward her, but she grabbed his arm and spun him around so she could get a better look at his back. One by one, she ran her fingers over the tattoos she remembered. The one she was looking for wasn't there.

North of my ass. Wasn't that what he'd said?

She put her arms around him and undid his pants. "Excuse me, but this is important."

"Go for it, baby," he growled enthusiastically. "I like a woman who knows that she wants. No wonder we're friends."

She rolled her eyes, but didn't stop what she was doing.

Fortunately, he stood patiently as she pulled the back of his pants down enough to see his entire lower back. It wasn't there.

"Well?" he asked.

"It's not there. Your key tattoo. It's missing."

A look of alarm crossed his face as they both turned

toward the portal opening. Darius quickly pulled up his pants and came to stand beside her as a crack appeared and a hand slipped out holding Darius's golden key.

Before either of them could do a thing, the magic that had been floating at the ceiling suddenly stretched toward the key.

Above them, in the domed ceiling, the circle of light representing the full moon began to glow, and slowly a beam of light stretched downward until it merged with the magic streaming toward the key.

"So that's your plan," Darius whispered just loud enough for Lexi to hear.

"What?" she asked, turning to him.

"Amadja's plan." He grabbed her by the arms. "That isn't just any portal. I have to stop them before they get the gate open."

"What gate?" She was confused.

So much living magic was flowing through, the crack in the portal opened wider.

He started running for it. "Satan's Gate."

"Oh, my Goddess," she swore. "Wait," she shouted, running after him. "You can't go in there."

"I have to," Darius shouted back. "Stay here." He reached the portal and dove through the opening.

When he landed on the other side, he jumped to his feet. White light stretched out all around him. He squinted against it and finally spotted Amadja and Tain at the back, where the prison holding 666 demons had been built. Already, Amadja looked pale and drawn. Being trapped in a living-magic portal was taking its toll. Sadly, it wouldn't destroy him. It would just deplete his strength, which explained why he'd needed Tain.

The prison, like the portal, had been built by Re and could only be opened by another deity—or by someone with strong living magic, like an Immortal.

Darius raced forward to stop Tain, but before he could reach him, the prison gate opened and the first demon slipped out, a formless dark shade that sailed past him, sending tendrils of cold evil prickling along his skin. Two more demons followed, and then more poured through. Darius had no idea how he could possibly stop them all.

An ache over his chest told him that Fury was straining to get free. Darius knew the Bocca demon would track down each shade demon he could and destroy it.

He touched his chest, and Fury sprang to life, growing to the size of a large dog. Then he darted off after the nearest escaping demon. Darius was only half aware of Fury snapping up the first shade and swallowing it. His attention was concentrated solely on reaching the prison. Amadja and Tain, however, stood blocking his way. Without pausing, Darius stormed forward and punched Amadja, catching him by surprise.

The demon lord staggered but didn't go down. He retaliated with a formidable strike of his own. As Darius fell back, Amadja gathered his magic and let loose a black bolt of power. Inside the living-magic portal, the death magic's impact was muted, but still it seared every nerve in Darius's body. Dragging his hand along the wall of the portal, Darius scooped up a handful of magic and returned fire on the demon lord. The blast knocked him across the narrow opening and he lay there, dazed.

Darius sprang for the gate, intent on closing it, but Tain stepped in his way.

"I can't let you do that," he said.

"What?" Darius could hardly believe what he was hearing. "Step aside."

Tain shook his head. "I can't."

"You have no idea what you're doing," Darius said. "If those demons get out, most of New York City will die."

"That's the plan, big brother," Tain said. "To end this miserable, fucking existence."

At that moment, a recovered Amadja stood, wiping a drop of blood from his split lip. The glare he gave Darius was so evil, Darius felt a chill. He reacted with all the anger in him—anger for what Amadja had done to his brother and Lexi, anger for what Amadja was trying to do to the world.

"I'm going to destroy you," he vowed to the demon, promising him so much more in his gaze than words would allow.

"Then let's get to it," Amadja said.

Out in the chamber, Lexi watched the opening, wondering what was happening inside. She moved closer, thinking maybe she could find some way to help. Just then, she heard a sound on the other side of the chamber. She turned to see Daphne walk in. Her skin glowed with a brilliant radiance from the living magic she'd stolen from her unfortunate partners. Lexi's own heightened state of magic paled by comparison, and she felt sick thinking about how many men had been sacrificed. She seethed remembering how this creature had targeted Darius. It was payback time.

Lexi didn't move as the pink-haired seductress approached the collection pool, seemingly oblivious to her surroundings. Moving with the grace of a practiced lover, she stroked her hand down the length of her arm, starting at her shoulder. An opalescent substance gathered and clung to her fingers, and when she reached her wrist, she released the magic into the pool.

Sounds of fighting erupted from the portal, and the succubus jerked her head up, finally seeming to notice a brilliant vertical beam of light hanging in midair. She stared at it for a long time before stroking her arm once more. A swooshing noise was followed by a flash of black as a dark shadow escaped the portal to sail about the room.

A second later, another shadow joined the first, flying haphazardly. Then a third and a fourth, and so on, until a dozen or more shapes swarmed around the room like dark ghosts. When one sailed past Lexi, she felt the icy cold of death magic and realized these were the shade demons that had been trapped for centuries.

A cry brought her attention back to the succubus just in time to see a demon fly by and brush against her arm. Daphne cried out again, and this time, Lexi caught the odor of burnt flesh. As the demon flew back to the others, Lexi noticed that it was no longer as transparent as it had been. In fact, it seemed to be taking on substance and form. Then it hit her: The shades were feeding off the succubus's living magic—just as she had done with her human victims.

Soon the succubus was ducking to avoid the demons as they dove at her. There were so many. Like bats rushing from a cave at the first sign of light, they swarmed all around. Daphne turned to run out of the room, but Lexi stepped into her path.

"Going somewhere?"

Daphne's eyes widened at the sight of her, but she quickly recovered and offered a friendly smile. "Hello, love," she said in dulcet tones.

Lexi felt her gaze pulled to the deep blue eyes of the woman before her. She'd never noticed how beautiful the woman was. She was feminine perfection, and Lexi ached to be close to her.

"I could make you so happy," Daphne said in a seductive tone that promised to deliver everything Lexi was looking for in life. "Let me make you happy," she continued, taking another step toward her.

"Yes," Lexi whispered, oblivious now to the demons around them.

Daphne reached out to her, and her fingers brushed across Lexi's cheek. Lexi smiled tenderly—then grabbed the succubus by the wrist and hauled her forward while planting her fist in the creature's jaw. "That's for all the men you've killed," Lexi said.

The succubus recovered quickly and shot a bolt of magic at Lexi, trying to get her to let go, but Lexi held tight and kicked her in the ribs. "That's for messing with my man," she muttered.

"I'm going to kill you," Daphne screamed. She twisted and jerked, trying to pull free, but Lexi held on and delivered another kick to Daphne's kidneys. Then she needed both fists to deliver punches. She was driven by a primal need to get even with the woman for all the times she'd seduced Darius. It never occurred to her to use magic. She was a she-wolf, defending her territory with her bare hands.

With her next punch, she shattered Daphne's nose, and blood poured forth. The light in the succubus's eyes took on an unnatural glow, and the beauty that had been so obvious faded. "I'm going to kill you, bitch!" Daphne screamed in an inhuman voice that was accompanied by a violent blast of magic. Lexi felt like she'd been slammed into a wall.

She shook her head, trying to clear her vision. "Don't count on it." Pooling her lupine strength, she hit the succubus so hard in the head that she thought she'd broken the bones in her hand.

Daphne's head snapped back, and for a long second she seemed to totter on her heels. Then she collapsed on the floor, unconscious. Before Lexi could do anything, the circling demons dove from the ceiling to cover the body. Soon all Lexi heard was the sound of scores of demons sucking the life force from the succubus.

It was over almost as quickly as it started, and when the demons scattered seconds later, all that was left of the succubus was a dried, withered shell.

Lexi stared at it, feeling no remorse. "That'll teach you to fuck with a bitch in heat," she muttered.

Then a burning pain in her arm distracted her, and she swatted at the demon who had bitten her. Now that the succubus was dead, Lexi was the next best source of magic. They still hadn't discovered the collection pool.

A roaring sound temporarily distracted her, and Fury shot from the portal in hot pursuit of a demon. Even as Lexi watched, the beast caught a shade and swallowed it whole. It seemed to her that Fury then grew a bit in size, but wasn't weighed down at all. In the next instant, he was shooting after another shade.

Then she had no time to watch Fury because the demons started attacking her en masse.

Instinctively she placed the palms of her hands together and fashioned a hasty fireball, which she hurled at the approaching demons. She hit one and it burst into flames. Encouraged, she formed another ball and threw it. Fortunately, her aim didn't have to be the greatest. There were so many demons flying about that almost anywhere she threw the ball, it was bound to hit one.

Gradually, she noticed the intensity of her fireballs was getting weaker. It took a great deal of magic and energy to form a fireball, and, thanks to Darius's efforts to keep her from imploding on her own magic earlier, she no longer had that much left in reserve.

The thought of Darius fighting alone in the portal stiffened her resolve, and she released another fireball into the demons circling above. It hit its mark, but didn't kill it. The demon came straight at her, its face a twisted mask of fury.

Lexi lashed out, desperate to divert the creature. Although it looked nearly transparent, it wasn't. The impact of her punch knocked the demon into the collection pool.

Horrified, she watched the shade splashing around, drinking the magic. It showed no signs of stopping; any minute she expected to see it grow into a formidable beast.

Then she heard a loud popping noise as the demon burst like a huge water balloon, spilling magic back into the pool. She waited to see if it would emerge, but after a second, there was still nothing. She jumped when she felt a burning on her arm, the result of another fly-by. The demon in the pool, however, never reappeared. Perhaps the living magic had been too powerful. Instead of feeding the demon, such a large dose had killed it. The thought filled her with hope.

Lexi started trying to knock the demons into the pool, but there were just too many. They continued to swarm around her, burning her wherever they touched, further draining her magic. She fought them as best she could, but she was weak and growing tired.

Just then, the door to the chamber opened, and Ricco walked in, followed by Mai, Heather and at least twenty vampires.

"Thank the Goddess," she sighed. "Hurry," she shouted at him. "Darius is in the portal. We need to help him."

Ricco sprang into action, ordering several of his men to follow him to the portal's opening. But without a powerful creature of living magic to help, it repelled them. "We can't get in," Ricco shouted.

"I'll go," Lexi hollered. "You stay out here."

She reached Ricco's side, covering her head to keep one of the demons from burning her face. Ricco's hand shot out and smacked the offending demon back.

She was about to tell Ricco and his party about the pool when an arrow buzzed by her head. It had to be Mai's thornalis. Instead of killing the demon, the arrow passed clean through its body. "No, no," Lexi told her protectors. "Knock them into the pool. It'll kill them."

When the next shade reached them, Ricco hit it again, adjusting the angle of the blow so the demon shot away and hit the water with a resounding plop. It started lapping at the magic and in less than ten seconds, it burst into nothingness.

"Cool," Ricco said as another demon flew at him. Ricco's vampire reflexes were much faster than Lexi's, and he had no problem connecting with the shades as they darted about. Ricco's team quickly picked up on the technique, and soon demons were sailing into the pool.

With Ricco and his boys busy dealing with the

shades, Lexi motioned to Heather and Mai to join her. Maybe together they could open the portal enough to help Darius.

Amadja was winning. That was the thought that raced through Darius's mind as he lay paralyzed in a heap against the far wall of the portal where the demon's latest magic bolt had sent him. He tried to catch his breath as he struggled to his feet. He glanced at Tain, but knew he'd get no help from that quarter. He was on his own.

He turned back to Amadja and saw the demon was already preparing his next attack. When the next volley of magic came at him, Darius dove out of the way.

The bolt flew past and hit Tain, who hadn't moved fast enough. He cried out in pain, and Darius knew from personal experience that the magic was spreading through Tain's body, searing every nerve. He felt only a moment's remorse for his brother's agony. Tain's eyes rolled back in his head, and he collapsed, unconscious.

Amadja roared with anger and hurled another bolt of magic at Darius, hitting him in the chest. He fell back, nearly tripping over Tain's body. When he touched the side of the portal, living magic poured into him, giving him the strength to fire a return volley at Amadja. He could tell it stunned the demon, but that was all.

As Amadja gathered his power to unleash another bolt of magic, Darius reached up and pulled off the shield, wishing he'd thought of it sooner. He almost had it in front of him when the black magic struck his arm and sent the shield flying. Before he could react, Amadja began a continuous assault.

"Give up, Immortal," Amadja said with a knowing smile. "I'm going to give you a chance to experience death."

Darius's foot hit Tain's prone body, and when he looked down, he noticed Tain's head was turned and the pentacle tattoo on his cheek was facing up. It was the sign of the Immortal, a reminder of who he was. Give up? "Don't count on it," he muttered.

Reaching down, he hauled Tain's unconscious body up and slammed him into the side of the cell, holding him there with his body. He lifted Tain's arm and propped it against the cell. As soon as he could, he grabbed Tain's hand, palm-to-palm, and interlaced their fingers, locking their hands together. Immediately the pentacle tattoo on the back of his neck began to burn. Power welled up inside him: Immortal magic.

When Amadja came rushing at him, Darius lowered his hand, interlaced with Tain's, and a brilliant beam of living magic shot forth, hitting Amadja square in the chest. He screamed as the bolt blasted him across the portal and out the opening.

Darius knew he should go after him, but first he had to see to Satan's Gate.

Lexi, Heather and Mai had just managed to open the portal a little when a flash of light arced out of it and across the domed ceiling. It happened so quickly, Lexi wasn't sure what she'd seen, but it made her worry all the more about Darius.

She jumped through the opening and saw Darius holding Tain and leaning against some kind of gate. She could tell that Darius was tired and hurt—but he continued to struggle to close the gate.

Hundreds of demons pushed against the other side, shoving and fighting to get out of their prison. Though the number of escaping demons had slowed significantly, they were still slipping out in massive numbers and would continue to until the gate was completely shut and locked.

"Want some help?" she asked, giving him a thorough visual inspection as she hurried forward.

"I'm not sure I have enough magic left to do this," Darius told her.

She put her shoulder to the gate and pushed with all her might. The gate budged the tiniest amount, and they stopped to catch their breath.

Lexi saw him reach out and touch the side of the portal. It seemed to restore him a little, so she did the same and felt magic surge through her. It gave her the strength she needed, and between them, they got the gate closed.

"Help me with Tain," Darius instructed as he hefted his brother's body away from the gate and propped him against the wall of the portal. "Hold him here."

Curious about what he was doing, she did as he asked. Slowly she felt the magic slipping through Tain. It seemed to travel through his body and into Darius through their clasped hands. For a full minute, the brothers simply stood there while the magic built. Then Darius reached for his key, still inserted in the lock of the gate.

As soon as he touched it, magic surged from the portal, through the men and into the key.

"No!" Tain came fully awake, shouting. He was clearly distressed. Lexi glanced at Darius for guidance, but his face was twisted with pain as well. The key shone so brightly it seemed to burn, but if it really did,

Darius gave no indication. He held on to it and slowly turned it.

It seemed to take forever, and as she watched, Tain's agitation grew more pronounced. Then she heard the snap of the lock sliding into place, followed by Darius's sigh.

"Done," he said.

Lexi glanced at Tain, who had suddenly quieted. His expression was unreadable. Something about him worried her; something she felt she should remember but couldn't.

"Are you all right?" Darius asked her, concern written on his face.

She nodded. "Ricco and some of his gang showed up. They're out there dealing with the demons who escaped."

"Good."

"What about Amadja?" she asked.

Darius looked dismal. "He escaped."

Lexi remembered the arc of light moments before. "What should we do about Tain?"

"He'll be fine. Once I get him home."

Home. Lexi didn't want to think about Darius leaving.

"Let's get out of here," Darius said, letting go of Tain's hand but urging him forward. Soon they were standing outside the portal, looking around the chamber. It seemed empty, except for Ricco, who was walking toward them.

"Everything all right?" Ricco asked.

Lexi hurried to intercept him, knowing that Darius wouldn't remember the vampire.

"Ricco's a friend of mine," she told him, standing between the two. "He and his friends helped me fight the demons while you were inside."

Ricco looked confused.

"Darius lost his memory," she hurried to explain. "But he seems to remember bits and pieces." Just not her.

"Oh, well, no problem," Ricco said. "We got it under control."

Darius smiled and held out his hand. "Thank you."

"No problem. I got your message, not that there was any question about where you were."

"What do you mean?" Darius asked.

"At the stroke of midnight, suddenly all the magic in New York was being pulled to the same point—the spire at the top of this building. Standing outside, it looked like hundreds of bolts of lightning were touching the top. When I took a closer look, I saw that the spire was actually absorbing the magic, presumably funneling it down the building to some point below ground. That much magic couldn't be good."

Lexi gasped. "Oh, my Goddess." She looked around. "Where are Heather and Mai?"

"They're fine. Once we destroyed the last of the demons, Heather said she had to contact the Coven of Light and tell them what was going on. Mai ran off talking about this all making a great story." He smiled. "I sent a couple of my boys with them, although I'm thinking about going to check on Mai personally a little later. She gave me her address." He looked from Lexi to Darius. "I assume that's all right with both of you?"

Lexi smiled, glad that Mai had finally gotten what she had been wanting—Ricco, all to herself. It suddenly made her own situation that much harder to take. She glanced at Darius, wondering if he remembered anything of what they had shared.

"What about the Vlads?" Darius asked, and Lexi

wondered how he had remembered the name of Ricco's rival gang.

"Looks like O'Rourke and his gang left town as soon as they realized what was going down. I don't think we'll have to worry about them for a while, but we'll keep our eyes open just the same." Ricco nodded toward Tain. "Do you need any more help?"

"No," Darius said. "I think I've got it under control."

"All right, then. I guess I'll be on my way." Ricco shook hands with Darius, bent forward to give Lexi a quick kiss on the cheek and left.

She watched Ricco walk out of the chamber, and as the door closed behind him, a large, plump dragon flew past, heading straight for Darius. It startled her so much, she took a step back before recognizing Fury. There was a shimmer of magic, and then, in the blink of an eye, the demon was gone and the dragon tattoo was back on Darius's chest.

"Let's close the portal," he said, bringing her attention back to the matter at hand. "The sooner we close it, the sooner we can go home."

Home. He was leaving and taking Tain with him. She felt her heart breaking. Maybe it was better this way, she told herself. What future could a mortal and immortal possibly have together?

He started walking toward the portal, and she followed behind him to help. They'd almost reached it when something plowed into her from behind, knocking her over. She hit her head on the hard floor and slid several feet before coming to a stop.

Dazed, she looked up and saw Tain pointing Mai's thornalis at Darius.

"What are you doing, Tain?" Darius asked, keeping his voice level.

"I can't let you close the portal."

"Why not?"

"Aja can't come back if you close the portal."

"Aja isn't who you think she is," Darius said, sounding like a parent doing his best to deal with an unreasonable child. "She's not a real woman. She's using you."

"No," Tain shouted. "She loves me. She's the only one who ever cared about me."

"That's not true, Tain," Darius said. "Adrian, Kalen, Hunter and I all love you—as does Cerridwen, your mother. She misses you greatly. Come home with me, Tain. Come home to Ravenscroft."

"No," Tain said in a saner, more reasonable tone. "I won't go back."

Lexi started to get to her feet, but a sharp shake of Darius's head made her hold still.

"Tain, even if you shoot me, I won't die. So you're wasting your time."

"You're forgetting about that new tattoo over your heart." Tain's smile was sinister and the hand holding the thornalis was frighteningly steady. "You didn't think I knew about that, did you? That's the problem with a psychic summoning—it's hard to control who gets the call. You didn't even know we were there, did you? Aja and I. Listening to your conversation with Whitley."

"I don't care that you heard the conversation," Darius said. "You won't shoot me. I'm your brother."

Lexi didn't share his conviction. She wasn't sure that Darius knew his brother as well as he thought he did. The old Tain might not have shot his brother, but the Tain who'd been tortured for centuries might.

She let her eyes morph to lupine so she could get a closer view of his trigger finger. She saw the barely imperceptible movement as he tested the resistance without actually pulling the trigger.

She looked at his face and saw the hate and determination there. Darius, on the other hand, seemed oblivious to it.

Then, to her surprise, Tain's hand fell to his side. She saw Darius visibly relax.

"Let me close this and we'll go home." Darius turned his back and started walking toward the portal.

The hairs on the back of Lexi's neck stood on end, she didn't even question why. She simply reacted, morphing into her wolf form as she leapt through the air.

Time slowed. The sound of the thornalis going off resounded loudly in her ears, but she barely noticed. She saw the thorn emerge from the muzzle and elongate into a four-inch wooden arrow. On its current trajectory she knew it would enter Darius's back, right below his left shoulder blade and pass through his heart before exiting through the center of his serpent tattoo. He would die.

Then, just as suddenly as time had slowed, everything went back to normal speed. She was leaping through the air, front legs stretched out as far as she could reach in an effort to put herself between the arrow and Darius.

She felt the arrow pierce her body. The pain was excruciating, worse than anything she'd felt in her life.

She fell to the ground. Her legs buckled beneath her, and she slumped to the floor, in too much agony to even lift her head. Things started to grow fuzzy as blood seeped from her body. She tried to gather enough magic to shift, hoping to close the wound, but she'd spent the last of it changing in midair.

As her vision narrowed, she thought of her sister and finally understood why Bev had been willing to sacrifice herself for the man she loved. It would have been too painful to go on without him.

From far away, she heard the thornalis fire again. It was followed by a man's roar of pain. Darius. She knew then that there was no longer any point in trying to hang on to life.

Her attempt to save Darius had been for nothing. Tain had shot him anyway. She stopped fighting and closed her eyes, letting the pain and darkness swallow her completely.

Chapter Twenty-three

At the first sound of a weapon being discharged, Darius whipped around just in time to see a black wolf leaping through the air before him. He heard the sickening thud as an arrow, intended for him, impaled the wolf instead. He knew then that Tain would stop at nothing to kill him. That was the first shock.

The second came when he took another look at the wolf and realized where it had come from. Lying on the floor, slowly bleeding to death, was the woman he loved. A horror unlike any he'd faced before in his life hit him, nearly crippling him.

Consumed by an overwhelming rage, he gave a primal roar, startling Tain, whose eyes went wide.

Tain stared at the weapon in his hand, then at the wolf at his feet. "I didn't mean . . ."

Darius raced forward. "If death is what you seek, then death is what you'll get," he snarled, pulling off each of the weapons tattooed on his arms and chest and hurling them at Tain. If he'd thought about it, he would have known it was impossible to kill his brother, but he was beyond thinking.

He heard the weapon go off a second time, but the shot went wild—and still Darius bore down on Tain. His rage was such that he would not stop until Tain lay dead at his feet. It took him no time to reach Tain and grab him by the throat. He lifted his brother off the floor, squeezing with all his might.

"You killed her," Darius growled.

Tain clawed at Darius's hands. "No," he gasped. "She still lives. You can save her."

Slowly the words pierced his rage, and he turned to see that the wolf was still breathing. Barely. He dropped Tain and hurried to Lexi's side. Tain took advantage of the opportunity to make his escape. Darius let him go. If Lexi died, he had the rest of eternity to hunt his brother and exact revenge.

But now he had more immediate concerns.

"Lexi, my love. Can you hear me?"

He saw the wolf's eyes open slowly.

"Baby, it's me, Darius."

A faint whimper was the only response he got.

"Hang on, love." He searched the room, searching for some means to save her life. Maybe if she morphed. He hurried to the pool, now nearly empty, and dipped his hand into it. He felt the warmth of the living magic and carried it to Lexi. He wasn't sure of the best way to help her, so he simply laid his hand on her and willed the magic into her.

The transformation was slow, but she started to change. He hurried several more times to the pool to carry magic back to her. At one point, he considered placing her in the pool, but wasn't sure what that might do to her.

Once she was human, the wound appeared as a tiny hole in her chest. Darius thought that changing would have healed it and couldn't understand why it hadn't. He bent close and finally saw the protruding small piece of wood. He knew he had to get it out, even though he hated to cause her even more pain. Grabbing the end of it, he pulled.

Lexi cried out, but he didn't stop until he'd fully extracted the arrow. Blood flowed freely, spilling over her bare breasts and down her stomach. The bright red against her pale complexion was stark and horrifying.

"Oh, Lexi, baby. I'm so sorry." He lifted her onto his lap, rocking her as he looked around the room, desperate for a way to save her. He didn't think, even given all the magic in the pool, that she had the strength to morph again.

She couldn't even generate a tiny fireball to cauterize the wound, as she'd done for him.

It wasn't fair that the life of the woman he loved should be snatched away from him like this. He didn't want to live without her—not another day, not another hour, not another second. He sure as hell didn't want to spend eternity without her.

But what if he could join her?

He remembered the serpent tattoo on his chest. His life force. He hadn't tried to remove it, wasn't sure he could. He touched the tattoo and felt the shimmer of magic. He found the edge and slipped his finger beneath it. When he gave it an experimental tug, he felt the pull of it all the way to his core. Taking this off could very well kill him, but he was prepared for that. He accepted that. What he couldn't accept was Lexi dying.

But maybe she didn't have to.

Knowing her time was almost up, he bent over and, tilting her head back, he pressed his lips to hers. "I never forgot you," he told her. "And I never will." He only hoped she would understand.

Then he grabbed the edge of the serpent tattoo and ripped it from his chest. The pain tore at his very soul, and he couldn't suppress crying out. Almost immediately he felt himself slipping away. Quickly he slapped the tattoo over Lexi's wound. Maybe his immortal life force would be enough to save her.

He watched in amazement as the bleeding stopped and the wound started to close. Lexi's breathing started coming easier and color seeped back into her complexion. She seemed to be getting stronger.

Darius, on the other hand, wasn't doing so well. The ringing in his head was getting louder by the second. He felt himself being pulled by unknown forces, but he fought to resist them. He wanted to stay with Lexi for as long as he could.

When her eyelids fluttered open, he smiled down at her.

"Darius?" Her voice was little more than a croak. "What happened?"

"Tain shot you, but you're going to be all right."

"I thought you were dead." Her voice cracked with emotion.

He wanted to tell her he was fine, but he wouldn't lie. Instead, he smiled down at her, willing her to see the love he felt because talking was becoming too difficult.

The pull on him increased, and he shook from the effort of resisting. Afraid she would feel it, he laid her down on the floor, though she whimpered in protest. "Don't leave me," she pleaded. "Please don't leave me."

He knew it was a promise he couldn't keep. He

bent and pressed a final kiss to her lips. "I'm sorry," he whispered.

Then suddenly he was torn from Earth's dimension, hurtling through space and time. Lights streaked past him, blinding him. He closed his eyes, praying that death would come quickly.

Suddenly he was no longer moving, but lying on something cold and hard. Maybe he was still in the chamber, on the floor next to Lexi? His heart leapt at the possibility, and he opened his eyes.

Quickly he closed them again, to block out the blinding light. It was harder to block out his disappointment.

After several long seconds, he sat up, and this time shielded his eyes before opening them. He found himself on the balcony of his home, surrounded by a familiar clear blue sky and the lush green woods on each side of the sapphire-blue water of Lake Pax. The sense of déjà vu was so strong that at first he doubted whether he'd ever left Ravenscroft.

The memory of Lexi's light gray eyes when she looked up at him—of her lush, firm body pressed against his was too real to have been imagined.

"Darius!" Sekhmet cried as she and Whitley rushed out to him. "Are you all right?"

Whitley helped him to his feet, and his mother pulled him into a fierce embrace. He fought to be free. "Send me back," he demanded. He grabbed his mother by the arms and shook her. "Please, Mother," he cried. "I beg you. Send me back. Now."

"I can't," she told him, tears springing to her eyes. "It was everything I could do to bring you back."

"Come inside," Whitley suggested. "Everything will be better in time."

An icy cold enveloped Darius, and he dropped his

hands to his sides, stepping away from Sekhmet and Whitley. He left them staring after him and walked through the mansion until he found his room. It was as stark and bare of emotion as he now felt. At some point, the numbness would wear off and he'd be left with nothing but pain. So for now, he welcomed the numbness.

Darius had no idea how long he slept. For all he knew, it could have been months. He had no interest in living, so there was no point in getting out of bed.

When he finally did venture forth from his room, Whitley and his mother were waiting for him in the family room. She was sitting in her favorite chair, doing something with two metal sticks and a roll of yarn. It was so unexpected to see her doing something as mundane as knitting that for a moment he actually felt a spark of curiosity. It quickly passed.

"How are you?" she asked, her concern obvious by the tone of her voice and the look on her face.

"Hello, Mother." He walked over to her and placed a kiss on her head. "I'm . . ." *Miserable*. "Fine."

She cupped his face with her hand and kissed his cheek. "We were worried about you."

He walked over to sit in a chair beside Whitley and waited for the barrage of questions. He didn't wait long.

"Tell us everything," Sekhmet said. "Were you able to stop Amadja? What about Tain? Did you see him? Is he all right?"

"Whoa. You're overwhelming the boy," Whitley said. "Darius, just tell us what happened. We were worried about you."

Darius tried to consider how they felt. How he would have felt if he and Lexi had had a son.

A fresh new pain shot through him, but with it a small hope. Taking a deep breath, he swallowed hard. Then, slowly, he told them everything.

Lexi felt the tendrils of dawn urging her to wake up. She wasn't ready to face the day just yet, so she rolled over and willed herself back to sleep.

She woke hours later to the sound of Mai walking through her apartment, but kept her eyes closed, hoping Mai would take the hint and go away.

"You can't sleep your life away," Mai told her, not unsympathetically. "Eventually, you'll have to get out of bed and start living again."

Lexi knew she was right. "I don't think I can," she said, no longer pretending to sleep. "I hurt so bad."

Mai came over and sat down on the edge of the bed. "I thought the wound had completely healed. Maybe I'd better check it."

Lexi sighed. "The wound healed. The heart didn't."

She felt the cool touch of Mai's hand on her head. "I know, honey. It's not easy. I was talking to Ricco and he was saying . . . well, he was wondering, you know . . . maybe Darius will come back?"

Lexi had thought so too. Each day for the first two weeks after he disappeared, she'd thought he would come back for her. Each day that he didn't return, though, was further proof that her worst fear had been realized. He really had forgotten her. For him, there was nothing to return for.

She still saw him, though. Every time she closed her eyes, he was there beside her, telling her that he loved her, that he'd never forget her. Her heart ached so badly for him that she'd taken to sleeping later and later, just so she could spend more time with him.

It was pathetic, she knew. But it was all she had.

"Lexi," Mai said, apparently not for the first time. "Are you listening to me?"

"What?" She felt so tired.

"There's someone here to see you."

For one brief moment, Lexi thought that maybe Darius had come back, but then logic exerted itself.

"Sit up," Mai ordered, doing her best to straighten Lexi's hair. "Okay!" she hollered.

Lexi looked at the door expectantly and was mildly surprised when her brother-in-law, Derrick, appeared.

He gave her an apologetic smile. "I know I'm probably the last person you want to see right now, but Ricco told me what happened, and under the circumstances, I thought . . ." He paused and took a deep breath. "I thought it might help to talk to someone who'd been through the same thing."

Someone who knew what it was like to lose the person they loved. Like he'd lost Bev.

He came into the room, and Lexi gestured to the side of the bed. He sat down while she considered all the questions she wanted to ask him and settled on the most important. "Does it ever stop hurting?"

"I'll let you know," he said, his voice cracking a little.

She realized now how much he must have suffered when Bev died. "I'm so, so sorry for all the things I said," she apologized. "I shouldn't have blamed you. It wasn't your fault."

He shook his head. "There was nothing you said that I hadn't said to myself at least a million times."

She reached out and took his hand. "But you have to know that it wasn't your fault."

He covered her hand with his. "Thanks, but it doesn't make the day any easier to get through—does it?"

"No, it doesn't." Lexi tried to smile but couldn't. And then it was like a dam bursting. Her pain and heartache came rushing out. And Derrick held her, letting her cry until she thought there were no tears left. They talked well into the night. She never even noticed that Mai had snuck out early to leave them alone.

When Derrick finally decided to leave, she was starting to feel better. They made plans to see each other again because he was, after all, her brother-in-law. Then she went into the kitchen and, for the first time in days, ate because she was hungry.

Afterwards, she went to her room to lie down again. The dreams she had that night when she slept were mostly the same ones she'd been having, with Darius holding her and telling her how much he loved her.

At one point, a beautiful woman appeared in her dream. Lexi had never seen her before, but she wasn't frightened. The woman looked on her with kindly eyes, and when she waved her hand, the dreams changed. She relived each moment from the time Darius had appeared to her to the moment she'd realized Tain was about to shoot Darius and she'd morphed into a wolf to save him. Had saved him. Her last image was of waking up and seeing Darius's face one last time, just before some force snatched him from her. "I love you," she called to him, but he didn't come back. "I'll always love you."

She woke up in tears and saw that it was morning. With the sun shining brightly through her window, she forced herself to get out of bed and headed for the bathroom. It was time to start living again.

When she undressed and looked in the mirror, the coiled serpent tattoo over her heart stared back at her. She touched it, as she did so often, tentatively testing its permanency. It didn't move or rub off. It was one of the two things Darius had left her to remember him by.

She touched her stomach and wondered how the Mother Goddess could gift her with a child while robbing her of its father. It was too much to think about, so she stepped in the shower and let the steam carry her thoughts away.

An hour later, she walked into the office. Marge looked up from her desk and gave her a sympathetic smile. Lexi groaned.

"I must really look bad if you feel like you have to be nice to me."

"Actually," the older woman said, "you've got a little glow underneath the dark circles. How ya doing, sugar?"

"Honestly? I've been better," Lexi admitted, going over to the case files. She had several stacked up and she flipped through them. Finally she picked one out and handed the rest to Marge. "Tell TJ that I appreciate what he's trying to do, but I'm fine. I don't need all the light cases." She held up the file in her hand. "I'm going after this one, but when I come back, we'll divide up the rest of the cases a little more evenly."

Marge gave her a critical look and then accepted the files from her. "You got it. Welcome back."

"Thanks." She turned and left the office, managing to keep her composure until she reached the street. She had to fake a serious interest in the display case of the bakery next door while she took several deep breaths. One of the case files had been for Paddy Darby, leprechaun. He'd missed his second court hearing, and Lexi had a feeling no one would ever see the little man again. In any event, she couldn't bring herself to look for him.

Pulling herself together, she walked several blocks north to an OTB. The skip she was looking for was a repeat offender, and she knew this was where he liked to bet on the day's horse races.

She made herself comfortable waiting outside. The last two times she'd brought him in, he'd shown up right around this time.

He appeared five minutes later, walking down the street alone. When he saw her, he didn't bother to run, like he normally did. Instead, he gave Lexi a knowing smile, pulled out a gun and shot her.

At first she didn't even feel the pain. Her next thought was that he'd better not have shot her in the abdomen, because if he harmed her baby, she was going to kill him. Finally, she took note of the horrified expression on his face as he stared at her.

Then she realized why he looked that way. He'd shot her in the right shoulder, and, since she wasn't wearing sleeves, a bullet wound should have been clearly visible. But there was only a small pucker in the flesh, and even that quickly disappeared.

She was as shocked as the skip was, but there wasn't time to think about it. Already he was aiming again. Suddenly there was a flash of light on the ground between them, and when the accompanying smoke cleared, a man dressed in black pants and a black sleeveless duster stood there, his upper torso covered in tattoos.

Lexi's heart skipped a beat as she stared at Darius. His attention was fixed on the skip, whose hand holding the gun was shaking so badly, Lexi wasn't sure he would be able to hit anything should he pull the trigger. Darius didn't give him the chance to try.

He tapped Fury, and the small demon shot forth and chased the skip down the street. Lexi didn't even mind that the skip was getting away. Her entire focus was on the man before her.

He strolled forward, and she waited, hardly daring to breathe as he stopped before her. She stared into his eyes, willing him to remember her.

"Darius." His name escaped her in a breathless rush.

"I missed you," he told her, cupping her face. He dipped his head and kissed her. It was a long time before either of them was able to speak.

"I thought you'd forgotten me," she said with a shaky laugh after they finally came up for air.

"I never did. Back in the chamber, after we made love, everything started to go blank, but I kept thinking how much I loved you. It seemed to work, because after several minutes passed, I remembered everything—including the fact that some force, probably Amadja and Tain, had eavesdropped on the dream I had when Whitley summoned me. They would know that I was destined to forget everything should I climax during lovemaking. I knew that had to be part of their plan. Why else would they have given *you*, specifically, Demon Fire? It was part of their plan all along that we make love. That's when I knew I had to pretend to lose my memory. I'm just sorry I didn't have a chance to tell you. I love you, Lexi. More than life itself. I want you to know that."

"I do," she assured him. "That arrow Tain shot should have killed me. When it didn't, I knew there had to be a reason why, because I remembered being too weak to morph. That's when I noticed your tattoo. I had your tattoo, but you were gone. I thought . . ." She hesitated, because even now, the thought brought pain. "I thought by giving me your tattoo, you had killed yourself."

He rested his forehead against hers, still holding her close. "Don't you realize that you're the most important thing in my life? I couldn't sit there and watch you die—not if there was anything I could do to save you. I gladly gave you my life-force tattoo—even if it meant my own death." He pressed his fingers to her mouth when she would have argued with him. "Shh. Instead of dying, I was pulled back to Ravenscroft." He gave a short laugh. "It seems that my mother spent my entire absence working on spells to safeguard me—including one that would return me to Ravenscroft should I lose my life force." He pulled her to him for a quick hug. "I was a crazy man when I got there. I was wild with worry about you—whether you lived or died. I didn't want to leave you, so I demanded to be sent back to Earth—to no avail. My only means of getting to Earth lay with the life-force tattoo—which I no longer had. I was trapped in Ravenscroft."

"What changed?"

He gave a little chuckle. "Nothing." When she looked at him confused, he went on. "As the weeks passed, my love for you never faded. If anything, it grew stronger—just as yours did for me." He smiled. "One day, I woke up and my life-force tattoo was back. At first, I was horrified. I thought it meant that you had died. My mother begged me not to do anything rash until she could discover the truth, which she did, apparently, by coming to you in a dream." He smiled. "She liked you very much, by the way."

Lexi thought back to the dream she'd had and the woman in it. "I think I remember her."

"Once she learned that you were alive and still very much in love with me, she knew what had happened." He smiled. "My life-force tattoo can only attach itself to me or something as precious to me as my own life—in this case, you. It just took time for the tattoo to reappear over my heart." He pulled back from her enough to flip open the left side of his duster where she saw the life-force serpent tattoo over his heart.

Surprised, she unbuttoned her shirt enough to verify that her own tattoo was still in place. She looked up at him, confused. "I don't get it. Are we sharing the same life force now?"

"Sounds poetic, doesn't it? Two souls merged into one through the power of love? Mother said she couldn't risk losing either one of us and merged our immortal life forces into our souls. That gives us the ability to travel back and forth from Earth to Ravenscroft whenever we want."

It was all a little overwhelming for Lexi. "Our *immortal* life forces?"

"Yes. I'm afraid you're stuck with me for the rest of eternity." Taking her hand, he led her toward the street. "Now, unless you don't mind a very public display of affection, I suggest we go someplace private."

Lexi couldn't remember much about the cab ride to her apartment except that she spent most of it in Darius's arms.

When they finally walked into her apartment, he kicked the door shut and, picking her up, carried her into the bedroom.

"I've been fantasizing for the longest time about making love to you in a real bed," he told her, setting her on the bed.

She smiled and pulled him down beside her. "I can't

believe you're here," she whispered, leaning over to kiss him. "I'm so afraid that all of this will turn out to be a dream and when I wake up, you'll be gone." She shuddered. "I never want to go through that again."

"I'll never make you. I promise."

He kissed her then—slowly, sweetly—as if they had all the time in the world. When they came up for air, it was only so he could get rid of their clothing. Lying naked, facing each other, it was strange to see their twin tattoos. Two halves of one greater love. Lexi, who had never been one for sappy stuff, thought it was romantically poetic.

Darius didn't give her much time to think about it before he had her beneath him on the bed. Holding himself above her, he looked strong and capable. When he dipped his head to tease first one nipple and then the other, liquid desire pooled deep in her abdomen, and she felt her pulse quicken.

The blunt tip of his erection probed her swollen flesh at the juncture of her legs, and she shifted her hips in anticipation. When his cock finally pushed into her, filling her, Lexi thought she'd never felt anything quite so exquisite. As if realizing the effect he was having on her, Darius started moving with deliberate slowness. It caused the tension in her to quickly build. Soon she was skating on the edge of a powerful orgasm, waiting for that last driving stroke that would send her crashing over the edge. She tightened her inner muscles, and when Darius surged into her one last time, together they found their release.

Afterward, they lay in each other's arms for a long time, spent yet satisfied.

Lexi thought she had everything in the world that she wanted—the man of her dreams, a child on the way . . .

Reality raised its ugly head. What if Darius didn't want children?

"I need to tell you something," she said tentatively. "And I hope it won't spoil things between us."

Darius look at her with obvious concern. "What is it, love?"

"I'm pregnant."

He grinned. "I know."

"What . . . How . . . ?"

He took a deep breath. "As an Immortal, I can control the release of my seed. When we made love that time in the chamber, I didn't know if the spell to forget would claim me again. If it did, I wanted to leave you with something to remember me by—something as precious to me as my life or yours. I'm sorry we didn't talk about it first, but there was no time."

She felt her heart swell. "When I found out I was pregnant, it was like getting a part of you back in my life. I had a reason to live again. I could never regret being pregnant with *our* child."

Darius smiled. "Whew." He dipped his head and kissed her. "But if I seem extra protective in the coming days, you would do best to humor me."

"Why? What's happening?"

"We leave for Seattle tomorrow—to meet up with Amber and Adrian."

"We?" she asked, not sure she'd heard correctly.

He smiled at her. "You don't seriously think I'd go without you?"

"So Amadja is still out there?"

He frowned. "I'm afraid so."

"And Tain?" She almost hated to mention his name.

Darius sighed. "He's out there as well."

"Will you and Adrian be enough to defeat them?"

"We're still hoping that Kalen and Hunter can be found, but if not, it still won't be just me and Adrian. Amber and you will be there, as well as the Coven of Light witches and some of Amber and Adrian's friends."

"And Ricco and Mai," she added.

Darius gave her a startled look. "What?"

She nodded. "Mai called me last night and told me she and Ricco—who have been seeing a lot of each other, by the way—made plans to join forces with the others in Seattle. I hadn't decided yet whether or not I was going."

"And now?" Darius asked.

"I go where you go," Lexi said, leaning close to kiss him. "*Wherever* you go, my love."

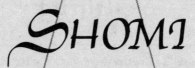

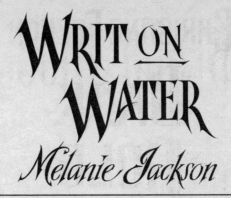